EX IN THE CITY

PORTIA MACINTOSH

Boldwood

First published in Great Britain in 2024 by Boldwood Books Ltd.

Copyright © Portia MacIntosh, 2024

Cover Design by Alexandra Allden

Cover Illustration: Shutterstock

A CIP catalogue record for this book is available from the British Library.

Paperback ISBN 978-1-80426-697-7

Large Print ISBN 978-1-80426-700-4

Hardback ISBN 978-1-80426-701-1

Ebook ISBN 978-1-80426-699-1

Kindle ISBN 978-1-80426-698-4

Audio CD ISBN 978-1-80426-706-6

MP3 CD ISBN 978-1-80426-704-2

Digital audio download ISBN 978-1-80426-702-8

Boldwood Books Ltd
23 Bowerdean Street
London SW6 3TN
www.boldwoodbooks.com

For my incredible family, for their unconditional support. Here's to the next ten years!

1

'Come on, Nicole, smile,' Robert, the photographer, insists. 'Cheer up – it might never happen.'

They say a picture is worth a thousand words. I can't even imagine what the look on my face is going to say in this one.

I wince. I hate that phrase – cheer up, it might never happen. It's one of those phrases you only ever really hear men say to women, and I can't imagine it ever being all that well received. With phrases like that being barked at me, when I'm trying my best to relax, I'm not going to be able to muster up anything beyond a Mona Lisa smile. It's strange how I never quite get used to this.

You would just know Robert was a photographer

the second you laid eyes on him. Robert, who must be in his forties, is clearly an arty type, the kind of guy you would expect to see clutching a vintage camera in one hand while sipping espresso outside a Parisian café with the other. His flowing brown hair, streaked with a few strands of silver, is twisted into a bun that sits on the top of his head. Still, he likes to whip his head, as though he's moving loose strands from his eyes – it must be a force of habit – but it all adds to this air of snobbery he's not only exuding, it feels as though he's actively fostering it.

'Rowan, put your arm around her, show the world how in love you are,' Robert demands as he pushes his round-rimmed tortoiseshell glasses up his nose.

Rowan, who is standing next to me, looks at me for a second before doing as he is told. I shuffle slightly, trying to find a comfortable position with his arm across my back, his hand squeezing my shoulder.

'And, children, if you could stand a little closer to Mother,' he continues. 'Nicole, put a hand on the smallest one's shoulder.'

Ned – the 'smallest one' – stares at me.

'Go on,' Rowan encourages him with a smile.

Ned, who is five, is standing in front of me, while Archie, who is eight, is standing in front of his dad. We're all standing in our kitchen, in front of the bifold doors that open out into the back garden, but it's hard to feel at home right now.

'These photos are to show what a happy family you are – smile,' Robert reminds us all. 'The loved-up couple, the beautiful kids, the big house. The dream!'

Rowan looks so relaxed for the camera, so effortlessly handsome. He's a lifestyle influencer, making a living through sponsored content and ads on his videos. He made a name for himself as one of those gymfluencer types – you know the guys, the ones posting photos from the gym, flogging protein powders – but has evolved his brand into something more family-friendly these days. He went viral, years ago, when someone took a photo of him with his shirt off, hanging off the monkey bars at the playgroup with the kids, while a bunch of mums sat on a nearby bench, all gawping at his abs. He was dubbed 'Hot Dad' and ever since he's focused on making family content, showing what a happy life he lives, how he entertains his kids, how he renovates his huge house in picture-perfect suburbia. For his male followers, his content is aspirational. They want to be him, to live his life, to copy his style. As for his female followers, well, the fact that he's handsome and posts a lot of shirtless photos doesn't hurt.

Rowan is a really good-looking guy. It was his good

looks that caught my attention on the day we met. He has short, wavy brown hair that he always neatly blows back, bright blue eyes, and a jaw so sharp it could cut glass. You can tell that he takes care of himself – that he moisturises his skin and conditions his hair – and that he goes to the gym every day. Even his perfectly formed muscles have muscles, that's the kind of shape he's in. But while it was his looks that caught my eye, it was his personality that stole my heart. At thirty-seven, he's a few years older than me, but his maturity was another thing that appealed to me. He seemed so kind, so caring, so family-orientated, and that's exactly what I wanted. A nice quiet life, with a man I loved, and a happy family, ideally in a beautiful home in a lovely part of the country.

'Perfect smiles, boys, good work,' Robert tells the kids.

Growing up with a dad whose entire life is on social media has turned them into naturals. They're so at home with the camera, so used to all of their big moments being documented. I always joke that Ned, who is naturally accident-prone, didn't break his first bone until he was on camera, given that he'd taken so many tumbles without a scratch – prior to breaking his leg as Rowan filmed him running through a field.

I, on the other hand, have never been great in the spotlight. Still, I am part of this circus, and as such I seem to have gathered a bit of a following, as Rowan's 'mumfluencer' counterpart – although to me Instagram is just for fun, not a place for my content, but as an extension of Rowan people seem to want to follow me, to see what I'm doing, to access all areas of our dream life. I might be able to keep my own account private but, on Rowan's, I'm part of the cast of characters. It's not my day job, though, I have a real job – sometimes it feels like I'm the only person in this village who does. Little Harehill isn't really the sort of village where people have jobs (especially not the parents who take care of the kids), which is ironic because it is so expensive to live here. It's basically the kind of place you move to have a family and a big house, if you don't want to live in central London (or even if you do want to, but you want to have a big house with a nice garden that doesn't cost thirty million pounds), and the kind of place where everyone is competing with everyone – whether they want to or not.

'Oh, look at you all, so beautiful, so happy, the world will be so jealous,' Robert practically sings as he snaps away.

Yes, because that's the goal.

Rowan squeezes me and I can't help but squirm again.

A picture might be worth a thousand words, and this might look like a picture-perfect life, but don't believe everything you see online.

Things here are far from perfect – but not today, not in this photo, at least.

2

I always joke that you can tell how much a private school costs by how excessive the uniforms are. Here at Little Harehill School, where the boys go, not only are straw hats part of the official get-up, but girls aren't even allowed to tie their hair up with anything other than the official school scrunchie, which comes in their chosen shade of forest green. Perhaps it's good for kids to be given such strict uniform rules to adhere to, but at such a young age it feels excessive to me. When I was Ned's age, I probably spent many of my school days with ketchup in my hair, because I was forever accidentally dipping my unruly long blonde locks in my dinner. To be honest with you, this still happens sometimes, and I'm thirty-four now.

The school building, a towering stone structure that looks like it's been plucked from the pages of a novel set in Victorian times, is the kind of place where the PTA meetings have a menu and the tea is served in porcelain cups. The actual teaching of the actual children feels like a really small part of what we've got going on here. For the parents of Little Harehill – aka the land of perfectly pruned hedges and extravagantly landscaped gardens – socialising, partying and most importantly having an arena for competing against one another appears to be far more important. And it isn't just about parents competing over who has the most impressive child, oh no, that's such a small part of the Middle-Class Olympics. Medals are also up for grabs for who has the most expensive car, the biggest house, and bizarrely (and in a completely sexist way) who has either the youngest wife or the wealthiest husband.

I shift my weight back and forth between my feet as I loiter in the playground, trying to avoid making eye contact with anyone as I wait for Archie and Ned to come out. Honestly, you run out of things to talk about, every day, twice a day, as you stand out here with the same people – people who are all just wanting to get on with their day too. And then it's home with the boys, for more repetitiveness, as we have the inevitable twenty-minute conversation about what dinner they're both willing to eat this evening. Honestly, they change their minds about what foods they like, and what foods they consider to be poison, all the time, which would be fine, but they never seem to like the same things at the same time. Kids are like mood rings, changing on a whim, due to some un-known (but teeny-tiny) variable. They are either the sweetest boys or – if I'm allowed to say this about kids – the biggest dickheads. They're kind of like their dad in that respect.

I notice all of the usual suspects lining up along-side me. Mostly au pairs – because even the mums that don't work don't always pick their kids up, al-though they more than make up for it by being in-credibly full-on in other ways. There's very much a mummy club, one I suspect I will never truly infil-trate, but it seems like a full-time job. To be honest, I think it's my actual full-time job that keeps me from becoming a fully-fledged member, but the constant coffee mornings, party planning committees, the gath-ering to judge people and look down their noses at them (Felicia Hickman painted her front door pink last year and I don't think anyone has forgiven her yet) – it's not the kind of stuff I have time for, in both respects.

But then, amidst the sea of frazzled-looking nannies, I spot a woman in her thirties, smiling warmly – far too warmly for a cold, miserable day like today. She seems like she's smiling at me, her eyes friendly as they lock on to mine – she looks at me as though she knows me. I don't think I've ever seen her before in my life.

Not wanting to be impolite – and just in case I have met her, but for some reason seem to have forgotten about it – I flash a friendly grin back at her. Interestingly, she takes this as an invitation and starts to make her way over.

'Hi, I'm Lisa,' she says, her voice as warm and welcoming as her smile.

'Nice to meet you, I'm Nicole,' I reply.

'Sorry, I know this is weird, but I feel like I know you,' Lisa continues.

I cock my head curiously, studying her face carefully. Lisa looks like she's in her early thirties, the same sort of age as me, but otherwise, I still can't find any familiarity in her face. She's tall – distinctively so – with long, glossy red hair. She makes a good impression that I can't imagine forgetting.

'Lots of people around here know Rowan Nutter, my partner,' I suggest because everyone in the village knows and adores Rowan.

'And we all see Nicole all over his Instagram,' Suzanne, one of the au pairs, pipes up, joining the conversation out of nowhere, keen to help solve the mystery.

Lisa's brow furrows as she visibly racks her brains.

'No, it's not that,' Lisa replies, sighing lightly. 'Hmm, weird, perhaps you just have one of those faces. I could have sworn I knew you – maybe in another life, hey?'

'Maybe,' I reply with a smile. 'Either way, it's lovely to meet you.'

'Yeah, I don't usually pick the kids up,' she begins to explain. 'We're new to the area and the au pair usually...'

I try to focus on what Lisa is saying but my brain wanders off. Lisa and I are around the same age but she has a local accent (the same London-suburb yummy-mummy accent everyone has here apart from me) and I grew up nearly 200 miles away in Leeds, so it's not like we crossed paths when we were much younger. But there are lots of years between when we were kids and now and that's what is worrying me, that and her choice of words, that perhaps we knew one another in another life, because I did very much used to live another life, one worlds away from the one I'm living now, and I've not only worked really hard to put it behind me, but I've done everything in my power to keep this lot – the village locals, who will get their pitchforks out for next to nothing – from finding out about it.

I wonder if Lisa knew me back then, if our paths crossed, or if she maybe saw me somewhere at some point – somewhere I probably shouldn't have been. Whatever the explanation, if she did know me back in the day, I need to do whatever it takes to keep her from remembering.

The last thing I need is for my new friends – or Rowan, for that matter – to be introduced to the old Nicole. Here's hoping my secret is still safe. For now...

3

As I wake up, my body instinctively stretches out in my bed. Slowly, I begin to open my eyes, allowing them to adjust to the light, my senses not quite awake yet. But something feels off, and then my legs collide with someone else's, and as I squint through my tired eyes, I realise that I am not alone in my bed.

I panic, obviously not expecting anyone else to be under the covers with me, as my body deliberates: fight or flight? My heart beats so fast it feels like it might burst – so does my face, as I realise I'm holding my breath. But then, as I allow myself a moment to focus, I realise it's just Rowan and I settle down – but not quite all the way.

'Rowan,' I say, practically gasping for air, semi-relieved to see that it's him. 'What the hell are you doing?'

'Shh, relax,' Rowan insists. 'It's Mother's Day, the boys wanted to bring you breakfast in bed.'

'What?' I reply in disbelief. 'So, what, you get in bed with me while I'm sleeping?'

'They wanted to wake you up with breakfast, and I don't want them catching wind of the fact we no longer sleep in the same bed. It makes sense that I'm in here,' he explains. 'Come on, Nicole, you're lucky they even want to do this.'

Wow, in one sentence he's managed to make me feel guilty about two things. Firstly, the fact that we no longer share a bedroom and, secondly, that I am not really Archie and Ned's mum.

'You could have woken me up, without getting in bed with me,' I point out.

'Ah, come on, Nicole, let them have their moment,' Rowan insists. 'Don't let how you're currently feeling about me ruin this for them.'

He uses the word 'currently' as though my feelings are likely to change but I really, really can't see that happening. He's well and truly done it this time.

Archie and Ned shuffle into the room, their faces beaming with pride, and I can't help but smile. Archie carries a tray with a cold-looking cup of tea on it (not that I want to see an eight-year-old navigating boiling water), which he balances with so much careful concentration it almost looks as though he is more likely to spill it. Meanwhile, Ned hands me a bowl containing what appears to be a combination of several different cereals – a mishmash including bran flakes and Coco Pops, which I can't imagine going all that well together, although adding anything to bran flakes has to improve them, surely?

As I look at the breakfast they've prepared, I bite my lip, trying not to laugh. It's a cold cup of tea and a bowl of congealed cereals but they've clearly put thought and effort into it, and their happy expressions are too adorable to disappoint. Plus, I know they're only young – and I'm not even sure how well they remember their mum, given that Ned wasn't even one when she passed away – but days like today must be hard for them. I'll eat every bite.

'Wow, thank you, boys,' I say with genuine gratitude as I pick up a spoon and take a cautious mouthful.

The varying tastes and textures mean that there is a lot going on in each bite. Sometimes it works, sometimes it really doesn't. I think it's when I catch something like a Weetabix with a Honey Monster Puff and a sprinkling of Coco Pops that it's a bit of an overload.

I take a big swig of tea to clear my palate.

Archie, even at the age of eight, looks like a miniature version of Rowan. He has inherited Rowan's dark, tousled hair, and his eyes mirror Rowan's, with that almost cold shade of blue. He has his dad's adventurous spirit too, as well as his boundless energy for all activities – anything outdoorsy. He's already so sporty, and I know Rowan is keen to get him into playing several sports more seriously as he gets older.

Ned, on the other hand, is the baby of the family at five years old. He has that classic blonde baby hair that frames his cute, rounded face. His eyes are bright and expressive, and he's interested in absolutely everything, so he's always picking things up, asking questions, and being read to might just be his favourite thing.

I smile brightly back at them, my heart warmed by their gesture.

'Thank you, boys. You've made my day,' I tell them.

Archie, with his mini-Rowan demeanour, leans forward, his curiosity getting the better of him.

'Do you like your breakfast?' he asks, his eyes fixed on mine.

I've never dated a man with kids before. It is strange, seeing these small, cute versions of him around all the time, so sweet and innocent – but so easy for said man to use as a shield in all sorts of situations, it turns out.

I nod, trying to maintain a straight face despite the bizarre combination of cereals. Thankfully, my expression doesn't betray me.

'It's delicious, Archie,' I tell him. 'You guys make the best breakfast.'

'Is it better than the breakfast Daddy makes?' Ned asks, his blonde locks bouncing as he tilts his head inquisitively.

Ha. Not that Daddy ever makes any of the meals in this house – not unless it's some dumb Instagram thing someone is paying him to film himself cooking, but even then that's never anything the kids – or even I – want to eat.

'Oh, absolutely,' I reply. 'In fact, I think you guys should start making breakfast for Daddy.'

Rowan grins at my suggestion. He knows it can't be as nice as I'm making it out to be. I hope he also knows that there is no combination of cereal known to man that he could eat that would make me forgive him for what he's done.

'Okay, boys, how about we give Nicole her present?' Rowan suggests, his voice packed with excitement.

The boys cheer, excited too, so I smile and do my

best to seem like everything is okay. I'm doing all of this for myself, and for the boys, because we shouldn't have to suffer, just because Rowan is a wanker.

'Nicole, put this on,' Rowan instructs, his voice a mixture of anticipation and excited impatience, as he throws me my dressing gown. 'And meet us downstairs. We'll go make sure your present is ready.'

I raise an eyebrow.

'Okay,' I say simply.

I get out of bed, as I'm told, but instead of throwing on my dressing gown, I grab a pair of trackies and a hoodie from my drawers to put on instead. I just don't feel comfortable here any more, this doesn't feel like my house, I don't feel like I can walk around in a dressing gown.

My bedroom, the one I used to share with Rowan before everything went tits up, is a room that I worked long and hard on. I redecorated it myself, with contemporary panelling, trendy muted tones, new furniture and a large bed at its centre. I wanted to make the ultimate bedroom, a tranquil space, somewhere that guaranteed a good night's sleep. And I succeeded, I made it perfect, but I soon found out that you can make the room as perfect as you like, but you will still find that you have very little control over what goes on inside it. Now it's simply a reminder of what used to be, a space that once felt like 'ours' but now hardly feels like mine, and with my plan being to move out as soon as the mess Rowan made is cleared up, soon it won't be mine at all. I'll never sleep in it again, I'll no longer be able to dig my toes into the plush rug as I read in the snuggler chair I deliberated over for weeks because I wanted to make sure I got one that was perfect for both of us. And while, yes, I could take the chair and the rug with me when I eventually leave, I don't actually know where I will be going when I do move out, so I can't exactly plan to take the furniture with me.

I wind my long blonde locks into a messy bun on the top of my head, take a deep breath, and leave the sanctuary of my bedroom. Right now, it's the one space where Rowan isn't (usually) allowed, the one place where I can drop the act. But out here, in the hallway, in the rest of the house – in the rest of the world, even – it's all about keeping up appearances. The show must go on, and I'm the leader of this particular shitshow. The ringmaster in the circus that is my life, and just when I thought I'd finally put my silly, messy days behind me, and that I could live a normal life, happy ever after.

I step out onto the landing. It's a large space with a polished wooden floor that gleams in the soft lighting coming in from the south-facing floor-to-ceiling window. Even on a cold March day like today, the room is flooded with natural light, which is something I'm really going to miss about living here. Four bedrooms branch off from the landing, and with two more bedrooms up another flight of stairs (we call the top floor the kids' floor) and more bathrooms than we could possibly use, the house feels so big, and kind of empty. It's as though, since my and Rowan's relationship went sour, the love that filled the rooms is gone, leaving cold, open spaces in its wake. Still, there's always the natural light, and even on the dark days it keeps me here, pushing on, until I can make things right.

The grand staircase is the centrepiece of the house, winding elegantly from the landing, its mahogany banister curving ever so smoothly as it leads the way downstairs. The steps themselves are made of rich, dark wood, covered with a cream carpet that runs down the centre. Most of the steps creak as you step on them, because this is an old house, and no amount of trendy paint colours or smart lighting can remove decades and decades of memories from a well-used staircase. It survived the renovation. It's too beautiful to replace, even if a new one might be silent, with a glass balustrade that would be far easier to take care of. As corny as it sounds, this staircase is kind of like my relationship with Rowan now. It looks perfect but get too close and you'll see how broken and tired it is.

I almost lovingly glide my hand down the banister as I head downstairs, as though I'm going to miss it, hoping that Rowan will care for its wood like I have been doing for the coming-up-to three years I've been living here – happy for a bit more than two of them, so it's not so bad.

As I reach the bottom of the stairs, I find Rowan and the boys eagerly waiting for me by the front door.

'Are you ready?' Rowan asks excitedly.

'I am,' I reply, mustering up as much enthusiasm as I can, as I pull on my Ugg boots.

'Okay, boys, let's do it,' Rowan announces.

He practically throws open the large front doors and the boys charge out. Rowan hangs back for me and, as the two of us walk outside together, my jaw drops.

There, parked on our front driveway, is a shiny white Porsche, wrapped up in a red ribbon, with the biggest golden bow I've ever seen stuck to the bonnet, like some kind of extreme hood ornament.

'Happy Mother's Day,' Rowan practically sings as

he snaps a photo of my reaction on his phone. Christ, no doubt that will be on his Instagram later.

He's bought me a car. Why the hell has he bought me a car?

'Do you like it?' Archie asks me, probably puzzled by my seemingly muted – but actually stunned – reaction.

'I love it,' I tell them, turning on my smile, running over to give them both a big hug.

Rowan takes another photo.

'Sorry, I'm just in shock,' I tell them. 'I really do love it. It's gorgeous, it's just such a surprise.'

'We just wanted to show you how much we love and appreciate you,' Rowan says as he crashes our hug, wrapping us all up in his big arms.

'Let's get in,' Archie says.

'Yeah,' Ned says, hot on his heels.

Rowan keeps his arm around me for a moment and lowers his voice.

'*I* want to show you how much I love you,' he adds, keeping the smile firmly fixed on his face for the boys' benefit.

I smile, ever so slightly, keeping up the act for the boys, but with no idea what else to say or do.

A car. A fucking car. He knows we're over, he knows I'm moving out just as soon as I can, and yet he's buying me a car? Like a car can fix what he's done. Ha. Not even a Porsche, buddy. I'm not accepting it – in fact, I'm not even going to drive it, not even once.

Except...

'Where is my car?' I ask, rather naively, because I've no sooner asked the question than the answer has occurred to me.

'This is your car,' Rowan insists.

I stare at him expectantly, not saying another word until he gives me a real answer.

'I got rid of it, obviously,' Rowan replies. 'Well, you don't need it now, you have a Porsche! The other mums are going to be so jealous!'

'And where is your car?' I ask, realising his Jag is nowhere to be seen.

'I'm picking it up tomorrow morning,' he tells me. 'While I was getting the, you know, paintwork cleaned, I thought I might as well get a valet and a service. Don't worry, I know you'll be taking the kids to school, so I'll get a taxi.'

Okay, so maybe I am going to have to drive it. For fuck's sake. Why on earth would he think that, with the way things are between us, swapping my car for this new one would be something I would respond well to? And that comment about making the other mums jealous – I hate being lumped in with the mums. Why can't I make the men jealous? Why do I need to make anyone jealous? Why can't we all just have what we have, what we've worked hard for, and enjoy it? Why does life in this stupid village have to be a competition? And, of course, I moved in with the most competitive man here.

I know what you're thinking, I sound like an ungrateful cow, because someone just bought me a Porsche and I'm whining, but you don't know what I've been through. Yes, okay, he's trying to make things right, I suppose, and that's something, but it's just not going to work, unfortunately. The damage is already done.

4

Do you ever have one of those days where you think, I know, I'll do some sorting out, but then you totally pull everything out of place in the room you plan to sort, only to find yourself amongst the mess, sitting in the middle of the floor, thinking to yourself: why did I do this? When will I learn that, when I think the mood is striking where I want to have a big clear-out and clean-out, I don't actually want that at all, and I would do well to just wait for the feeling to pass? It's never worth opening up a messy box, because you're only going to have to sort it out to get it all back inside.

I'm sitting in my bedroom, surrounded by a sea of things that I know I'll have to pack when the time comes for me to move out. It's a strange sensation, knowing that I'm basically living here on borrowed time now, and naturally knowing this means that my patience for all the silly village formalities isn't what it used to be. The endless brunch meetings and coffee mornings with the yummy mummies no longer feel all that important to endure. After all, they won't be my problem for much longer (it's an unstated but widely known fact that only families fit their wanky social aesthetic), so if pretty soon I'm going to be alone, just me, no Rowan, no kids – none of them are going to have time for me anyway. So I'm pretty much checked out, unless it's something for the boys, of course, and then I'll be there with bells on.

One thing I'm certain of in all of this mess is that I want to make sure the boys will be okay when I'm not around any more. I may have only been their mother-type figure for a couple of years or so, but I love them.

As I sort through my belongings, I spot one of the boxes that I pulled out of the cupboard. I say 'spot', but, if I'm being honest, I know deep down that the only reason I'm even sorting my things to begin with is because I want to open this particular box.

Ever since Lisa potentially recognised me at the school gates, my old life has been on my mind – and deep-diving into this box of memories has been all I could think about. But opening this box is about more than simply opening a box because it opens up so much more than the cardboard. It's about unlocking a compartment in my mind that I usually keep tightly locked, but every now and then, something small wiggles its way in, prying open the door, and I allow myself a moment to gaze into my old life, and think about what could have been, before slamming the box shut and returning to reality.

And just like that, it's in front of me, and I'm opening it up, and taking out the first item: a copy of a magazine. *My* magazine.

I was fresh out of uni when I started *Starstruck*, a music magazine – one that I wanted to be different from all the other music mags out at the time. Back then, when I was in my early twenties, I had lots of friends who were in bands and so I wanted the magazine to be something more personal than the gossipy pieces I was used to reading. I wanted it to feel like it was made by the fans, for the fans, with a dose of insider info you just didn't get anywhere else. Yes, I was a journalist, but that almost felt like it came second to what I really was, I was practically one of the band when I was on tour, part of the family even, with the bands that I was especially close with. I loved nothing more than disappearing on tour for days at a time, getting to live that rock-star life, but not actually needing to have any music talent (that said, that never seems to hold most gigging musicians back). Often I would be there under the guise of writing a review, or doing an interview, but the reality is that those things rarely took more than an hour, and the truth is that I was there because I wanted to be, and because people wanted me there too. God, I loved it. I lived for it, just counting down the days until the next time I could jump on that tour bus and head off with my friends.

It's funny, I think everyone thought I was some kind of groupie given that there were a handful of bands I was on touring terms with, but we really were a family, everyone had their roles, and I loved being the (usually only) steady female influence on board. If the tour manager was the daddy – the one in charge, telling everyone what to do, keeping everyone in check – then I was the mummy, the soft touch, the one who cared for the guys when they were drunk rather than yelling at them. I like to think that's why I know what I'm doing with Archie and Ned, despite not being their mum, because I had a lot of practice with much bigger kids. Rock stars made kids seem quite easy to take care of.

The next thing I pull out is another magazine, this one from a later date, when my little magazine was taken under the wing of a tabloid newspaper, the

Daily Scoop, after I made the move from Leeds to London and I started writing it for them to give away as a supplement with their paper. I have every copy at my parents' house in Leeds, but in this box of memories, I keep two magazines, one from our humble beginnings, and one from when we hit the big time. I wish I'd known, when I made the change, that it would be the beginning of the end.

There are all sorts of things in this box. Signed CDs, plectrums and drumsticks given to me by various musicians after their shows – I could probably clean up on eBay, and I may well need to, when I'm out on my arse here. But the thing I'm looking for, the main reason I'm opening this box, is for the photos. Yes, I know I sound like I am one thousand years old, but it was still cool (although only just about) to take a disposable camera around with you back then – and even when we made the switch to digital, it didn't feel right, not printing them out, not holding the photos in your hands to look through them or put them on the walls. It's funny because these days we pretty much accept that all of our photos are just data that we push around in the digital world. I'll take pictures on my phone, post them to Instagram, and then leave them to live happily in the cloud. I miss having real photos, when I realise that.

I pull the photos out and the first thing I see are pictures from the last time I toured with Two For The Road. Wow, you never hear of them any more, they were one of those bands who got way too big way too fast and they let it go to their heads. There was Eddie, the sexy frontman, a guy who had so much charisma he needed multiple girlfriends to help him manage it. Well, when I say girlfriends, I don't mean that they were his girlfriends – although more often than not they were someone else's. Then there was Ben, the guitarist, Mark, the bassist, and then Luke, the drummer.

I hold my breath for a moment as I look at a photo of me and Luke, him with his arm around my waist as we both pose for a photo in some dimly lit, grubby backstage room. I had the biggest crush on Luke for years and years, and I never thought he would ever like me back until one tour, when Two For The Road were just starting to hit the big time, when he told me that he felt the same way. It took us a while to get together, thanks to all sorts of reasons, but eventually we did.

I actually lived with him, in London, for a little while when I first moved there – that's the first time I felt like I was getting my happy ever after. I thought I had a good job at a big newspaper, a cool flat where I lived with my boyfriend and our dog – but it was actually Buddy, my chihuahua, who lasted the longest out of all of the above. He sadly passed away last year but having him in my life for a decade made everything feel so much easier. All of the bad times feel better when you have a dog around, someone who loves you unconditionally, something to care for when you don't even feel like caring for yourself.

Luke Fox, on the other hand, was a different kind of dog. I thought he was great, he was there for me when I needed him, and I stood by him through his problems with drugs, and when we were out the other side of it all I thought that was it, the bad stuff was behind us, it was all going to be okay. However, the first tour he went on without me, it turned out that he not only loved doing drugs more than he loved me, but he loved doing random groupies even more than he loved doing drugs. He's not so much my one that got away, more the one I was lucky to get away from. Honestly, it was a really strange moment, when my editor thought it would be a good idea for me to be the person who broke the story about him. It was therapeutic, in a way, and deeply traumatic in others.

Ah, well, good riddance to that lot, they were all dirtbags anyway. So were most bands back then – definitely all of the ones that I knew, or had to work with.

I flick through more photos, looking at my younger self, seeing how happy I looked. We all thought we were so cool back then, that we were living the dream, that our lifestyle was this amazing thing that everyone else wished they had. Looking back now, we weren't living the dream at all, it was a nightmare at times.

Things that seemed so normal at the time are so obviously the biggest red flags now. In this day and age, with so many people coming forward to expose their past bad experiences with celebrities, I often see people asking the question: why didn't they say anything sooner? Honestly, I was there, and believe me when I say that none of us realised that we actually could.

The things I experienced, or that I saw, were all things that we were made to feel were normal. It was just a given, that the rich, handsome celebrity was going to pick someone to go back to his hotel room, and you were supposed to hope you'd be chosen as the lucky one. Oftentimes things didn't even feel like a choice you were making, it was just the done thing, and everyone made you feel like you were so, so fortunate to be there. That's the thing, when you're in a bad situation, but you can see so many girls so willing to take your place, it tricks your brain into thinking that maybe things aren't bad, maybe you're just being silly. My blood boils when I think of some of the men I encountered back then, and some of the stories I heard from others, and I'm so happy that people are being called out now.

I find one picture in particular, of me and Luke, and I can tell from the state of him that he was fresh out of the hospital (an accident, courtesy of his drug problem), and we're both smiling, like we're on top of the world, and I just want to grab that poor girl and hug her and take her away from it all. I went through so much, so young, and if I ever have kids, I would hate to think of them experiencing the same.

It wasn't all bad memories. Sure, there are lots of them dotted along the timeline, but when things were good, they were great. I had so much fun – I've probably forgotten more than I remember – and I made the kind of memories that most people don't get the chance to. I remember back when I was at school, and I was first getting into music in a big way (assuming we don't count how obsessed I was with the Spice Girls back in the nineties), I would put posters on my walls and lie on my bed listening to albums on my allegedly portable CD player (which seems laughably unportable, compared to the iPod I eventually got for my sixteenth birthday) and I would fantasise, dreaming up all these different scenarios, imagining them playing out like movies in my head. I would think about my favourite bands, me going to see them, my favourite band member spotting me in the crowd, picking me – a socially awkward teenage mosher still in school – out of a sea of other dorky teenage girls, him totally falling for me – despite him being rich, famous and ultimately able to get any girl he wanted. I would think about touring with them, being on the bus, hanging out backstage at their shows. I never thought in a million years that any of it would happen but I did it, I made it, I got myself there.

It's funny, when I was a kid I would look at photos of my parents and cringe at their outfits. I could never get my head around how painfully uncool they were, how they must have known, at the time, that they looked like dorks with their silly hairstyles and their not-at-all stylish clothing. Now, however, I am willing to admit that they may well have been the height of style and coolness at the time, because I am looking at pictures that span enough years to see the same in myself. I mean, come on, there's a whole chunk of time where I wore what was basically a school uniform – for fun. Even if I wasn't in full fake school uniform, I still loved a tie. When I was at school, I would whinge about having to wear my dull uniform every day, but then I would wear fashion ties basically all of the time. In fact, if I remember rightly, I used to wear ties on non-uniform days, except I would pair them with enormously oversized baggy jeans (the kind that completely hide your feet) and whatever Tammy Girl fishnet top I had recently acquired. I remember a time when I used to go to this tattoo and piercing place, and what I really wanted was to get cool tattoos and a nose ring, and an eyebrow bar, and maybe my lip done – but I was of course too scared, and my mum and dad would have killed me, so instead I used to get these rainbow-coloured hair extensions done there. It was just some guy, with a glue gun, who would attach these brightly coloured pieces of rainbow. These days I won't blow-dry my hair without using heat protection spray, and back then I was letting random guys put glue in my hair.

I'm not quite sure if wearing a pair of jeans under a dress with a seriously tacky belt is better or worse and, if I were to try to say something nice about the emo fringe that I rocked for a while (you know, the big thick one that swept in from the side and made it impossible to see where you were going), at least it covered my eyebrows. My eyebrows, over the years, went on a real journey, and not a nice one like a holiday, a chaotic one, like *Lord of the Rings*.

Eventually, I get to the photos of Dylan King – yes, *the* Dylan King, the frontman of The Burnouts. If anyone (let's say human, otherwise Buddy the chihuahua would have it in the bag) could claim the title of 'love of my life' then it would be Dylan King.

The first photo shows me smiling almost manically as Dylan squeezes my face and kisses me on the cheek. With Dylan, I really do look happy, and do you want to know the secret (and this might only apply to musicians, although I can't say gymfluencers are any less complicated)? The fact that things between us were platonic. Dylan and I were best friends, together through thick and thin, and the fact that I was potentially the only woman on the planet who he wanted around him but didn't want to sleep with made me feel more special than any man who has ever actually desired me has.

The thing you need to know about Dylan is that he was a nightmare at the height of his fame. He drank too much, he slept with lots of girls, he was a true bad boy with no respect for the rules, a rock-star rebel, and his antics probably paid the mortgages of half of Fleet Street – there will be journalists who retired on the money they made while the legendary Dylan King was at large. Not this one, though, oh no, because I was his friend, so I spent my days trying to help him. If he went missing, I found him. If he fucked up, I cleaned up his mess. I remember one night, in the middle of nowhere, running around some town all night trying to find him, to make sure he was sober and on the tour bus the next day. But I found him, and I got him where he needed to be, and okay, he wasn't sober, but the point is I had his back.

Things were great between us until one day, back in 2014, when he called me up with some shocking news. He told me he had got someone pregnant, although that wasn't the shocking news because, with the number of girls he slept with, statistically it seemed like there should have already been a few Little Dylans running amok – if you don't count the Little Dylan in his pants, to use the name we all so lovingly gave his penis.

The shocking part of the tale was that he had hired a publicist to manage the 'crisis' and that somehow this publicist had convinced him to get married to the pregnant girl – a wannabe glamour model called Crystal Slater – whom he hardly knew! I'm sure it goes without saying but that turned out to be a terrible idea, the twins turned out not to be his, and while all of this felt pretty on-brand for the infamous Dylan King, the original top shagger, my accidental involvement – and subsequent brief brush with tabloid fame – pretty much marked the beginning of the end for me. I wonder if that's why Lisa recognised me, if somewhere in the back of her mind she recalls seeing me on the front of a newspaper, branded (wrongly, of course, but that never seems to bother tabloid journalists) as the woman whom Dylan was cheating on his wife with.

It was such a silly thing, a non-event, the kind of night out we had all the time. Still, the press ran with it, and for a while I went from being someone who silently reported the news to actually being the news. Nicole Wilde: Homewrecker. I cleared my name, of course, and life did get a little better before it got worse. It wasn't too long after that when I realised I needed to get out, I couldn't live that lifestyle, or in that world, any more, I just wanted to be normal and happy and secure – although that hasn't exactly materialised either.

Looking back, it all seems like such a mess. So much of it was so wrong. I chew my lip thoughtfully for a second. I was happy, though, for the most part, and that's the part I miss. I miss the excitement, the buzz of being with the band, living on tour buses, sleeping in beautiful hotels, and having my tour family. Did you ever have a sleepover, when you were a kid? All of your best friends piled into your bedroom, your poor parents frazzled looking after you all, none of you wanting to sleep, laughing and screaming and having a blast all night long. It was like time didn't exist, like a normal tomorrow wasn't coming, the only thing that existed was the night. That's exactly what life on tour was like. When things were great, I loved it.

Of course, that's easy to say now, when I'm so, so unhappy. Everyone on the outside gawps in at me and thinks I have the most perfect life. They see the big house, the dream man, the gorgeous kids and every part of our Instagrammable existence and they think it's a dream come true – but it's just a dream. A nightmare at times. Right now, and for the foreseeable future, I am trapped here. This isn't a life, it's a show, and I'm playing a part – but I am working on writing myself out of it.

I stare at the photo of me and Dylan, looking deep into the eyes of my much younger, fresh-faced self, and for all the mess and the chaos and the bad people I was surrounded by, I see a sparkle in my eyes. A genuine happiness – I look like I'm home, unlike when I'm here, my actual home, and I just feel this huge hole inside, one that I can't seem to fill.

I place the pile of photos back inside the box, followed by the access-all-areas passes, the signed CDs –

all of it – one item at a time, slowly returning my memories to the confines of the box, to never be thought of again – well, until the next time my past life pops into my brain. Today feels different, though, somehow, I don't quite seem to be able to close the memory box in my brain quite as easily as I return the cardboard lid, securing it in place before popping the box back inside the wardrobe.

I turn around and see that I've left the photo of me and Dylan lying there on the carpet. I pick it up again and stare at it, almost accusingly, as though it re-moved itself from the box to mess with me. I run my fingers over the edges of the photo, remembering the good times, the secrets we shared, the bond we had with each other – one that I know I've never been able to find with anyone since. And then I think about what happened between us, how our decisions tore us apart, and the pain of losing his friendship still makes my heart ache.

I head towards the wardrobe before almost imme-diately stopping in my tracks, turning around again, and heading for my bed. Instead of returning the photo to the memory box, I decide to put it in my bed-side table drawer, hiding it under various bits and pieces – why? I don't know. I have no idea why I'm not only keeping it from the box, but hiding it too.

The past is the past, and it's not good for me to be constantly raking it up, but my present is a mess and my future is so uncertain. Right now, letting my brain wander back to happier times is a welcome break from reality.

But reality is what it is, and the past is the past, so it's time to close the drawer and crack on with things.

For now, at least.

5

I used to dread Monday mornings when I was a kid. Sometime, usually around Sunday lunchtime, the impending sense of doom would set in, and that would be it, my weekend would be over, and I would just miserably count down the minutes until the school week started. But then, when I grew up, that feeling just sort of went away. Sure, I had work, but I never dreaded it like I did school. In hindsight, I suspect the reason it felt so stressful was because school – at least when I went – was so needlessly strict. There was no benefit of the doubt, no reasonable excuse for being late, no leeway for accidentally leaving something in the car. It was that fear, that I might displease one of the militant sticklers for the rules, that had me panicking every day. Mondays in particular, though, because, after two days off, it always felt so much worse.

Interestingly, even though I don't have to go to school any more, I get that feeling on a Sunday again, now that I'm the school-run chauffeur to Archie and Ned.

Obviously I don't have to go to school but my mornings are a chaotic whirlwind of getting the kids ready, making sure they have everything, and making sure they get there on time – because it's me who gets it in the neck if they don't.

The school run is always chaotic. The boys scamper around the house, searching for misplaced shoes, backpacks and homework – and I help them as my much-needed cup of coffee grows cold. I feel like my own mum, as I shout out half-hearted empty threats about what will happen if they're late, but they always seems to fall on deaf ears.

But while I'm usually delighted that I never have to go to school again, I would probably happily swap where I'm heading right now for PE and double science – I've been called for a meeting with some of the other mums.

I was accosted at the school gates by Rafe's au pair, telling me that Rebecca, his mum, would like to see me at Lily's café for a meeting about the kids.

Knowing that my days in this village are numbered, I've been doing a great job of winding down my strictly social obligations, but when it's about the kids, I show up, so that's where I am now, at Lily's, to find out what fresh hell today has in store.

I park outside the café and practically scowl at *the* car – which I don't really want to refer to as my car – as I lock it. I don't mean to sound ungrateful, really I don't, and an I'm-sorry Porsche is definitely leagues above an I'm-sorry bunch of flowers, but somehow that just makes me even angrier, because it implies that if the sorry is expensive enough, it can cancel out even the most despicable of betrayals. Spilled a cup of coffee on the carpet? That's a box of chocolates, at least. Forgot an anniversary? Breakfast in bed will do it. Kissed the au pair behind your back? Oof, that's big no-no, that's got to be a trip to Italy, at least. All I'm saying is, it's interesting that what Rowan did to me is something that he thinks a Porsche can cancel out. It doesn't even come close.

Lily's is a quaint little café, the kind of place that is always warm and welcoming. The aroma of freshly brewed coffee mixed with the comforting scent of baked pastries wafts through the air – it's hard not to follow the scent, heading for the counter, where the urge to order everything is overwhelming. Sunlight streams in through the large windows – even on cold days like today – casting a golden glow over the cosy, mismatched furniture.

But then my eyes land on their table, the mums, all waiting patiently for me so that the meeting can start. I swear it's darker over there, where they're sitting, because even the sun finds them a bit much. It's almost as though they've drawn an invisible circle around themselves, creating an impenetrable bubble of hostility and drama. I can see them talking between themselves, in hushed tones, their body language intense as I approach them. Of course, as I rock up at the table, it's fake smiles as far as the eye can see. I suppose it's easy to be two-faced, when you have Botox and fillers and a face full of make-up. Everyone looks perfect, always, like the scene at the end of *The Stepford Wives* – but these women are the baddies, in my universe.

Rebecca Rollins – Rafe's mum – has assigned herself the role as queen bee, and as such has positioned herself in the centre of the table. To her left there is Carolyn and Teresa, and on her right Deanna. Their kids are in Archie's main friendship group, so not only do I see a lot of them, but it's often about dumb, unimportant shit – even completely made-up things like setting boundaries over what levels of pollution the kids will be exposed to at different people's houses *in the same village.*

Rebecca, Carolyn, Teresa and Deanna are the busiest, nosiest and most involved mums in the village, but with Rebecca presenting herself as some sort of boss-level mum, the others have always sort of blurred into one for me. They're like her henchmen, and willingly so – the kind of extras you see killed off in movies because they do nothing for the plot. To be honest, I think that only makes them more dangerous, they're like Rebecca's spies, all reporting back to her. They are always in the know – and even if they're not, they believe they are, which is often worse – deeply entangled in the school activities, village events and the lives of other families. And while Archie is friends with their kids, and they involve me in all of their never-ending lists of things, I don't feel like they've ever really accepted me as one of them – one of the mums. I often wonder if it is because they don't see me as a real mum, given that I'm not Archie and Ned's birth mum (which would be silly and infuriating), but then other times I wonder if it's a class thing, because for some reason, to them, being a northerner is regarded as some kind of social disadvantage. Whatever it was, it always made sense to keep my past life a big secret from them, because imagine if they knew I used to run around with rock stars.

Why should any of it matter, in the grand scheme of things? I would never judge anyone for their past, or their accent – but I guess a floozy of a northerner like me would say that, wouldn't I?

I take a deep breath and force a smile on my face as I join them.

'Hello, ladies,' I say brightly – even I'm impressed by how genuine that sounded.

'You're late, Nicole,' Rebecca remarks with an obnoxious hint of self-satisfaction.

I look at my watch. I'm not late, I'm just not early.

'I'm here,' I say simply, in no mood for additional drama. Rebecca might have nothing better to do today but I need to get home and get some work done.

Rebecca, ever the centre of gravity, clears her throat before she gets started.

'Well, you're here now, and we have something very important to discuss,' she begins. 'It has come to my attention that our children have learned a swear word – the W word.'

The other women gasp. I, on the other hand...

'Which one?' I ask curiously.

Rebecca's eyes widen.

'Some of us only know the one,' she points out. 'It

rhymes with anchor, and I certainly don't use it. We need to work out which child learned it and where they learned it from.'

Oh my God, this is some sort of witch hunt. That's why we're here, to try to work out which child learned a bad word, and where they picked it up. I cannot believe I'm taking time from my work to do this. And surely it's impossible to work out where it came from, right?

As Rebecca turns to Teresa, with a serious look on her face, I guess not.

'Teresa, you recently took Art to that grotesque indoor playground, in the city, didn't you?' she says accusingly.

Ahh, yes, because any child who visits London is automatically enrolled in Fagin's gang.

'It was his cousin's birthday party,' Teresa says in her own defence.

'Perhaps he picked it up there,' Rebecca suggests.

I frown at the suggestion that Art must have picked up the swear word from an inner-city kid – what a snobby, gross insinuation.

'Absolutely not,' Teresa insists.

'Maybe they heard a parent say it,' Deanna reasons, trying to defuse the tension that is growing around the table already.

'Not in my house,' Carolyn insists firmly.

'Nor mine,' Rebecca adds. 'Deanna, are we to take this as an admission of guilt?'

'Obviously not,' she replies, her voice wobbling, horrified to have been accused for simply speaking.

That's when everyone realises I'm yet to say anything, so all eyes land on me. I've made myself seem suspicious by simply refusing to participate.

'Look, I don't know where they've learned it either,' I reply calmly, keeping my voice steady. 'But surely all that matters is that we tell them it's a bad word and that they shouldn't use it – does it really matter where they learned it, if they know that it's wrong?'

'Sounds like something a guilty party would say,' Rebecca tells me, clicking her tongue. She pauses for a moment, her gaze moving around the table before landing on Deanna again. 'But I suppose you're right – unless, Deanna, didn't you have family visiting from Stoke?'

Carolyn gasps, as though Rebecca has just uncovered the smoking gun.

I cringe. What the hell is wrong with these women?

As I pushed my chair back, I force a smile across my face, hiding my irritation.

'Listen, I need to head out,' I tell them, the tension in the air still thick. 'But I'll have a word with Archie and make sure he knows it's a naughty word – not that I've heard him say it – but perhaps you can all do the same. But I need to go now. I have work to do.'

'Oh, Nicole, always working,' Rebecca points out with a sigh. 'Perhaps you need to focus a little more on that family.'

I notice her choice of words – 'that family' instead of 'your family'. It's like she's always reminding me that they're not my kids.

'Never mind that,' Deanna says, clearly gearing up for gossip. 'Nicole, did I see you getting out of a new Porsche?'

I bite my lip, feeling slightly embarrassed.

'Oh, yes,' I say casually, almost as though I'd for-gotten already. 'Rowan and the boys got me it for Mother's Day.'

Rebecca gives me a knowing smile.

'Come on then, what has he done?' she asks.

'What do you mean?' I reply.

'Rowan,' she continues. 'What has he done wrong? He must have done something if he's buying you a nice car like that.'

Her eyes sparkle with curiosity as she persists.

'When Martin pranged my Bentley, he bought me

a diamond ring,' she tells me.

'I got this Rolex when Thomas ran over the cat,' Deanna joins in, showing me the watch on her wrist.

'And Carolyn, when there was that big misunderstanding with your Keith, and that horrible girl from his office, he bought you that villa in the south of France, didn't he?' Rebecca says on Carolyn's behalf. Carolyn just nods.

Bloody hell, I should hope he did.

I let out a polite laugh and bat my hand, my forced smile still holding strong.

'No, nothing,' I reply firmly. 'Rowan hasn't done anything wrong. It was just a lovely Mother's Day present from him and the boys, that's all – see you ladies later.'

I keep my smile firmly in place as I head for my new car, knowing full well that the ladies think I'm deluded, that Rowan has done something terrible behind my back, and that I'm kidding myself that he hasn't. Well, the joke is on them, because I know exactly what Rowan has done, and why he's bought me this car. Then again, that doesn't exactly make it much better, does it? And how cliché of Rowan, to tackle a problem by doing exactly what his rich mates would do. Ergh, I hate that the other mums are right, but there is no way it's going to work on me.

6

I can't believe it's lunchtime as I finally pull up at home. I feel frustrated that I haven't been able to start work yet. See, this is the problem when you work from home, especially when you're self-employed, everyone seems to think you have unlimited time and ultimate flexibility to do whatever you want, whenever you want.

The driveway stretches out from the main road, smoothly paved and lined with neatly pruned mature trees. It's nice to see spring creeping up on the branches, and to think that summer will be here before we know it.

It's a long driveway with space to park several cars outside the house – not that anyone pays much attention to the cars when they're standing in front of the main event.

The house itself is an impressive, huge and modern renovation with a minimalist design. The smooth white render contrasts beautifully with the anthracite-grey frames of the windows and doors – and with so much of the house being glass, not only does natural light flood the place, but the modern lighting inside carries out into the garden, making the place glow in such an inviting way.

The house is surrounded by a large garden, which is edged with more mature greenery, meaning that when you're here, it feels like there is nowhere else in the world, as though nothing exists beyond the boundary of the garden. It used to feel soothing but now it just makes me feel isolated.

As I pull up, I'm surprised to see Rowan standing on the driveway, inspecting his car with a frown on his face, because he told me he was out all day today. He catches sight of me, so I can't really drive off and wait for him to leave, not without making things more awkward, anyway. It's funny how, aside from the public appearances and putting on a happy front for the kids, Rowan and I feel like complete strangers now. It's hard to believe that just a couple of months ago, we were sharing a bed, planning our future together. In hindsight, I suppose we had our fair share of problems in our relationship, but then again, no relationship is perfect, is it? I was willing to accept the bumps and obstacles, to persevere and build a happy life together. I was in this for keeps. He was the one who fucked it all up.

I park my car next to his and, as I step out, I can't help but feel my stress levels creeping up.

'Hi,' he says, his voice a mix of hope and worry. 'Where have you been?'

His question sounds almost accusatory, as though he was expecting to find me here and it's rattled him that I didn't come straight home.

'Rebecca summoned me to a meeting about the kids,' I reply matter-of-factly, my eyes momentarily darting towards his car. 'Is your car sorted?'

Rowan nods, but there's an air of frustration around him.

'Yeah, I think so.'

I walk around the car to have a look for myself.

'What do you think? Can you see any sign of it?' he asks.

I inspect the door closely, searching for any remnants of the damage.

'No, no sign of it,' I confirm, keeping my expression neutral.

Rowan's brows knit together as he shakes his head angrily.

'I still can't think who might have done it,' he says – he's been saying this ever since it happened last week.

'Have you double-checked the video doorbell?' I ask him. 'There must be something on there.'

'Yeah,' Rowan answers, growing more frustrated by the second. 'But there's nothing there. Hopefully, this is an end to it and no one saw it. You don't think they'll come back, do you?'

I bite my lip, knowing that this situation might not be as put to bed as he is hoping.

'Oh, I'm sure they won't come back, it was probably just kids messing around,' I reply. 'But you might need to explain to people what happened, if it comes to it. The reason Rebecca called me to a meeting is because apparently the kids are running around saying the word "wanker" and she's trying to work out where they've learned it.'

Rowan winces at the mention of the word. Not because he's a prude, but because someone graffitied his car with it last week – something he is mortified about – and he's only just had it removed.

'You don't think Archie saw it, do you?' he asks, clenching his jaw. 'As if it's not bad enough someone wrote it on my car, now they've got my kid running around saying it.'

'It will be fine,' I tell him, offering him a reassuring smile. 'No one knows where it came from, and I'll have a word with Archie so he knows it's a bad word. I can sort it, I just thought I should let you know.'

I turn to head inside, leaving Rowan with the car he cares so much about – honestly, he seemed more upset about it getting graffitied than he did about basically everything else that has happened recently.

'Wait,' Rowan calls after me. 'Can we talk?'

'Can we talk inside?' I reply. 'It's cold out here.'

Rowan follows me into the hallway, and as soon as we're through the door, he starts.

'Nicole, come on, how long are you going to keep this up?' he pleads. 'I've done what you asked, I've given you space – surely you must forgive me by now?'

'Rowan, this isn't going to blow over,' I stress. 'I'll never be able to trust you again.'

'But I'm trying to make it right,' Rowan insists, as though that should be good enough.

'No, *I'm* trying to make it right,' I correct him. 'I mean, as if it wasn't bad enough that you've got yourself mixed up in some kind of protein Ponzi scheme, but to put my name down on the paperwork without telling me – to think you could drag me down with you and that I would be chill about it – is just un-hinged. Bloody Carrie knew more than I did.'

Carrie, a business acquaintance of Rowan's, wasn't someone I knew well, although I did make her dinner a couple of times. Ever so slightly in Rowan's defence, it seems like Carrie might have manipulated him, in-volving him in promoting some ridiculous protein powder that claimed to do all sorts of magical things, but surely did none of them. She even had him help recruit more investors – more people for her to scam money out of. I suppose that's how these things work, not that I'm an expert, but it seems like there isn't re-ally anything to invest in. The people at the top get the money and the fools like Rowan hand it over. The only real way to not be out of pocket is to find someone else to 'invest', to pay yourself.

At the start, I don't think Rowan knew that it was a scam, I think he really did think he was investing in something with a supposedly high return, which is why he put not only his own but also a big chunk of my savings into it. And then, I guess when he realised he was being scammed, he started working with Carrie to make our money back before I found out about it.

Oh, but I did find out about it – pretty much by accident, which made it all the more of a shock. I knew he was up to something, that's why I was sneaking around in his office, looking for clues, or evidence. To be totally honest, I thought he and Carrie were having an affair, rather than just being the business associates he claimed they were. When I found the paperwork, I didn't know what I was looking at but it led to me looking at the bank statements, and then I started to piece together what was happening.

I was furious at Rowan for putting me in such a shitty situation – especially given my job – but I knew I had to clean up the mess. He had mostly replaced our money, but that was with scammed money, so we figured the best thing to do was for him to take on more work, to not only replace our money but to pay back the people he had taken money from. For weeks, I've put my job on hold, turning away genuine clients to try to fix this mess, ensuring that no one Rowan recruited lost any money, and securing Archie and Ned's future by making sure that their stupid dad didn't damage his reputation or lose them their home. This is why I've had to stick around, because a big part of Rowan's brand is the family, and so all of his promotional work and sponsored content relies on me and the boys. I've been sticking around as a prop, to pick up the pieces, and it has worked. We're almost there.

Honestly, if this wasn't my job, I don't know how I would have handled it. I work with individuals and businesses that are entangled in scandals or struggling with their public image. It's my responsibility to transform the public's perception of them – but not by making them look good, by making them be good, genuinely, sometimes through unconventional methods. Well, after years working with rock stars, I got quite good at putting out fires – sometimes quite literally. While it's a good thing that this is my job, because it's put me in the best position to tackle what Rowan has done, it would be devastating for my career – the girl who cleans up the scandals, caught up in one of her own.

My hope is that, once the mess is cleaned up, Rowan and I can part amicably, avoiding any scandal, drama, and anyone digging up my past dalliances with the tabloid press. All I want – all I've ever wanted since I left showbiz – is a low-key life, and for Rowan to blow it up so spectacularly is infuriating and unforgivable.

'I made a mistake,' Rowan admits, his voice tinged with regret, but I've heard it so many times now. 'I just wanted to make more money, for us, for the family, for our future – so you don't have to work.'

'I like to work,' I tell him firmly. 'I like to help people. I don't like ripping people off.'

'Look, Carrie had me all confused about it, I didn't realise it was wrong, and I didn't mean to get you involved, I just saw it as our money, our investment,' he explains.

I can't help but roll my eyes.

'It still makes me laugh to think that, at first, I thought you and Carrie were sneaking around together because you were having an affair,' I say wryly. 'Now I almost wish you had been.'

'You don't mean that,' Rowan says, panic creeping into his voice. 'And look, I need you, look how you've fixed everything – we make a great team.'

'Rowan, please, just let me get on with this,' I beg. 'And then let me go. We both need a fresh start.'

'But the boys,' he insists.

'The main reason I'm still here is for the boys,' I snap back. 'So that when I do leave, they still have a house.'

Rowan lets out a sigh, puffing air from his cheeks. But then he finds his confidence again, his voice getting stronger as his determination grows.

'Look, I know I messed up, big time, and I know I've hurt you, but I'm going to make it up to you. I'm going to show you that you can trust me, that I'm working hard for this family, and that I love you. I'm going to win you back, Nicole. I'm going to show you that I'm the man you fell in love with.'

I really wish he wouldn't.

'Rowan, it's too late,' I tell him firmly.

'It's never too late,' he insists. 'I'm holding up my hands, dropping to my knees and begging for forgiveness, but I know that actions speak louder than words, so, just, let me show you, okay? I have a work meeting to get to, but let me make dinner tonight. When I get home, you do nothing today.'

'I have to work,' I remind him *again*. 'Now that our crisis is almost wrapped up, I need to figure out which new clients I'm taking on, get started with that...'

'Okay, okay,' Rowan says, relenting. 'But then, after that, let me spoil you and the boys tonight. Let's have a great family night. Dinner, a movie, hot chocolate and warm blankets on the sofa.'

I take a deep breath and try to be reasonable.

'I'll do it for the boys,' I tell him. 'They'll really like that – and it might take the sting out of the difficult conversation I need to have with them about appropriate language.'

Not that I'm one to fucking talk.

'Great,' Rowan says with a hopeful smile, clearly thinking he's making progress. 'And I'll even drop the boys at school in the morning, so that you can have a lie-in. You deserve it. See you later.'

He kisses me on the cheek as he passes me on his way to the door. I finally put my bag down. I head to the kitchen, switching on the coffee machine, ready to make myself a much-needed drink. As I gaze out of the bifold doors into the back garden, I can't help but think about the colossal mess we're in. Gosh, it could have been such a nice life, here, in picture-perfect suburbia, with everything any family could ever want.

It would be nice to forgive Rowan, and go back to how things were, but how happy could I really be, knowing that I couldn't trust him? I'd forever be worrying, snooping on his business, checking the bank account, questioning his friendships and business acquaintances. Even thinking about it sounds exhausting.

While I'd love to fix things, to make things right for the boys, it just isn't going to happen. I need to be happy and comfortable too, and that's not going to happen here, not with Rowan. I've accepted it. Now, Rowan needs to do the same.

7

I sink into my plush chair, behind my desk in the garden office. I love it in here, it's my one true escape from the house, which I need more than ever these days. It's one of those fancy garden rooms – the kind that feels like a real room, almost as though it has been chopped from the main house – proudly perched at the bottom of our long back garden. With its glass front, it has a view of the lawn, then the patio, and then the house itself. Not only does it give me a little distance from the house, but the wide-open view means that I can see if anyone is coming. It's impossible for anyone to get here, from the house, without me seeing them coming, so it buys me a little time to mentally prepare for unwanted visitors.

The reason I have an office out here is because my job often involves client meetings, and so having my own space away from the house is ideal for that – even if they're online meetings. Well, with kids running amok and Rowan constantly busy filming (usually noisy) content for his YouTube channel, the house can sometimes feel like a never-ending storm of chaos. At least out here I can maintain a shred of professionalism, even if I feel like a bit of a fraud, given my own recent (albeit accidental) almost-scandal.

I sit in front of my large pine desk, staring at my computer screen, thinking about my next move. I'm a one-woman show, so I can only devote my efforts to one or two clients at a time, but my services are always sought after (although I don't imagine they would be, if people found out I had almost been caught up in a scam) so I have a few to choose from.

I glance at the two proposals resting on my desk – the shortlist that I've decided to choose between, to get me back into the swing of things. One is a confectionery company and the other a musician manager, both looking for someone to help them get their businesses back on track. The confectionery company seems like it could be a good challenge because it's the kind of drama you couldn't make up. After years of having a particular celebrity front their ad campaigns for a particular box of chocolates – campaigns that focus around the slogan 'impossible not to steal' – said celebrity has been sent to prison. For stealing. The headlines are writing themselves. Then there's the musician manager, someone who has engaged in a series of relationships with female singers he has managed, none of which have lasted, so now no one wants to work with him. It's maybe not as interesting as the confectionery company, but the music industry is my area of expertise.

I have years of experience behind me now. I'm the reason Ellie-Anne Foy didn't lose the fashion collaborations she landed after appearing on reality show *Welcome to Singledom*, when someone unearthed bullying social media posts from when she was at school. It's thanks to me that Starr Haul, the haulage company, was able to turn things around when it turned out one of the higher-ups was sleeping his way through the secretaries. I've turned plenty of potential clients down too, though, because I'm not interested in enabling people, or helping them look like they're doing better – what I do is so effective because I don't simply smooth things over, I repair them. If I don't think I can genuinely clean a person or a company up, I don't work with them.

I sigh. God, after spending so much time and effort sorting out Rowan's crisis, the thought of going back to sorting out other people's messes sounds exhausting. I just need to get back into the swing of things, to find my mojo again, and it will be fine.

I lean back in my chair, closing my eyes for a moment while I think about what to do. My mind begins to drift, already thinking about things other than work, when suddenly the doorbell rings, snapping me from my thoughts – and distracting me from my work.

I jolt upright and glance around the desk for my phone.

I quickly load up the app for the video doorbell. My connection, however, decides to act up, and as I watch the little buffering wheel spin and spin, I realise it's not going to work. I let out a little groan of frustration. The whole point of having a bloody video doorbell was so that we could answer the door from the garden room, the top floor, or even the bath, without having to make a dash for the door. And yet here I am, still running to the door, hoping I make it in time before whoever it is gets tired of waiting and leaves. I usually find that delivery men are leaving before their finger has even made contact with the doorbell, and given that I'm in a bit of a mood today, I have no patience for it.

I bolt from my chair and hurry through the garden, finally making a beeline for the front door via the kitchen, only to find that, as expected, there is no one there. I've obviously missed whoever it was. Amazing. Just what I need.

I let out an exasperated, seriously overdramatic sigh as I grab my phone from my pocket, once again launching the doorbell app, only to see that it is working perfectly now. Of course it is, because I'm standing next to the bloody thing.

I replay the footage, hoping for a glimpse of something that will show me if I've missed anything important, secretly hoping I haven't so that I can get back to work. I really don't need these distractions right now. The video shows a man, casually dressed in black jeans and a blue denim jacket. A black beanie perches atop his head, obscuring his features, making it nearly impossible to discern any meaningful details about him.

He presses the bell and then, curiously, turns around to survey the garden. Eventually, he gives up waiting and strolls away. He doesn't seem like a delivery person, nor does he look like any of the neighbours or parents from school.

Satisfied I haven't missed anything important, I'm

about to close the app when he glances back at the camera, only for a fleeting moment, before he continues on his way.

I drop my phone, as though I can't stand to look at it, like it's the midday sun burning my eyes. But the phone has no sooner hit the ground when I snatch it back up to take another look.

I rewind the footage and watch it again. I gasp.

The eyes, undoubtedly familiar but frustratingly blurry, almost feel like they are haunting me. I know those eyes.

Panic flits through my mind before I manage to talk some sense into myself. No, it's not a ghost from my past, and beyond those eyes, there's nothing else to connect this stranger to the person I initially thought it might be.

With a deep exhale, I let out the tension that had momentarily gripped me. My past is on my mind at the moment, and given recent events it's not surprising that my brain is trying to retreat to a time when I was happier.

As I make my way back to the garden room, I psych myself up about work, getting back to the task of choosing a client to help next.

I'm just being paranoid. That's what it is. I need to

focus on the present and then the future. The past is the past. See, this is what happens, when you open a box of memories. It all comes flooding back, whether you want it to or not.

8

It's just a photo. It's meant to be looked at.

That's what I tell myself, as I step out of my dress, kicking it to one side, as I get ready for bed. It's been a long evening, with Rowan and the kids, playing happy families.

I sit on the edge of my bed and stare at my bedside table, and it almost feels as though the top drawer stares back at me.

I feel my breathing deepen as my heartbeat picks up the pace. Okay, this is just silly, why do I feel like I'm doing something wrong? I'm not doing anything wrong, I'm just going to look at the photo again. That's it.

Before I can talk myself out of it again, I open the

drawer, grab the photo of me and Dylan, and climb into bed with it.

For a moment, I just stare at it. At him. At myself.

It's funny. When you're younger, you tell yourself that you'll never be the kind of person who looks back at their old photos with a strange sadness. And yet here I am, doing the exact thing I swore I'd never do, but I guess it's inevitable. I suppose it gets us all, at some point, a snapshot of a different time, and when you look at it, all you think about is how you felt back then. It sounds silly but I wish, back then, that I'd known how happy I was, and my God, I was in the best shape of my life, and I genuinely thought I was chubby. What I would give to wind my body back ten years. They say your body changes when you have kids, which is fair enough, except I didn't even have Archie and Ned, and yet I feel so mumsy and frumpy in comparison to how I looked back then. I wish I'd known that I looked okay, that I shouldn't have felt so self-conscious at the time.

I suppose the funniest thing of all is that I won't learn from this. I'm in my early thirties now, and when I'm in my forties, my fifties, my sixties and so on, I'll probably keep looking back, thinking the same thing about my photos from ten years previous. You will never be younger than you are right now. It's always worth remembering that. Just, you know, not right now, because right now we are dwelling. Let's not ruin a good pity party.

Dylan was one of those men who somehow possessed endless sex appeal. He was gorgeous, sexy and seriously charming, and he did it all in a way that didn't tick the usual boxes. He had what I guess you would call an average body, not that muscular, but not carrying much extra weight either. He loved to eat, drink and enjoy himself. Like any rock star, he loved women, but I always appreciated that he didn't just go for the same young, skinny thing all the other celebrities were after – Dylan certainly didn't have a type, or care all that much about the superficial things. The tabloids always used to pitch him as the kind of guy who could make any woman weak at the knees, and the kind of lad any fella would love to go to the pub with. He had some tattoos back then, getting more and more as the years went on, which only added to his rough-and-ready bad-boy good looks. There was no denying that he was attractive.

I fancied him before I met him, because of course I did, I'm only human. Surprisingly, I didn't encounter him through work, though. I actually won a competition to meet his band, The Burnouts, backstage before one of their gigs. I was so nervous, and so excited, and then so, so disappointed when I found myself in a room with the man himself. Mikey, his brother/the guitarist in the band, seemed nice and down to earth, and the other band members seemed fine too, but when Dylan came in, giving it the big I-am, so obviously trying to impress me, I decided that I would be anything but impressed, because I didn't want to give him the satisfaction. I acted completely unbothered by his presence and, when he played me a sneak preview of their new album, I made out like I thought it was trash (even though it was really good). Dylan was shocked, then amused, and then his barriers were down. Suddenly we were getting on like a house on fire and, just like that, we became instant best friends – and we completely friend-zoned one another in the process, because that was just the way it had to be. Sleeping with Dylan wasn't the way to stick around in his life, not sleeping with him was the key to that.

In a way, I always felt special, being a constant female presence in Dylan's life, but one who wasn't there to hook up with him. We fell in this sort of strange, deep platonic love with each other, and being best friends with Dylan King not only helped my career, but he could always count on me to give him a bit of good press when the rest of the media were piling on him for something. We were always there for each other, come rain or shine, through thick and thin, whether we were in different countries or relationships – none of it mattered. Until it all went wrong, obviously.

I try not to think about it, day to day, but I miss it, I miss us, I miss him. And while I'm usually pretty good at batting away the feeling and getting on with my life, tonight I just can't seem to do it. Suddenly a few stolen glances, or even a long, lingering look at a photo, aren't hitting the spot. I need more.

I grab my laptop and set it down on my lap on top of the duvet, and then I grab my phone, because this is a two-screen military operation. One of the downsides to being friends with musicians, or even meeting them and seeing what they are really like, is that it really shapes what you listen to. Genuinely, the bands I met when I was a journalist, seeing how awful most of them were, it did what I like to refer to as 'morally curate' my playlists. Similarly, when Dylan and I fell out, I suddenly found it impossible to listen to his music any more, listening to that sexy, beautiful voice just felt too much like hanging out with him, being on tour with him, the way he would always sing me to sleep on the tour bus. Tonight, though, I don't know, something has shifted. I need to hear him, to look him up, to see how he's doing.

I fire up Instagram on my phone and look him up – something I've always been able to stop myself from doing – and see that he abandoned it, along with his other socials, years ago. He doesn't look much different in the most recent ones, a little older, with a lot more tattoos, but he's still my Dylan. From the latest photos it looks like he's still partying hard, even though it's been a long time since he was touring. I suppose, for a while, he was just famous for being famous, after he and his brother, Mikey, fell out and The Burnouts subsequently disbanded. I remember at first he did a few naff celebrity reality TV shows, and the tabloids carried on hounding him, reporting on his exploits, and I guess I just found it too hard to watch him going off the rails so I just pretended he didn't exist.

Seeing him basically drop off the face of the earth makes me feel guilty, like I should have stayed in touch, because who knows where he is now, or what he's doing?

I switch to my laptop, opening YouTube, and typing in his name. One of the first things I spot is that about six years ago he did an episode of *Step Inside*, which was a sort of *Cribs*-type show that took you inside celebrities' houses.

I chew my thumbnail as I think about opening it.

It's fine, right? It's not like I'm actually going inside his house, and it's not like he's going to know. I guess it just feels kind of voyeuristic, and weirdly intrusive, like I'm breaching his privacy, because it's not like he's going to get to see inside my house, is it? It feels unfair.

I click it and the first thing I see is a familiar front door. It's Dylan's house – obviously – the one in Primrose Hill, that I've been to countless times. It's a big, white, double-fronted detached house tucked away behind electronic gates. I watch the black front door open about an inch before I hit pause. Why am I being such a baby about this? Perhaps stepping into his house, even via an old clip of a TV show, feels too much like retreading my own steps.

In the related videos, I notice a live performance of one of their big hits, 'In the Night', from the height of their fame, so I click that. A music video feels like a better place to start.

I see Taz, the drummer, and then Jamie, who played bass. Then the camera pans to Mikey King, the quiet but super-talented guitarist – well, he was quiet back then, but after the band broke up he managed to forge himself a career as a TV presenter, so he's not all that shy these days from what I've seen on the TV now and then. Then Dylan runs out onto the stage, a blur of charisma and confidence, grabbing the mic stand as he begins belting out the lyrics. He smiles and his eyes twinkle as an arena of adoring fans sing his lyrics loudly back at him. Watching him strutting around, his shirt unbuttoned enough for his body to peek out at the crowd, his skinny jeans so tight and riding so low his boxers are pretty much the only thing keeping his bum covered up – God, it all feels like it was only yesterday.

A bra appears out of nowhere, obviously launched by someone in the crowd. Dylan picks it up, his vocals briefly interrupted by his dirty laugh as his slips his arms through the straps – much to the delight of the audience. I know, I'm probably biased because I was his friend, but they were the best band to go see live. So much fun, so much energy, such infectiously catchy songs that seemed to transcend genre. Everyone loved The Burnouts.

Watching Dylan running around on stage, doing what he does best, is like seeing a ghost, or watching an old episode of a TV show you used to love. It feels like it happened to someone else, or like it was a dream – not at all like I was there, and I was quite literally there, watching from the wings on that particular night. The memories are so vivid, but they are just so far removed from the life I have now that it all feels like it couldn't possibly have happened to me. I feel like that teenage girl again, the one who used to fantasise about running away with her favourite bands, just in a sort of strange, reversed way. Rather than thinking it will never happen, it feels like it never did, and like it certainly never will again.

I laugh quietly to myself as I watch Dylan having the time of his life, working the crowd, and the more I watch, the more I relax, the more I find myself enjoying it – and the more videos I want to watch. Perhaps this is what I need, to watch a bunch of clips, get it all out of my system, and then go back to my quiet little life – or what's left of it, anyway.

I sigh. It's hard to say, because who knows what might have happened if things had played out differently – I might have still quit the business, Dylan might still be making music, and the two of us might still be friends. But we ruined it. How? With sex, obviously. Nothing ruins a friendship like sex – no matter how good it was.

9

'Stop it,' I whisper in a breathy voice, not meaning it for a second. There's no way I want him to stop.

I squirm in my bed, making myself more comfortable on my side as he presses his body up against the back of mine, teasing me with kisses on my shoulder.

'Mmm,' I groan.

'You want me to stop doing this?' he asks playfully as his hand runs over my hip, then onto my stomach, then slowly further down my body.

'You heard me, Dylan King,' I flirtatiously tick him off – again, in no way wanting him to stop.

'Okay, I'll stop,' he says simply.

As he pulls away, taking his hand with him, his

lips no longer lightly brushing across my skin, it feels like someone has taken oxygen away from me.

I jolt up in my bed, gasping for breath, eventually realising where I am. I'm in my own bed, alone – unless you count my laptop. I must have fallen asleep, watching videos of Dylan, and then had a sex dream about him which is just, wow, an extra-special, extra-torturous way of teasing myself.

All of a sudden, I notice the doorbell ringing, which must be what woke me up, given that I turned my alarm off last night because Rowan offered to take the boys to school for a change.

I grab my phone but it's dead so, still half asleep and totally disorientated, I grab my fluffy bright-pink dressing gown, throw it on over the underwear I slept in, and hurry down to answer the door.

'Okay, okay,' I call out moodily as I fuss with the lock. I know that it's going to sound pathetic but, whoever it is, I'm actually annoyed with them for waking me up from my dream, because not only was it shaping up to be a good one, but it meant that I actually got to spend time – even imagined time – with...

'Dylan,' I blurt.

Then I slam the door shut as fast as I opened it.

I hear his laughter on the other side.

It's not Dylan. It can't be. I mean, it looked like

him, sort of, before I slammed the door in his face but... surely not? I really have plummeted to the deepest depths of rock bottom this time.

'Hello?' I call out through the door.

'Hello,' he calls back. 'I already got a good look at the dressing gown, if that's what you're worried about, so you might as well let me in.'

He laughs again.

I chew the nails on my left hand as I open the door again with my right. Then I slowly back away, as though something dangerous might be lurking on the other side of the door. Well, it's like vampires, right? If you invite them in, it's over for you.

The man opens the door the rest of the way and steps inside.

'Hello,' he says with a smile, his south London accent as friendly and cheeky-sounding as ever.

'Are you real?' I ask him.

I mean, of course he's fucking real, he's standing right there, but I don't know what else to say.

'I think so,' he laughs, patting his body down with his hands.

For a second, I just stare at him. It's Dylan, *my* Dylan, but so much about him is so different. I mean, for one thing, he's absolutely jacked. Wherever he's been, while he's been out of the public eye, one thing I can tell you is that it definitely has a gym. He's swapped his dark, messy hair for a super-short style – practically a buzz cut – which connects to his stubbly beard. I've never seen him look so... so... well, macho. He's wearing black jeans and a white T-shirt, with a black leather jacket over the top. Tattoos creep out from his sleeves, and above his neckline. He looks so stylish. I can't believe it's him. It's like someone took a photo of Dylan, who was arguably already a seriously sexy individual, and ran it through some sort of AI that makes perfect-looking men. My jaw is on the floor.

'It's been the best part of a decade,' he reminds me. 'Don't I get a hug?'

I'm not kidding, I launch myself at him. I jump into his arms, hooking my own arms around his neck, and squeeze him as though he's come back from the dead.

Dylan laughs as he holds me tightly.

'I've missed you too,' he says.

For a moment, I just stay there, in his new freakishly strong arms, smelling his aftershave, because for all the changes to his appearance, that familiarity is still there and it feels so comforting. I've never needed it more.

I force myself to let him go and then I take a step back, looking him up and down again.

'I just... can't believe you're you,' I tell him.

'Nicole Wilde, are you star-struck?' he teases. 'Are you still Wilde?'

No, I'm boring as hell. Oh, right, he means my surname. Thank God I realised that before I embarrassed myself. Well, embarrassed myself further, I am standing in here in a bright-pink fluffy dressing gown gawping at him like a fish, after all.

'Yes, still Wilde,' I reply.

He coughs and points to my dressing gown before politely looking away. I glance down and realise that, while I was violently hugging him, my belt must have loosened because one boob has popped out – thank God I fell asleep in a bra last night.

'Nothing like popping a tit to welcome guests,' I joke, trying to find myself again in all the chaos. 'Coffee?'

'Coffee is a good start,' he says with a laugh.

'The kitchen is this way,' I tell him, indicating for him to follow my lead.

As I walk ahead of him, I can't help but mouth the words 'what the fuck?' to myself as I go. I reach up and run a hand through my hair, my fingers getting tangled in the knots as I try to smooth it down. I can't even imagine how scruffy I must look right now – it's probably best I try not to think about it.

I grab my phone from my dressing gown pocket and place it on charge in the kitchen before turning the coffee machine on. Then I turn around and look at him again, Dylan King, sitting at my kitchen island.

'I'm trying to think where we were, the last time I saw you,' he says.

I mean, the last time I saw him was in my sex dream, before he woke me up with the doorbell, but I don't think that counts, does it?

'London,' I tell him.

'Right, of course,' he says. 'The last time we toured.'

My phone can't have been on again for long before it starts ringing.

'Shit, it's the school,' I tell him – not that it means anything to him.

'Go for it,' he says, encouraging me to answer.

'Hello?' I say, worried something might be wrong.

'Hello, Ms Wilde, this is Jo Morgan calling from Little Harehill School,' she says. 'We were expecting you and Mr Nutter this morning, for the career day...'

Shiiiiit.

'...thankfully the parents who were going after you arrived early, so they were able to take your slot. It means so much to Archie, that you and Mr Nutter were going to come in and talk about your jobs, the two of you both being in such fascinating lines of work – are you able to fill the 11 a.m. slot?'

I glance at my watch. Fifteen minutes – we're about ten from the school.

'Yes, of course,' I tell her. 'So sorry for the hold-up, we'll be right there.'

'Ah, fantastic,' she replies. 'I know a lot of the parents were looking forward to seeing you and your partner talk – you've got quite the crowd waiting for you.'

'Great, see you soon,' I say, trying to sound as calm as possible. Then I hang up. 'Fuck, fuck, fuck, fuck...'

'Are you okay?' Dylan asks me, concerned.

'I'm okay,' I say as I try to call Rowan but he isn't picking up. 'I'm just... fuck. I'm fucked.'

He approaches me slowly.

'What's going on?' he asks.

'I'm supposed to be doing a careers talk at Archie's school, with Rowan, his dad, but I guess we both forgot, and he's not picking up, and they're expecting me at eleven and – look at me. I really, really don't want to let Archie down, not with everything...'

I let my sentence taper off. Dylan doesn't need to know what's going on here.

Dylan places his hands on my shoulders and gives them a squeeze.

'Go upstairs, grab your things and meet me out-side,' he instructs. 'My car is outside. I'll drive you there. You can get ready in the car, and try to call your fella, and I'll get you there on time.'

'Thank you,' I tell him sincerely before dashing upstairs.

I throw on a dress, blast my hair with dry shampoo and brush my teeth, and then stuff a few items of make-up and a pair of tights into a handbag before hurrying back downstairs.

Unbelievably I'm still almost as shocked as I was to see him the first time, when I see Dylan standing in the hallway, holding a reusable coffee cup.

'I had time to make one,' he says. 'And I think you need it more than me. Come on.'

'Thank you,' I tell him, taking a swig as we hurry down the drive, to where his Range Rover is parked.

I feel like I'm in a dream, as I hop into the passen-ger's seat. I try Rowan again but he still isn't an-swering.

'Of all the times to go radio-silent,' I say to myself as I throw my phone into my bag.

'Where are we going?' Dylan asks as he fusses with his navigation system. 'You just focus on getting ready.'

'Little Harehill School,' I tell him.

He sets off almost right away, leaving me to apply my make-up in the car sun-visor mirror.

'Ahh, it's just like old times,' he jokes. 'I don't know how many times I've seen you get ready in a moving vehicle.'

'It's been a while,' I say with a laugh. 'But... come on, look at that winged eyeliner. Flawless.'

He laughs.

I have my face on in a matter of minutes. Then I check my phone, but there's still no word from Rowan. As I try to swap my phone for the pair of tights I stuffed into my bag, I drop my phone into the footwell.

'Okay, maybe I'm not as good at this as I used to be,' I say, hitching up my dress so that I can pull up my tights.

I notice Dylan's eyes land on my thighs before he almost forcibly drags his gaze back to the road.

'We're here,' he tells me as we arrive. 'I'll wait here for you.'

'Erm, thanks,' I say with a laugh. 'Sorry. This is... all incredibly weird. I'll explain when I get back.'

'So will I,' he reassures me with a smile. 'Now, go, you've got a literal minute to spare.'

I grab my bag and hurry into the school reception.

'Hi, I'm here to see Mrs Morgan,' I tell the lady behind the desk. 'I'm doing one of the careers talks.'

'I'll call her now,' she replies.

I hover in the hallway for a second, as I wait for Jo Morgan, the head teacher here, to come and get me.

'Nicole,' Dylan calls out from the doorway.

I jump – still not expecting to hear his voice.

'You forgot your phone,' he says. 'I thought you might need it.'

'Oh, thank you,' I reply as I go to grab it.

'Ms Wilde, you're here.' I hear Jo's voice behind me. 'And... you're not Mr Nutter.'

I realise she's talking to Dylan.

'No, I'm not,' he says with a smile.

'Rowan can't make it, unfortunately, he has work,' I tell her, but she's looking through me.

'You're Dylan King,' she says.

'Er...' he laughs. 'I am indeed.'

Jo's voice trembles with excitement, her hands flapping.

'Oh, this is incredible!' she squeaks. 'If Mr Nutter can't make it, and we have two slots to fill, why don't you join Ms Wilde?' she suggests. 'You seem like you're here together – I assume you know one another?'

Dylan looks at me with an amused glint in his eye,

almost like he's seeking my permission before he says anything. I feel like I'm caught between a rock star and a hard place right now, because it should be Rowan here, and Jo seems more than keen to replace him with Dylan. But, then again, Rowan isn't here, or contactable. Dylan stepping up might just smooth all of this over, and no one will even be thinking about the fact that both Rowan and I forgot all about this – that's the kind of thing that gets you in all sorts of trouble in a village like this.

I nod, still a little bewildered but willing to go with it.

'Yeah, okay,' I reply. 'I don't want to let the kids down.'

Jo can hardly contain her excitement.

'This is fantastic! Come on, let's get you both set up in Archie's classroom. The kids are going to love this!' she continues. 'Actually, you know the way, walk ahead, I'm going to see if anyone else wants to sit in. A genuine celebrity, I can't believe it.'

Walking into the classroom with Dylan by my side feels like stepping out onto a stage. The room is filled with parents, teachers and curious kids, and the moment we walk through the door, all eyes are on us. For the kids, it's not that they recognise Dylan because how could they, The Burnouts disbanded before any of them were born, but in a village like Little Harehill there aren't that many heavily tattooed rock stars strolling around.

Whispers and hushed conversations ripple through the crowd of adults at the back of the room – a crowd that is growing by the second. You can tell almost everyone recognises him and anyone who doesn't, well, I guess they're the people with their phones in their hands, frantically googling 'Dylan King'.

I sense the shift in the atmosphere as we head for the front of the classroom. All eyes are on us, and you could hear a pin drop right now. I feel like I'm in the epicentre of an unexpected storm – I just hope, whatever happens, it isn't as destructive.

I lean down to Archie as I pass him. He's looking up at me with a mix of surprise and disappointment.

'Sorry, kid, your dad got held up with work, but I've brought a friend of mine to help out instead,' I reassure him.

He nods, understanding, but it's a shame that he has to.

As we stand at the front of the classroom, even though we feel a little bit like lambs to the slaughter, I can't help but feel a sense of déjà vu too. It's me and Dylan against the world, just like it used to be – although, admittedly, it was usually me helping him clean up his messes. Still, the fact that he's here, now, returning the favour – it's as though our friendship never faded, like we never had a single day off from it, like we haven't spent a moment without one another over the last almost decade.

Jo eventually returns, an undeniable spring in her step, and she takes her place alongside us.

'Ladies and gentlemen, parents, and students,' she calls out, her voice carrying across the room and then some. 'Please give a warm welcome to our special guests today: Nicole Wilde and Dylan King!'

She introduces us like we're about to take to the Pyramid Stage at Glastonbury and, hilariously, a few of the mums 'whoop' and cheer like we are too.

I can't help but notice how some of the women's eyes follow Dylan's every move. It's like they're teenagers watching their favourite pop star. Dylan has always been a heart-throb, and time only seems to have enhanced his appeal. Then again, look at him, he's matured like a fine wine, whereas I'm maturing more like a cheese.

'Nicole is a businesswoman,' Jo tells the kids, giving them a pretty vague and totally boring description of my job – not that my job will be that interesting to kids, I suppose. '*But* Dylan is a musician.'

But! Okay, cool, she thinks I'm boring in comparison too.

'A famous musician,' Jo continues. 'One who has toured the world, been on TV, sold thousands and thousands of albums.'

Dylan clears his throat.

'Millions,' he corrects her, quite casually, given what a brag it is.

'Wow, millions,' Jo says. 'Very impressive.'

'You're not Archie's dad,' Rafe, one of Archie's friends, calls out.

'No, I'm not,' Dylan confirms. 'I'm Archie's mummy's special friend.'

He purses his lips for a second, trying not to laugh at his choice of words.

'Very special,' Jo continues. 'Ask your mummies and daddies and they will tell you that Dylan is a very talented singer.'

'What's the most people you have sang in front of?' Maggie, another kid in Archie's class, asks.

'Hmm, was it 100... maybe 120,' Dylan ponders out loud.

'That's not many,' Maggie tells him.

'Yeah, sorry, that's 120,000,' he says – again, quite plainly, given how impressive that is. 'It was at a festival.'

'You're famous?' Amelia calls out, her eyebrow raised sceptically. I'm trying to remember if I questioned a single thing when I was a child. 'I've never heard of you. Are you really famous, like Taylor Swift famous?'

'Is anyone, other than Taylor Swift, Taylor Swift famous?' he replies with a smile.

'Is it easy to make music?' Archie asks.

I don't know why it warms my heart to see him so engaged, asking questions, clearly interested in what Dylan has to say.

Dylan surveys the room before turning to Jo.

'Can I show them?' he asks her.

'Go right ahead,' she replies curiously.

'Great,' he says. 'Do you have any pencils? Oh, and some rubber bands too.'

'Store cupboard,' Ms Holmes, Archie's teacher, says as she goes to grab them.

Dylan starts gathering various boxes and containers from around the room. Some he turns upside down, and others he covers with elastic bands. He twangs and arranges different elastic bands on the containers, tuning them by ear to get the sound he wants from each one.

'Okay, here we are, musical instruments,' he tells the class. 'Who wants to try one?'

'They're not instruments,' Maggie insists with a roll of her eyes.

'They are,' Dylan says confidently. 'This whole room is full of musical instruments – the world is full of things you can make music with.'

'How do we play them?' Archie asks, clearly interested.

'However you want,' Dylan tells him. 'Like this...'

He demonstrates, grabbing a pencil and drumming out the iconic beat to Queen's 'We Will Rock You' on his makeshift drum kit. The kids burst into laughter at the familiar rhythm. I smile as I see how into it Archie is. I don't suppose he's had much exposure to music.

'Or,' Dylan continues, 'you can do this.'

He starts twanging different rubber bands, seemingly randomly, but the familiar notes of 'Twinkle, Twinkle' are there.

'Come on, give them a go,' he encourages the room. 'Parents and teachers too.'

Everyone rushes forwards to grab an instrument to try.

'I was such a big fan of yours, back in the day,' Talia, one of the mums, tells him, almost flirtatiously. 'It's nice to see you're still making music.'

Dylan laughs.

'Yeah, well, it's a little different to the old stuff,' he jokes.

'Is there any chance of the old stuff coming back?' she asks nosily. 'People would love to see The Burnouts back together.'

'And there's me thinking you really did like this,' he replies tactfully, holding up a cardboard guitar, playing a few notes.

Everyone knows that The Burnouts only broke up because Dylan and Mikey fell out. It's such a sore point, even I'm scared to mention it.

As Dylan watches the kids experiment and laugh, he turns to me, and there's a softness in his eyes that I like.

I still can't believe he's here, saving the day. He's somehow turned up right when I need him – in more ways than one – I just can't help but wonder why.

10

Dylan and I are sitting in the car together, finally alone after spending an hour with the kids. For a moment, we just sit in silence. I don't think either of us was expecting a day like today.

I grab the unfinished cup of coffee I abandoned earlier and take a swig.

'I can't believe you remember exactly how I like it,' I say.

'I can't believe you still do that,' he replies with a laugh.

I raise an eyebrow at him, feigning innocence.

'What? It's basically an iced coffee at this stage.'

Dylan laughs, shaking his head.

'It's not an iced coffee, it's a cold hot coffee,' he corrects me.

'Yeah, well, I've seen you drink "vodka surprise" from a shoe, so you can't say anything,' I tease.

Vodka surprise was a regular thing from back in the day. It was vodka with, well, whatever concoction the others fancied tossing into the glass – or the shoe, in the case of the infamous incident I'm referring to.

Dylan smiles.

'I'll take you home.'

'Thanks,' I reply, feeling a sudden rush of gratitude again.

As we set off, my curiosity gets the better of me.

'You know, I don't think I've ever seen you drive a car,' I point out. 'In fact, weren't you the man who refused to learn because you had to be sober to drive, and you weren't prepared to do that?'

Dylan laughs, and I can't get enough of hearing it.

'Yeah, well, we all have to grow up at some point, right?' he informs me. 'I mean, look at you, you've got a bloke, a big house, kids – I'm guessing that was your Porsche on the driveway, it's very nice.'

'Yeah,' I say with a heavy sigh that I can't quite mask.

'How old are the kids?' he asks.

'There's Ned, who is five, and Archie, who you met today, is nine soon,' I explain.

'Nine,' he murmurs, seemingly taken aback.

'Before you start getting your calendar out and sweating, Archie and Ned are Rowan's kids from a previous relationship,' I point out through a cheeky grin. 'I only met Rowan about three years ago.'

Dylan laughs, feigning relief.

'That's great, though,' he says. 'Family is family, right? You can see how much you care about them.'

'Thanks again for helping me out with things today,' I tell him sincerely. 'I didn't want to let Archie down.'

'Ah, it was nothing,' he insists as we drive back toward my house. 'It was actually a lot of fun.'

As we near home, suddenly, the thought of saying goodbye to him terrifies me, even if it isn't for years this time. I don't want to let him go.

'Come to ours for dinner tonight,' I insist, my voice eager. 'So we can all say thank you for saving the day.'

'Okay, sure,' he agrees. 'I'd love to. Although, I'm sure I didn't save the day.'

'Are you kidding? You were the star of the show,' I remind him, grateful for his presence. 'I didn't even end up talking about my job at all.'

'Would you like to?' he asks in an interesting tone.

I'm taken aback for a moment.

'What do you mean?' I ask.

'Would you like to talk about your job?' he repeats. 'That's why I'm here, Nic. I know all about what you do now, how you take people like me and make them look good again. That's what I need.'

I'm stunned.

'I mean... you look great,' I point out.

Although I know what he's getting at. Dylan's reputation wasn't all that great back in the day. He was known for being a bit of a tart – aren't all young male rock stars, though? – and for drinking too much, trashing hotel rooms, being a bit of a menace generally. I guess because I knew him, I knew he was a good person, under all the shit, but the world was turning on him, just before The Burnouts split. Courtesy of the tabloids, of course.

'We've been offered a reunion tour,' he tells me. 'Me, Mikey, Jamie and Taz – the original line-up back together again. But on one condition, that I clean up my act and show the world that I'm different now. And who better to help me than you?'

I shake my head, still trying to process it all.

'Of all the reasons I thought you were here, that's probably the only thing I didn't consider,' I say with a laugh. 'I would have put you needing a kidney higher up on the list than that.'

He laughs.

'Well, let's not rule that out at some point, but I'll be seeing you for dinner later, right?' he replies. 'Think about it and give me your answer then. No hard feelings if you don't think you're up to it. It's a big job. What time do you want me?'

I have to remind myself that he means for dinner.

'Six o'clock?' I suggest.

'Great,' he replies, his grin infectious. 'See you then. And think about it, yeah?'

I get out of the car, the possibilities spinning in my head. He's definitely given me a lot to think about.

11

I buzz around the kitchen, putting the finishing touches on dinner. The lasagne is baking in the oven, filling the room with that comforting home-cooked smell that goes hand in hand with such a crowd-pleasing dish. I slice through the fresh focaccia, trying to keep my nervous excitement in check. Dylan should be here any minute.

Rowan, however, isn't sharing my enthusiasm. After a barrage of questions about Dylan, our history, why he's here and so on, Rowan has gone uncharacteristically quiet, selecting wine glasses from the cupboard with an irked look on his face.

'I just don't understand why you never mentioned

that you were friends with him,' Rowan finally pipes up again.

I put down the knife and turn to face him, my patience wearing thin.

'Sorry, I guess I must not have been paying attention properly when you supplied me with the list of every friend you've ever had, ever,' I say sarcastically.

He sighs, his frustration growing too.

'I would tell you if my best friend was Kylie-bloody-Minogue,' he claps back. 'It just seems weird to me that you wouldn't ever mention it.'

'When I met you, I hadn't seen Dylan in years,' I remind him, exasperated, as I've been explaining this to him for over an hour now.

'Were you together?' Rowan asks, his tone more than a little suspicious.

My heart skips a beat.

'What do you mean?' I reply, knowing exactly what he means.

Rowan gives me a look, like he knows that I know what he means too.

'I mean, were you and him involved?' he says, slowly and clearly. 'Sexually.'

Rowan lowers his voice when he says the last word, because the kids are watching TV on the sofa at the other end of the open-plan living space. Thankfully, they're too engrossed in whatever show they're watching to pay attention to our 'boring adult talk'.

'Rowan, what part of "we were friends" are you struggling with?' I respond plainly.

'Okay, but, what, some guy turns up from your past and...?' Rowan's voice trails off, his eyebrows knitting together in that way they always do when he's stressed, confused or angry – right now, I think he's all of the above.

'...And wants to hire me to do my job, the one I'm good at,' I finish his sentence. 'I suppose if I take the job, he can just hang around for a while, we'll go through what he needs to do, and then that's it. It will be done. It's work.'

'Then why are you making him dinner?' Rowan asks.

'Because he is still an old friend,' I reply firmly.

'An old friend who you had replace me at the school today,' Rowan points out, his jealousy evident. 'It was supposed to be Archie's dad doing the talk.'

'Well, Archie's dad wasn't there, or answering his phone,' I explain, trying to maintain my composure.

Rowan's feelings, whether you think he's right or not, are totally null and void because we broke up months ago, and he knows where we stand. He has no right to be jealous.

'Tell me he isn't staying here, with us,' Rowan says, his voice almost pleading.

I pause, uncertain about Dylan's plans. Obviously, I haven't invited him to stay here, though.

'Oh, no, I would never impose like that,' Dylan's voice suddenly chimes in. Both Rowan and I turn to look at him, neither of us expecting him to be standing there.

'Oh, hello,' I say, mustering up my usual level of hospitality for any dinner guests we have.

'Sorry, I rang the doorbell, I don't think it's working,' Dylan points out.

He's wearing a pair of black jeans and a black T-shirt, with the leather jacket I saw him in earlier. Rowan, seemingly threatened, has dressed up for dinner too, in a pair of cream chinos with a white shirt, which only reminds me how different the two of them are.

'Yeah, sorry, the doorbell is rubbish,' I tell him. 'Dylan, this is Rowan. Rowan, this is Dylan.'

'Hi,' Rowan says simply, almost angrily even, as he reaches out and gives him one of those cringy manly handshakes.

'Hey,' Dylan replies – you can tell he's picking up on the awkwardness. 'Listen, I just overheard your conversation and, really, I would never overstep the mark like that. I don't want to stay here.'

'See, there you go,' I tell Rowan, hoping it chills him out a bit.

'I've actually rented the house across the street,' Dylan continues, as though it's the most normal thing in the world.

Oh, boy.

Rowan is briefly stunned into silence.

'What, Mr Campbell's house?' I ask as I lift the food from the oven.

'Is that the one with the green door?' Dylan checks.

'Yes,' I reply.

'Then yes,' he confirms with a smile. 'I thought it would be easier than travelling back and forth for like four hours a day or whatever.'

That does sound like a sensible idea, but for Rowan, the prospect of my secret rock-star bestie moving in across the street is obviously a bit much.

Mr Campbell, our cul-de-sac's octogenarian nosy neighbour, sadly passed away recently. While his grown kids are working out what to do with his house, they've been renting it out on one of those short-term letting sites.

'Are you fu—'

'Kids, dinner is ready,' I call out, cutting Rowan off. He seems seriously rattled by Dylan's presence. Definitely more so than I thought he would be, but then again Dylan has always had that effect on men, if they felt threatened by him. His confidence can be mistaken for arrogance, and his naturally flirtatious tone can be misconstrued for genuine romantic advances.

'Dylan,' Archie says, only just realising he's here, running over excitedly, grabbing Dylan for a hug.

'Hey, dude,' Dylan says, ruffling his hair.

'Dad, Dylan is the coolest,' Archie informs Rowan – much to Rowan's annoyance. 'He's a rock star and he's sold millions of songs and played gigs for loads of people and everyone at school thinks he's the best.'

'Boys, listen, how would you like to eat dinner in front of the TV?' Rowan asks them, ignoring every word Archie just said. 'The grown-ups need to talk.'

The kids can't believe their ears. Rowan usually insists on family meals at the table, without any distractions. Then again, Dylan is quite the distraction.

'Is this a trick?' Archie asks, one eyebrow raised suspiciously.

'No, boys, it's not a trick,' I reassure them. 'Go get comfortable, and I'll bring your food over.'

'And while she does that, why don't you and I take a seat?' Rowan suggests to Dylan.

'Sure,' Dylan replies.

While I serve up their dinner, Rowan steers Dylan towards the dining table.

'There you go,' he says, indicating a chair. 'Can I pour you some wine?'

'Just something soft for me, please,' Dylan requests. 'I'm trying to impress someone.'

I laugh. Rowan does not.

'With my good behaviour, obviously,' he clarifies after seeing Rowan's unimpressed expression.

I give the kids their meals and then join Rowan and Dylan at the table. I can't help but notice Rowan has seated himself opposite Dylan, next to me, rather than in his usual spot at the head of the table. I mentally roll my eyes.

Rowan takes the silver salt shaker from in front of him and sprinkles it over his food. He is terrible for putting extra seasoning on his food, before he's even tasted it.

Then he cuts his food, takes a big mouthful, and his face changes in a way I've never seen before. He coughs and splutters and then grabs his glass of wine and practically pours it straight down his throat.

'Are you okay, buddy?' Dylan asks him, concerned.

'The salt,' Rowan groans, his voice weak. 'It's not salt. It's sugar.'

I clap my hand over my mouth.

'Oh, my gosh,' I say guiltily. 'I didn't think, when I put the best shakers out, but on Pancake Day I filled it with sugar for the boys. I completely forgot, here, give me your plate, let me get you a fresh piece. You didn't use any, did you, Dill?' I check.

'No, I didn't,' he says, tucking into his food. 'I'm sweet enough.'

'So, this must be weird for you two, huh?' Rowan says, leading the conversation now that he's over the shock of the sugar. 'Friends for years, you see nothing of each other, no interaction at all, and then you just turn up out of the blue?'

He seems to be doubting our story – doubting me, not just Dylan's reasons for coming here, which annoys me, because how dare he think I'm the dishonest one?

'It was a surprise,' I say as I return to the table, 'but not weird. If anyone can help this guy turn his public image around, then who better than the person who already knows where all the skeletons are?'

'But isn't that because you helped me put them there?' Dylan teases, a mischievous glint in his eye. 'What was it we all used to say? Wilde by name...'

'Me?' I squeak playfully. 'Never.'

'Remember that night in Paris?' he says with a devilish grin.

I laugh, my mind racing back to a memory that these days feels more like something I saw in a movie.

'I'm sure everyone has been escorted from the Jardin des Tuileries at least once,' I protest.

Dylan's eyes twinkle with mischief.

'Not with their top off,' he adds.

Rowan's jaw lands right in his lasagne.

'He's exaggerating,' I insist to Rowan, trying to keep a straight face.

'I'm sure he is,' Rowan says. 'I know Nicole would never behave so appallingly in Paris.'

'Yeah, yeah, of course,' Dylan says, playing along. 'She did that in LA.'

My heart feels like it's going at a thousand beats per minute. Dylan and I only went to LA once. My mind flashes back to that night, remembering what his hands felt like on my body, the smell of his aftershave, the taste of his skin.

I glance at Dylan, the hint of a grin playing at the corners of my mouth. It's cheeky of him to bring it up here, now. It's also as though he's lit a match and flicked it into my lap. My entire body feels like it's on fire.

'Erm, your reputation is the one in question,' I remind him, getting our conversation back to where it should be.

'Does that mean you're taking me on?' Dylan asks. 'As a client.'

I'm glad he added that last part or Rowan might have boiled over.

I've been thinking about it, ever since he asked me earlier, and I have to do it. Not just because he's my friend, or because I already know him so well, which cuts out a lot of the legwork, or even because I know he's a good person deep down. I have to help him because he deserves it, and because I owe it to him. I can't help but feel responsible for him going fully off the rails, and for The Burnouts breaking up, so this is my chance to put things right.

'It does,' I confirm. 'Assuming you can still afford me. We can start tomorrow.'

'Great,' Dylan replies. 'Your place or mine?'

'Yours,' I say.

'What?' Rowan splutters in disbelief.

'You're using the garden room tomorrow, remember,' I refresh his memory. 'You've got that sponsorship meeting. Plus, it's only across the road. It's hardly a commute.'

'Perfect,' Dylan says. The he points at his food.

'Mmm, Nic, honestly, this lasagne is amazing. You've turned into a proper little housewife.'

'Thanks,' I reply, knowing he's teasing me – although I do make an amazing lasagne.

Rowan's arm suddenly wraps around me, pulling me closer to him. I feel incredibly awkward in his embrace but do my best to act normal.

'We're lucky to have her. Me and the boys,' he says proudly, as though to emphasise our set-up – or our pretend set-up, at least.

'Well, I'm easier than kids – these days, anyway,' Dylan insists.

'Then this will be a piece of cake,' I reply.

Well, I'm hoping it will be easy anyway, but if he brings up LA again, I'm not so sure.

12

I make my way across the street to Dylan's house – words I never thought I'd say.

Well, it's not his house, technically, it's the house where he's staying, but still. It felt so bizarre last night, lying in my bed, thinking about him sleeping just metres away. It's not quite the same as having him in the bunk next to me on the tour bus, but it's definitely a lot closer than the years of radio silence we endured for pushing a decade.

I'm a bag of nerves as I knock on his door. It's just Dylan, why am I letting the butterflies in my stomach get the better of me?

Eventually, Dylan answers, wearing a pair of plaid

pyjama bottoms – and nothing else. Seeing him without his shirt on sends me into shock. I can't help but admire his transformation – he's so physically fit, with bulging biceps and a body ripped with muscle. He has more tattoos than he did the last time I saw him without a shirt on. I used to know his ink like the back of my hand but now, not only has he filled in previously empty spaces, he's had lots of his scruffy old tattoos covered with new ones. They look a lot better than they used to, like they all come together, unlike before when he looked a bit like a wall that children of various ages had scribbled on when their parents weren't looking.

'Good morning,' he says with a welcoming smile.

'Good morning,' I reply, chuckling involuntarily. 'Sorry, this is just so... I don't know. Top optional, hmm?'

'Top optional,' he replies. 'Like Paris.'

I laugh. Honestly, that wasn't as bad as it sounds.

'I guess I had time to get used to the idea of us re-uniting,' he points out in an attempt to make me feel better. 'Whereas, for you, you just had me turning up at your door like Jacob Marley.'

'And yet, oddly, looking less like Jacob Marley than you used to,' I tease him.

Dylan laughs.

'I'm still going to let you in. Come on. The coffee is ready.'

I follow Dylan into the hallway that leads through to the kitchen. The house is a quirky mix of old-fashioned grandeur and the desperate need for modernisation. Perhaps that's why Mr Campbell's kids are holding off on selling it, hoping they'll make more money if they do it up first. Modern houses on this street sell for an absolute fortune.

It's a shame to see what would have been beautiful once upon a time looking so uncared for – kind of like the ends of my hair and the skin around my eyes that I really wish I'd started moisturising earlier in life. You can only see glimpses of the intricate pattern on the now faded wallpaper, and the chipped paintwork shows how long it has been since this house had any TLC.

The hallway is illuminated by an ornate chandelier that hangs from the ceiling which, again, even though it needs some attention, is undeniably beautiful and still casts a lovely warm glow over an otherwise dark room.

I can't resist checking out how I look in a tarnished antique wall mirror as I pass it. I don't think

I've ever worried about how I looked for a client before, so long as I looked smart, and I'm embarrassed to
say how long I spent getting ready today. I washed my
hair – on what would have been a non-hair-wash day
– and I changed my outfit at least three times. Only to
find Dylan in his PJs and without a top. Still, that
clearly takes a lot of competing with these days.

The kitchen is bathed in natural light, thanks to
large windows that overlook the garden. Again,
though, it's in need of a serious makeover to bring it
up to date. I like to see some original character in
houses but that feels like a luxury sometimes. When
you have jobs, kids and lots going on, it isn't realistic
to care for chandeliers and painted stairs. You need
that big open-plan living space, one that serves the
whole house, where you can fit everyone, keep an eye
on the kids while you cook and so on. The best way to
sell this house – and to appeal to the locals with the
money to afford it – would be to knock out a few walls
and then deck it out with a Scandi colour palette and
all the mod cons you can think of.

'It's fascinating, finally seeing inside here,' I tell
Dylan. 'I've been to the door many times, but never
inside. I used to bring Mr Campbell bits of shopping. I
think I was the only person on the street who didn't

hate him – and who he didn't totally despise. His kids didn't really bother with him; I guess he was quite hard work, and such a busybody, but I didn't mind picking him up the things he needed now and then.'

'It's nice to know you haven't changed,' Dylan replies through a smile. 'Still the same Nic, happy to help those who needed it.'

'Is that why I used to follow you around, wiping your arse?' I joke.

'I had my perks,' he insists, handing me a cup of coffee.

Huh, that's interesting. In an otherwise old-fashioned kitchen – with an aesthetic to match the rest of the house, and one that can only be described as The Shining – there is a sleek, shiny coffee machine with all the bells and whistles.

'I don't remember coffee beans being on his shopping list,' I say, puzzled.

'I brought this with me,' Dylan admits. 'And a few other necessities – things I can't live without.'

'Oh, God, don't tell me there are twenty-seven women upstairs,' I quip.

'Don't be silly,' Dylan replies. 'It's only a four-bed house.'

I can't help but smile.

'Were you that sure I would say yes?' I ask him curiously.

'I was that hopeful,' he replies. 'But not hopeful enough to bring twenty-seven women with me. However, I did find something interesting upstairs, though – want to see?' he asks.

'Always,' I reply.

I follow Dylan back into the hallway and up the creaky wooden stairs. As we reach the top, I can't help but feel an unusual flutter of nerves in my stomach, and I'm not sure if it's my building intrigue for what Dylan has unearthed in this old, mysterious house, or just Dylan's presence alone.

He leads me into a bedroom at the front of the house, which looks like it was being used as a study. The walls are adorned with shelves, and they're overflowing with books of all shapes and sizes. In one corner, a telescope stands by the window, silently observing the outside world.

'I never knew he was into astronomy,' I think out loud.

Dylan chuckles softly, his amusement evident.

'I don't think he was,' he replies. 'Look at this.'

He retrieves a red book from one of the shelves – one of many – and begins to read aloud from the pages.

'Lindy Mullings left her home at 11.20 a.m. – she also left her baby. No sign of the au pair until 11.48,' Dylan reads, his bemused disbelief present in every word. 'Returned home at 15.27. Bumped the car on the gatepost. Suspect she had too much to drink at lunch. Will continue to monitor the situation.'

My eyes widen with a mix of disbelief and horror.

'He's been spying on us?' I practically gasp.

Dylan nods, his expression mirroring my shock.

'It looks like it,' he replies. 'I came in here last night, looking for something to read, and I found all these.'

'Did you read them?' I ask, as curious as I am concerned.

'No,' he replies. 'Just this first bit of this first one, until I realised what I was reading. I suppose it's more interesting to you, because you know these people. I mean, look out of this window, he's got the best spot on the street, he can see everyone.'

I peer outside and he really does have a cracking view of the entire cul-de-sac, and I'm looking without the telescope. In fact, looking out from up here, it's probably the only spot on the street that can see in-side our front garden, with a view of the driveway right up to the front door. I suppose it's a good thing that we had an extra pair of eyes looking out for the place, but it makes me cringe at all the times I grabbed the milk from the step in my PJs.

'Hmm. As tempting as it is to read what he's written about everyone, it can only end in trouble, right?' I say, my lip caught between my teeth in thought. 'People deserve their privacy.'

'Says the journalist,' Dylan points out with a grin.

'Erm, former journalist, thank you,' I reply, keen to distance myself from the label. 'Which reminds me why I'm here in the first place.'

I try to push Mr Campbell's neighbourhood watch from my mind as I edge closer to the door.

'Come on,' I say firmly. 'Let's get to work.'

Back downstairs, I take a seat on Mr Campbell's tatty green sofa. Dylan sits down next to me, ready to get down to business.

'I can't believe you guys are getting back together,' I say, smiling, but still in shock. 'I thought The Burnouts were done.'

Dylan leans back on the sofa, a knowing smile on his face.

'Well, everyone is doing a comeback tour, right?' he points out. 'So anyone with any kind of financial interest in us wants it to happen, and Mikey and I have decided to put the past behind us, so that we can move on, because we both really want to get back to doing what we love, which is being on stage together.'

I can't help but smile at the idea of the two of them reuniting after all these years. Yes, it will be great to see the band back together, but seeing the two brothers back on good terms means so much more.

'Well, that's great,' I say sincerely. 'So now we just need to clean up your act, huh?'

Dylan flashes me a cheeky smile.

'Are you sure you're up to it?' he asks. 'Because I've forgotten most of what I've done.'

'Oh, I remember a lot, don't worry,' I say playfully. 'Actually, do worry.'

Dylan's laughter fills the room.

'Well, we're just putting the last bits and pieces in place for the comeback,' he explains. 'We're announcing the tour with some secret shows so I suppose that's when I'll need you to start, when I'm back out there.'

'Yeah, you've been doing a great job at keeping your head down,' I point out. 'I guess, in the meantime, I'll find you... something.'

'Like what?' he asks, his tone a little more serious.

'Something to make you look good,' I say simply. 'But, unfortunately, it's going to make you look good by making you actually good.'

'Boo,' he hisses jokily.

'Your makeover is a great start,' I tell him. 'There are glow-ups, and then there is... whatever this is. This will work really well. You look great, healthy, like you're taking care of yourself.'

'Thanks for noticing,' he replies.

'In my professional opinion,' I clarify, trying to maintain a semblance of professionalism. Then, I can't help myself, and a genuine smile creeps onto my face. 'I thought you looked great before too.'

'Well, thanks for noticing that too,' he replies.

I need to steer the conversation back to the task at hand. I guess, in my defence, I've never worked with anyone I already knew before.

'I'm going to need you to keep the drinking to a minimum, while we show people this different side of you – and definitely nothing stronger – and, whether there are twenty-seven girls upstairs, seven, or just two...'

'Just two?' Dylan interjects with a playful laugh, repeating my words back to me. 'A slow day.'

'Dill, you know what I mean,' I reply.

'I do,' he replies. 'And okay. That sounds fair.'

'And I was going to suggest swearing less but, now that I think about it, you already are,' I point out. The last time I saw Dylan it was like every other word.

'Thanks for fucking noticing,' he jokes. 'I do still swear, when the mood calls for it, but I'm getting ahead of the game, using them sparingly.'

I smile.

'That's good then,' I tell him. 'Good thinking. I'll come up with a list of ideas for things you can be seen doing, in the build-up to the announcement. But, again, they make you look good because they are good – I can't stress that enough.'

'Got it,' he confirms. 'Oh, one other thing, though, I was hoping, as part of the deal, before the announcement, if you might come with me to the meetings, the recordings, the rehearsals, and so on? I'll pay you, obviously, whatever you want. But I really don't want to mess this up, and if that means having you hold my hand every step of the way, then so be it.'

'Yeah, that makes sense,' I respond, trying to keep my excitement in check. Wow, it really does sound like old times.

'But I guess that means stepping back into your old shoes, going back to the world you left behind,' Dylan reminds me.

'I'm sure I can handle it,' I reply casually, although deep down, I'm really looking forward to it. A trip down memory lane feels like just what I need, back to my old life. I mean, come on, how many people get to time-travel like this? It's a chance to go back to the way things used to be, but to get it right this time. I'm older, wiser and more sensible now, and Dylan seems like he's in a much better place, and open to changing more, so it's not going to be anything like it used to be... is it?

I can't wait to find out.

13

As I finish my short stroll home, I can't help but sigh with playful exhaustion.

'Ahh, another hard day in the office,' I joke to Dylan as he joins me on my new commute – surely a contender for the record for the world's shortest commute ever?

He grins.

'I love that this is your job now,' he tells me. 'This is basically what you did, for free, back in the day. It's nice to see you getting compensated for it now.'

'You say that, but really, I should be thanking you,' I reply with a grin of my own. 'Because if it weren't for all the, shall we say, work experience you gave me, I probably wouldn't be so good at it.'

Dylan walks me to my front door, and I appreciate the company – his company – even if it is only a short trip.

'Thanks for escorting me home,' I tell him. 'What are you doing with yourself now?'

Dylan runs a hand through his newly short hair. Well, it's new to me, anyway. It really suits him, but I'm still not quite used to it. I'm not used to him being here generally, though, who am I kidding?

'I'm not sure,' he replies. 'What do people do for fun around here, in Little Cutesy Cutesy Name? Aside from keeping detailed files on everyone they can see from their window. You would never get that in London.'

'I mean, you are still technically in a borough of London,' I remind him with a laugh.

'Am I?' he says in disbelief. 'Wow, it seems so far away to me.'

'I know it does – you rented a house,' I remind him.

'Okay, I stand corrected then,' he concedes. 'So, what do people do for fun in this *borough* of London?'

'Fun? What's that?' I ask, cocking my head curiously for comedic effect.

'Cast your mind back far enough, and you'll remember,' Dylan replies, trying to hit me where it's nostalgic.

'You won't find any of that kind of fun here,' I inform him. 'The men like to play golf, talk about how much money they have, buy things with their money, complain about the price of things – although it's never the cost of electricity; it's things like how much extra they had to pay for twinkling lights in the roof of their car or whatever.'

Dylan chuckles at my description.

'So, not really my kind of hobbies,' he muses. 'Would I have more luck hanging out with the women?'

'Oh, yeah,' I quip. 'If you treat bitching and back-stabbing like Olympic sports, and you think you're a strong contender for the gold, they'll love you.'

'Then I shall stay away from them too,' he says with a laugh.

'I wish I could,' I tell him. 'But, speaking of the devils, I need to head to the school, to pick up the boys. No doubt I'll have an encounter with at least one or two of the mums...'

My voice trails off as I frantically search through my bag.

'Is everything okay?' Dylan asks.

'Shit,' I say as I realise what I've done. 'I forgot to

bring my keys with me today – which includes my house keys *and* my car keys. Rowan isn't home, and I need to pick up the boys.'

'I'll drive you,' he replies, quickly and helpfully.

'Really?' I ask, surprised by his offer.

'Of course,' he says. 'We've just established there is nothing else for me to do in this village.'

'You're a lifesaver. Thank you,' I say before letting my gratitude out via a huge sigh of relief.

'Back over to mine then,' he says as we head across the road again to retrieve his car. 'Thank God I'm living so close, hmm?'

'Indeed,' I reply with a smile.

'Rowan isn't happy about me being here, is he?' he says as we strap ourselves into the car.

'Oh, whatever gave you that impression?' I reply sarcastically.

'Hmm, I don't know,' Dylan replies in a similar tone. 'It might have been something to do with his generally hostile tone and the fact that he spent dessert stroking your hair.'

I can't help but laugh.

'Yeah, that will do it,' I reply. 'Sorry. I suppose, ever so slightly in his defence, you are Dylan King – and the new and improved, super-jacked version, no less.'

'I guess there's that,' he says, playing along.

We arrive at the school with time to spare.

'Thanks for the lift,' I tell him. 'I'll be five minutes, tops – and I promise not to make a habit of this.'

'It's okay, I'll come with you,' he insists.

'Yeah?' I reply, surprised – I'm constantly surprised at the moment.

'Yeah, why not?' Dylan says. 'I'm practically part of the PTA now.'

'Okay,' I chuckle. 'Let's do it.'

Walking into the school playground with Dylan, it's only a matter of seconds before all eyes are on us.

'I'd forgotten what it was like,' I say quietly, keeping my smile firmly on my face.

'What what was like?' Dylan replies.

'Standing next to you,' I tell him simply.

The playground feels different today, with significantly fewer au pairs and more mums around. The boss-level mums – Rebecca, Carolyn, Teresa and Deanna – are all here, although they've left their cauldrons, black cats and broomsticks at home. They all very much look like they're in the stance for causing trouble, though – the fact that they're here at all is bad vibes. They're like the four horsewomen of the apocalypse, although I don't dare to consider which one is which.

Lisa comes running toward us, her face bright red

as she bounds over like a hyperactive spaniel – confirming for me that when I met her earlier in the week and she thought she knew me, it probably was because she was a Dylan King fan.

I accept that I am affiliated with Dylan again, for lack of a better term, but I still desperately don't want anyone to recall why Lisa might remember me. My brief run-in with the tabloid press – with personal photos of me gracing the pages – was nothing but a big misunderstanding. Of course, if you only look at the first story they printed, and not the one where I proved my innocence, it looks bad. The last thing I need is for that scandal to rear its ugly head. No one in this village will care that I cleared my name, only that it got muddied in the first place.

'You're Dylan King,' Lisa informs him, rather pointlessly.

It's amazing how many people remind Dylan who he is – then again, back in the day, he often forgot.

'I am,' he says with a smile.

'I was in love with you,' she informs him, before leaning in closer, lowering her voice. 'I still am.'

'That's very nice of you to say,' he replies politely – a phrase he always used to use to reply to fans declaring this, and probably women he's dated too.

'Dylan,' another voice calls out. 'Dylan, hello.'

It's Jo Morgan, the boys' head teacher, who cannot hide her delight to be seeing Dylan again.

'We were hoping we might see you again,' she says, confirming my thoughts. 'I was going to ask Nicole if you might be in the area for any length of time.'

Dylan looks at me before answering the question.

'Yeah, sticking around for a little while,' he replies.

Jo's enthusiasm is palpable.

'The reason I ask... The children – the older children, that is, this is an all-through school – were so excited for their musical this year,' she explains. 'However, their music and drama teacher, Ms Telford, is off sick – we don't know for how long. What the kids need is some musical direction, even if it's just a talk, to help get the show back on the road.'

Dylan looks at me for guidance, and I nod with an encouraging smile. Helping the kids with their musical could only generate positive publicity – and it would genuinely help them out too.

'Okay, sure,' Dylan says.

'Okay, sure?' Jo repeats in astonishment. 'What shall I put you down for? A pep talk? A one-off lesson?'

'Happy to help in any way I can,' he says generously, but oh-so casually. 'I could meet the kids, see where they're at, maybe do a few rehearsals with them? That way, they can get everything together, and it's just a case of practising it until it's time to perform.'

Jo claps her hands so loudly that one of the older women at the other side of the playground ducks.

'The show will go on,' she declares. 'We were going to have a Parents and Teachers Society meeting in the morning – do you think you can attend?'

'I'll be there,' Dylan agrees. 'Can Nic come too?'

'Of course, she would be more than welcome,' Jo replies. 'I've been trying to get Ms Wilde to join PATS for some time now.'

I force a smile. Even the fact they call it 'pats' annoys me – I've avoided it like the plague.

'Marvellous, just marvellous,' Jo continues. 'Well, I'll leave you to collect your children, and I'll see you tomorrow.'

'Can I charge you extra for this?' I jokily ask Dylan once we're alone.

'Sure,' he says through a laugh. 'I actually think it might be fun.'

'The mums aren't all as friendly as Lisa,' I warn him.

Eventually, Archie and Ned come charging over to us.

'Dylan,' Archie exclaims excitedly.

'Hey, dude,' Dylan greets him. 'Good day?'

'It was okay,' Archie replies.

'Make any more music?' Dylan asks him.

'No, our music teacher has bluemonia,' Archie replies.

'Do you mean pneumonia?' I correct him.

Archie shrugs in indifference.

'That's what Bolt's mum says,' he informs us.

'Bolt,' Dylan says to himself, obviously having never heard of a child with that name before. Honestly, after a few years here, I don't think there is a single name that could surprise me any more.

'Yeah, well, Bolt's mum diagnosed me as "melancholic" when I had a bit of a limp from twisting my ankle,' I say. 'So I'd take what she says with a pinch of salt.'

'Or sugar,' Dylan adds, referring to the sugar incident at dinner last night.

'Or sugar,' I confirm with a smile.

'Maybe I can give you some music lessons,' Dylan suggests to Archie.

'Really?' Archie squeaks, excitement surging inside him. 'I want to be a drummer.'

'Really,' Dylan replies, then he turns his attention to Ned. 'What about you, little dude?'

'Yeah,' Ned says, agreeable as ever, joining in the excitement.

As we reach the car, I stop suddenly in my tracks.

'No car seats!' I exclaim. 'They have to be in car seats.'

'Then we'll walk,' Dylan says simply.

He takes Ned and lifts him onto his shoulders.

'Which way, little dude?' he asks him.

'That way.' Ned points confidently.

I smile.

'Come on then, Archie.' I offer my hand. 'I guess we're walking.'

'Okay,' Archie says. 'Can Dylan come for dinner again?'

'We'll see,' I reply. I'm not sure how into the idea Rowan would be.

'I really like having him around,' Archie confides in me.

'So do I,' I confess, knowing my revelation won't go any further.

I do, though. I really do. In fact, I love it.

14

I sigh heavily. I used to love coming here, to The Old Heifer, an upmarket pub and restaurant on the out-skirts of Little Harehill, back when things were good between me and Rowan. The boys love it too, and they usually find restaurants boring, but it could have something to do with the huge play area outside.

The casual, friendly atmosphere wraps around us as we all sit around our usual table. Archie and Ned fidget in their seats, polishing off the last of their chicken nuggets and chips, eager to go out and play as they often do before dessert.

Is it odd, that I'm going to miss the routine? I know, routine is boring, but there's something sort of nice about doing something that works. I've always loved bringing the boys here, seeing them enjoy their food, and the play area, and the ice cream station they have where kids can concoct their own creations. I don't suppose I'll ever enjoy it again, not in the way I used to. I mean, look at this evening, we're only here so that Rowan can take some pictures for his socials.

Rowan is on top form, armed with his phone, taking photos of every dish, of me, of the boys, of me and the boys – he even has a particular waiter, who he keeps getting to take candid photos of us. I'm no stranger to snapping a photo of my food, before I tuck in, but having someone take my photo while I'm eating makes it hard to relax.

'Smile, everyone!' Rowan insists as the waiter snaps another group shot.

I force myself to smile. I can't have many of these left to do now.

'Okay, boys, why don't you go hit up the play area while Nicole and I finish our food,' Rowan tells them. 'I'll come and get you, when it's time for ice cream.'

'Okay,' Archie says, speaking on behalf of them both.

'Let's let them burn off some energy,' he says to me with a smile, now that it's just the two of us.

I smile back dutifully as Rowan extends an arm, to take a selfie of us. But once the photo is captured, and his phone is back on the table, he looks at me with a sincerity that catches me off guard.

'Nicole, I'm sorry,' he tells me. 'I overreacted about Dylan showing up. It's just... it was a big shock, that's all. Yes, I still find it strange, that you never told me the two of you were friends, and it's bloody odd that he's just moved in across the road but, yeah, I get that this is your job, and it's important to you, and you've got to do what you've got to do.'

I appreciate him saying that, even if he is still banging on a little.

'Thank you,' I say simply, willing to be a grown-up about it. 'It is work – like how this is work for you, so I'm here, supporting you.'

Rowan's smile returns, a genuine one this time, as he looks past me. Suddenly, a waiter appears, carrying a chilled bottle of champagne which he places down in front of us.

'For the happy couple,' the waiter says.

Before I can say a word, a guitarist appears along-side our table, playing a medley of love songs on his acoustic as he sings the words – directing his set point-blank at me and Rowan.

Rowan reaches out across the table, taking my hand in his.

Oh, boy, is this awkward. Not only because, obviously, Rowan and I are no longer romantically involved, but also because it's uncomfortable, having someone play music just for us, up close, while everyone else in the room stares at us. I don't know where to look. Glancing around reminds me of all the eyes on us, I don't want to look at Rowan, and looking at the young man playing guitar while he sings is just cringe in a way I can't explain.

Just when I think it can't get any more surreal, I notice the waiter – the one who has been taking photos for Rowan all evening – discreetly recording the entire performance. My cringe intensifies, but I've got to keep my game face on, I just need to stick this out, it will be over soon.

Rowan tightens his grip on my hand.

'Nicole, I love you,' he tells me, and I'm not sure if he means it, or if it is for the cameras, but I can't bring myself to say it back. 'You're my world, and I'd do anything for you. You know that, right?'

I smile and nod.

'I mean it,' he insists. 'I am going to give you the best life, if you'll let me.'

A spark of panic ignites inside me as Rowan reaches into his pocket. My mind races, my God, tell me he isn't about to pull out a ring, because, let's face it, that's exactly the kind of thing Rowan would do.

Panicking at the prospect of Rowan giving me a ring, my mind races faster than my heartbeat.

'I'm just nipping to the loo,' I say, jumping to my feet, ready to dash off before he can even get his hand out of his pocket.

However – and this is just classic me – I'm in such a hurry that I'm not looking where I am going, so I collide with a waiter who was carrying two bowls of ice cream. The key word there being 'was' – they're on the floor now. The guitarist stops abruptly and, if Rowan was going to pull something from his pocket, he's clearly changed his mind now.

'Oh, my goodness, I am so sorry,' I tell the waiter.

'Not to worry,' the waiter kindly reassures me. 'I can take care of it.'

'One for the out-takes, hmm?' I say to Rowan, laughing awkwardly as I try in vain to lighten the situation. 'I'll be back in a sec – and I'll bring the boys for their dessert.'

I dash off, before he can say anything, retreating to the sanctuary of the ladies'.

I don't know for sure that Rowan was going to propose and, even if he was, I wouldn't know if he was doing it for show, or because he really wanted to. I guess, with someone like Rowan, you can never really know what they're doing for show, and what is genuine.

Either way, though, best not to risk it. And it's not like I'm going to be coming back here, is it? Not now that my days in Little Harehill are numbered.

15

There's a reason I didn't want to join PATS. Actually, there are several, but Rebecca bloody Rollins and her gaggle of mum minions – mumnions? – are right up there at the top.

Rebecca lives on our street, just a couple of doors away, and everything is a competition to her. Like, I never knew I was signed up for some sort of front door contest, or when she got their side hedges trimmed, and she spent two weeks berating our hedges – as though I gave a shit?

Honestly, I hate that I am forced to compete in such stupid things, whether I want to or not. It's easier to care less these days, knowing that my days here are numbered, but when I thought that this was it, for the rest of my life, wow. Sometimes I would literally count down the days until the boys would finish school, so that we could move away.

Today I am at the boys' school, surrounded by a mix of parents and teachers for the Parents and Teachers Society meeting, all gathered to discuss the musical that was teetering on the brink of cancellation until Dylan stepped in.

Around the table, we have the ever-present Rebecca, her loyal sidekicks, Jo, the head teacher, John, another teacher, and a couple of other parents I recognise but don't really know. They all sip tea from cups with saucers and nibble on minuscule cakes – the kind where you need to eat about five to feel like you've had one. I can't believe I'm at a PATS meeting, after all this time.

Dylan is in the next room, the drama studio, with the kids, having a chat with them about their progress so far, and what they think they can do moving forward. He's actually way into this, I'm really surprised.

'So, you and Dylan are old friends?' Jo asks curiously.

'Yes, since we were kids, really,' I reply.

Well, not *really* really. I was technically a teenager when I met Dylan, but bending the truth like this sounds so much more wholesome, doesn't it?

Rebecca, ever the sceptic, raises an eyebrow.

'So, he just, what, visits and helps you with the school run now and then?' she probes further.

'He isn't here to help with the school run,' I insist, laughing her comment off.

'And yet I've seen him here at the school with you three times in three days,' Rebecca points out. 'I don't think I've seen you and Rowan together three times this year.'

Well, yes, that's true, I suppose, but that's obviously because Rowan and I are like strangers now, and it's intentional on my part. I do everything I can to avoid being around him. Thankfully, showing my face in his photos is enough to convince people that we're still together. It's amazing, really, what people will believe, just because they see it on the internet.

'That's probably because I murdered him,' I say deadpan, but with a flicker of mischief in my eyes. 'That's why Dylan is here, to help me bury him under the patio.'

For a brief moment, everyone just stares at me.

'Or he's an old friend, and he's visiting, with no mysterious reason, no ulterior motive, and nothing that warrants any kind of conversation,' I add.

Jo holds her silence for a few more seconds before

laughing wildly, encouraging most of the others to join in.

Sassiness isn't rewarded in this village, in fact it's usually punished. But, come on, Rebecca is being a bit much today.

'While we're waiting for Dylan, why don't we talk about the fundfair for the production?' Jo suggests.

It's baffling that this school, which costs a small fortune per term, still heavily relies on fundraisers and donations. They call it a 'fundfair', but it's just another tactic to bleed more money from the parents. Extracurricular activities are quite clearly extra on top of the big bill for attending the school.

'We're doing a three-course dinner dance, black-tie attire, of course,' Rebecca informs the group.

Rebecca always plans these things and they are always the same – and they're always boring.

I sign heavily, maybe a bit too heavily, because Rebecca notices.

'What's wrong, Nicole?' she asks, her irritation clear.

'No, nothing, sorry,' I babble, desperately trying to deflect attention from my wandering mind.

'Were you thinking of something else?' Jo asks me curiously.

'No, not at all,' I insist, reminding myself to keep my head down moving on.

Jo thinks for a moment.

'I suppose we do have quite a lot of black-tie dinners,' Jo says. 'But what's the alternative? And could we make the changes in time?'

I contemplate whether or not it's worth speaking up, reminding myself that I won't be around for any more of these fundraisers. I don't need to get involved; I just need to endure it. But my better instincts take over, and...

'I guess we could do something more fun,' I suggest. 'But add it on to what we've already got planned, of course. Like... perhaps we could give the event a theme? Whatever it is, I know Dylan would love to be there.'

'A theme?' Rebecca replies with a look on her face that makes it seem like even the words taste bad in her mouth.

'The theme could be "celebrity",' I suggest, my courage and enthusiasm building with every word. 'Everyone could come dressed up as someone famous, we could lay out a red carpet, have fake paparazzi shooting photos as everyone arrives.'

'I hate it,' Rebecca says. 'I hate it so much.'

Jo, on the other hand, is smiling from ear to ear.

'Well, I love it,' she says.

'Me too,' John chimes in. 'It would be good to do something actually fun for a change. I'm sure more people would get involved too.'

Several other parents voice their support for the idea, and I can't help but smile, even though Rebecca's expression could spoil milk. The chances that there won't be consequences for this are slim.

'Hello,' Dylan says as he saunters in to join us.

Jo practically trips over herself as she rushes to him, guiding him to a seat, her arm wrapped around him.

'Hello, Dylan, come sit down,' she says. 'Can I make you a cup of tea?'

'That would be lovely,' Dylan replies, fully embracing the spirit of the occasion.

'So, how did it go?' Jo asks, cutting to the chase. 'Are they musically salvageable?'

'Yes, and no,' Dylan replies.

Jo is clearly intrigued.

'Oh?' she says simply, from the edge of her seat.

'So, the kids are excited about the musical,' Dylan tells the group. 'Just not this one.'

'What's wrong with *Joseph*?' Rebecca asks, in there like a flash, pissed off already.

I can't help but wonder if her reaction would be as intense if I hadn't already whipped her up.

'Nothing is wrong with *Joseph*,' Dylan replies. '*Joseph* is great. But you've got a great group of kids in there, a good split of boys and girls, and they want to have fun. *Joseph* just doesn't have enough roles to give the girls their time to shine. Plus, it sounds like they've done it before, so they're all a bit bored of it.'

'So, what do you suggest?' Jo asks him.

'*Bugsy Malone*,' Dylan says with an optimistic smile. 'Great roles for both the boys and the girls, a varied ensemble cast, lots of fun songs – I was in it, when I was at school, and it's just such a blast.'

Rebecca immediately dismisses Dylan's suggestion by chopping her hand through the air.

'Absolutely not,' she says firmly.

'Why not?' I ask.

'It's all guns and dancers,' Rebecca replies. 'It's not for kids.'

'It has an all-child cast,' Dylan reminds her with a laugh.

He's so cool, calm and collected – which only seems to make Rebecca angrier.

'I mean, the guns shoot cream,' I point out. 'I was in it when I was at school too, and we used shaving cream in our production. And, Rebecca, this might come as a huge shock to you, so thank goodness you're sitting down, but pretty much all musicals have dancers in them.'

I fake a gasp for good measure, knowing it will provoke her further.

For a moment, Rebecca is left speechless, her face slowly turning redder by the second. If she doesn't release the steam from her ears soon, she might spontaneously combust.

'I think *Bugsy Malone* is a wonderful idea,' Jo says, ignoring Rebecca's objections. 'But can it be done?'

'I know it like the back of my hand,' Dylan says simply. 'I can help them.'

I smile to myself because, not only would Dylan be helping them, but they would be helping him too. This is exactly the sort of thing he needs to be doing, to show people that he's changed. I was going to find something for him but the fact that he has put his own name down for this makes it mean all the more.

'Oh, Dylan, yes, that would be wonderful,' Jo tells him. 'And yes to the celebrity-themed fundfair. Thank you – from me and the kids.'

'I'm happy to organise the fundfair, if you like,' I suggest.

'No, that's my job, I'll do it,' Rebecca snaps. 'At

least that way I can ensure it's not totally classless and tacky.'

'Nic can help me with the show,' Dylan suggests. 'We used to sing songs from musicals on the bus all the time.'

'The bus?' Jo enquires.

'The school bus,' I quickly insist.

Dylan looks at her and gives her an interesting smile.

'Oh, I see, sorry, it makes sense now,' Jo replies. 'The two of you went to school together.'

'Right,' Dylan says, also learning this piece of 'information' for the first time.

'It feels like a lifetime ago,' I add, trying to style it out.

'Yeah,' Dylan agrees. 'Like it happened in another life, even.'

'Well, class dismissed,' Jo says with a smile. 'Dylan, we have your details, we'll make the arrangements and be in touch about when we can get this show on the road. Rebecca, you're in charge of the party, so assign jobs as you see fit. And I'll see you all later.'

As everyone filters out of the room, Dylan and I quickly head outside to the playground to escape the group.

'I know that I used to drink a lot back in the day,' Dylan starts. 'But I do not remember the two of us going to school together.'

'Sorry,' I say with a laugh. 'It's just that this lot doesn't know anything about the old me. And I want it to stay that way.'

'Why?' Dylan asks curiously.

'I mean, to outsiders, looking in – looking back at the old days – I just sort of looked like a bit of a groupie,' I say. 'Like I partied too much, drank too much, had a crazy time. And, I know, we all did. I just think that, because we have such good memories from those times, it's easy to forget that maybe not everything was that great – including us. I thought I was cool – we all did – but there's a reason we only choose to remember the good bits, right?'

Dylan wraps an arm around me, offering a comforting squeeze.

'Oh, Nic, I don't remember any of it, good or bad,' he jokes, making me laugh. 'But, on a serious note, you should never feel ashamed of your past. People do stupid things, especially when they're younger, when they're under the influence of drink or fame or whatever. We had our crazy days, but if there's one thing I do remember, it's that you always were, and always will be, one of the kindest, most caring, loyal friends

I've ever had. So you liked to get drunk, so you had a few shitty boyfriends – who cares? It doesn't take away from who you are. The past has no bearing on who you are now. People grow and they change and if we judge people by their past mistakes and behaviours forever, well, I'm screwed, right?'

His words hit home, and I place a hand on my chest, taking a deep breath as a smile forms on my face. I'm a little taken aback by Dylan's insight and how right he is. He's absolutely spot on – people do grow and change, and there's no need for me to be ashamed.

Nonetheless, everyone in this village is so judgemental, and if I can keep my wild-child days hidden from them, life will be much simpler. I'll be out of here soon.

'Anyway, what's the plan now?' he asks me. 'What are we doing with the rest of our day?'

I smile. It's been a long time since we were a 'we'. I like it.

'Well, I've got to get home,' I tell him. 'It's Archie's birthday today, so he's having some friends over after school, and we're having some parents over which is always *fun*. So, I need to go get the house ready.'

'I'll help you, if you like?' Dylan suggests.

'Dylan King wants to help set up a kids' party?' I

reply. 'You do know that the jelly is just jelly, and the lighter is only for lighting the candles on the cake, right?'

Dylan smiles widely as he laughs.

'Yes, I know all that,' he tells me. 'I need to go back to the house, to make a few phone calls, but that shouldn't take more than ten minutes. I would love to help you.'

'Okay, cool,' I reply. 'It's not the first party we've planned together, but it might just be the most surreal.'

'It will be fun,' he insists. 'Come on, let's go – I'm excited.'

I can't help but smile to myself. He really does seem excited.

Who is this man, and what has he done with the real Dylan King?

16

The house is alive with the sounds of laughter, music and chatter – oh, and screaming because, whether it's for good reasons or bad ones, there is always screaming.

Balloons of every colour adorn the living room – courtesy of Dylan, who said you could never have too many balloons. He was such a huge help, assisting me in setting everything up for the party, because Rowan certainly wasn't around to do it. I know, he's working hard, but the fact that he's only doing extra work to make up for scamming people makes it harder for me to be cool with picking up the slack.

Dylan left, to go back to the house and get changed, before Rowan got home, and when Rowan did arrive, he walked in, didn't compliment me on the house, or ask how I'd managed to do it all alone, or anything like that. Ah, well.

The party is in full swing now. We laid out the kitchen island with an assortment of goodies, from sandwiches and crisps to cupcakes to party bags. Everyone just keeps passing by the table, grazing, which is the best thing about a buffet. Even the adults are enjoying it, although I did notice Rebecca look over what was on offer and pull an unimpressed face. No doubt I'll be getting some sort of social penalty for putting out such a beige array of 'British tapas'.

Archie is having a great time, though, and that is all that matters. He's loving having his friends over, opening his presents and showing people what he's got. Rowan is schmoozing the parents, which to be honest I would rather not do, so I'm more than happy to play the dutiful host instead.

'Hello,' Dylan says, snapping me from my thoughts as I top up the crisps.

'Oh, hi,' I reply as I turn to face him.

Oh, wow, he's even dressed up for the party, in a pair of black jeans and a nicely fitting long-sleeved black T-shirt. I don't know why, but it gives me a bit of a lump in my throat.

'Dylan,' Archie screams as he charges over to greet him.

'Hey, dude, happy birthday,' Dylan tells him.

'You came to my party,' Archie points out, his eyes wide, his jaw slightly dropped.

'I wouldn't miss it for the world, little man,' Dylan replies. 'And I brought you a birthday present. It's in the hallway.'

'Cool,' Archie replies before running off in that direction.

I feel a sense of uneasiness before I clock Rowan staring at us. I feel like he's keeping an eye on me, like I'm one of the kids.

'Let's go see this present,' I suggest with a smile, although we've hardly made a move when I notice Rowan heading over to join us. He catches us up as we arrive in the hallway, where Archie is standing in silence, staring in wonderment at his shiny new drum kit.

'This is mine?' Archie blurts in disbelief.

'I figured, you seemed to enjoy making music at school the other day,' Dylan explains. 'And you've got a good sense of rhythm, dude. I thought this might help you explore it.'

'You bought a child a whole drum kit because he

enjoyed drumming once?' Rowan says, every word loaded.

'Well, there's only so much you can do with just a snare,' Dylan says, and it's not that I don't think he's detecting Rowan's tone, I think he's just choosing to rise above it.

'What do we say to Dylan?' I prompt Archie.

'Thanks, Dylan.' He beams. 'Can we play now?'

'I thought you wanted to play your new football game on the PlayStation?' Rowan says. 'I just set it up for you.'

'We can play drums any time,' Dylan tells Archie. 'I'll even give you lessons.'

'Okay,' Archie replies excitedly. 'Do you want to play my new game with me?'

'I thought you wanted me to play with you,' Rowan practically whines, like a petulant child.

You can tell he's rattled by Dylan's presence, and the fact that the kids love him, but he really needs to grow up. He's being so cringy right now.

'It's all right, I can play later,' Dylan tells Archie. 'You guys go ahead.'

Archie sighs.

'I'll just play later,' he says with a shrug. 'I'm going to get another cupcake.'

Another? Lord, how many has he had?

I notice Rowan running his tongue across his teeth, under his lip – something he often does when he's wound up. It's almost as though, the more reasonable Dylan is, the more unreasonable it makes Rowan feel.

'Okay, why don't we play?' Rowan suggests to Dylan.

Dylan laughs.

'I'm serious,' Rowan insists. 'Come on, me and you, head to head.'

I look at Dylan, my eyes wide, then back at Rowan, then to Dylan again as they pause in a silent stand-off. Surely this is a terrible idea.

'Okay, sure,' Dylan replies. 'Let's do it.'

I follow them to the sofa, nibbling at my thumbnail. Oh, boy, do we really have to do this now? At a kids' party? In front of all the village busybodies?

As Rowan sets up the game, Dylan examines the controller, looking at it as though he's never seen one before. Rowan glances over at him and smirks.

'Right, all set up – are you good to go?' Rowan asks him.

'Let's give it a go,' Dylan replies with a hopeful smile.

You can tell, from the look on Rowan's face, that he is confident he's going to win this one. Well, he plays with Archie all the time, so he's got a lot of experience under his belt. I don't like it, that smug look, that certainty that he's going to beat Dylan and, when he does, he thinks it'll prove something significant, like he's the better man. It's a bloody football game (and not only that, but a virtual one), for crying out loud.

A small crowd of parents gathers around the sofa – the dads because it is almost like sport and the mums because it is Dylan.

I don't think anyone is expecting to see Dylan effortlessly manoeuvre his on-screen players, executing swift passes and strategic moves, scoring goal after goal – well, anyone except me. On the other side, Rowan is struggling to keep up, his side floundering in comparison. The tension in the room thickens with every goal that Dylan scores. No one says a word, everyone just watches the game go on.

Thankfully, matches are significantly quicker than they are in real life – although it probably felt like ninety minutes – and the game comes to an end. Dylan has well and truly spanked him.

The room is suspended in a charged silence, broken only by the simulated cheers from the game. Dylan grins, enjoying the victory, but when he looks over at Rowan, he sees something unexpected – genuine fury etched across Rowan's face.

'You play a lot of video games, when you spend a lot of time on tour buses,' Dylan says, kindly feeling the need to explain. 'So, I've probably played more than most.'

Rowan takes to his feet.

'That's okay,' Rowan replies. 'You won, fair and square, and it's just a game. It's hard to be mad, when you know you've got the real prize.'

My body stiffens as Rowan takes me in his arms and kisses me on the lips. It feels like a violation, not just because we're no longer a couple, but because he knows that I know I have no choice but to play along. I don't know how long I let it go on for, it can only be a second or two, before I playfully push him away and laugh it off.

'Isn't he cheesy?' I say to the crowd of onlookers, who all laugh too.

Well, everyone but Dylan, who isn't even looking at us, he's kind of awkwardly looking at the screen, as he clicks through the motions to end the match.

What on earth is Rowan playing at? Showing off like that, just because he lost at a stupid video game. And why is Dylan so quiet? I guess he's on his best behaviour but, I don't know, it's all feeling a bit tense.

17

Saturday morning, a time when younger me would be nursing hangovers, enjoying leisurely lie-ins, savouring endless breakfasts, and making fun plans for the weekend ahead. Nowadays, with two energetic kids in the house, the weekends belong to them.

The kitchen is alive with activity as I rush around, preparing breakfast for Archie and Ned. Preparing their meals really keeps me on my toes, trying to cater to their very specific desires – their most and least favourite foods seem to change on a day-to-day basis. Archie wants his toast perfectly golden – with his Nutella spread in stripes – while Ned insists his cereal should be served in a particular bowl, and that I should pick out the misshapen ones – they taste bad, apparently.

Just as I'm painting my final freehand stripe of Nutella, on perfectly browned toast, Rowan saunters in, all dressed up smart.

He places a washing basket down on the floor before slapping a single bright red sock down on the island in front of me.

'What's that?' I ask him.

'My white shirts to wash,' he tells me. 'And that's the red sock I found in the basket. You need to be more careful – that would have ruined them.'

I pull a face to myself and resist telling him that he can do his own washing, if he thinks he'll do it so perfectly.

'Where are you taking the boys, all dolled up like that?' I ask as I glance over at him.

'Ah, I can't take them out today,' he replies so only I can hear. 'I've got a work opportunity and they've just called a meeting.'

'On a Saturday,' I say.

'An emergency meeting,' he replies.

I don't bother prying into the specifics of these 'emergency meetings' he's always rushing off to because I honestly don't care about what he does any more. All I care about is that he promised to spend time with the kids. The words don't come out, but the frustration's written all over my face.

'You'll have to take them,' he says, oblivious to my frustration. 'How about Jungle Jim's? It's a new play centre they've been wanting to visit.'

'Rowan...'

'Look, I've got to go,' he says, snatching up the toast I just finished working on before dashing to the door.

Is he serious? Is he really dumping the kids on me? We both agreed he would take them out today – I've been looking after them all week.

No sooner has the door closed behind him when there's an unexpected knock. I open it to find Dylan standing there, smiling widely.

'Hello, neighbour,' I joke. 'Come in. I'm trying to spread stripes of chocolate on toast.'

'Sounds fun,' he says with a laugh as he follows me through to the kitchen.

'Who's having the sock for breakfast?' he asks, nodding to Archie's red football sock that is still sitting where Rowan left it.

'Oh, Rowan put it there,' I tell him. 'He found it in the washing basket with his white shirts. Good job he spotted it. Anyway, what is the elusive Dylan King doing with his weekend?' I ask.

'I'm off to the recording studio,' he tells me, keeping his cool, but you can tell he's excited. 'I'm meeting up with the band to lay down a couple of our old tracks. Fancy joining me?'

My breath catches in my throat. It has been years since I was inside a recording studio. I want to say yes, of course I do, but family life has other plans for me.

'Ah, I'd love to, but I've got the kids today,' I tell him, unable to hide my disappointment. 'I wasn't supposed to be having them but Rowan pretty much just walked in, announced he was going out and then left, so...'

'So, the kids can come with us,' Dylan says with a shrug.

I'm taken aback by his offer but terrified he might take it back, so I bite his hand off.

'Can they really?' I reply. 'Because I would love, love, love to come.'

'Of course,' he says.

'But, this is going to sound silly, but you know that kids are kids, right?' I point out. 'They can't hold your beer or roll your joints or...'

My mind jumps back to the old days and the sights I saw that freaked even me out.

'Nic, I know that kids are kids,' he says with a laugh. 'Never met one that could roll a decent joint.'

I laugh at his joke. Okay, I'm being ridiculous. I guess I do have a bit of mum energy lurking inside me somewhere.

'Hey, dude, little dude,' Dylan calls out to them. 'How do you guys fancy visiting a real recording studio?'

'Yeah, cool,' Archie calls out.

'Yeah, cool,' Ned says, copying his brother.

'Cool,' Dylan says, then he turns to me. 'Problem solved. But you guys need to get ready, like, now.'

'Getting ready really quickly is still my number one skill,' I tell him excitedly. 'Come on, boys, we need to get dressed, double time.'

'I'll make the toast while you're getting them ready,' Dylan calls after me. 'I think I know what you mean.'

I practically charge upstairs, grabbing outfits for the boys, before flinging open my own wardrobe and looking for something to wear. There are the bones of my old look in here, I've just always watered them down, but black skinny jeans, a red vest top, a black leather jacket and big chunky pair of black boots together will make me feel right at home.

It's been so long since I was in a recording studio. Back in the day I would spend hours in them, like it was nothing, but suddenly the novelty is back. I'm excited to go, to reunite with the rest of the band, and to get to hear Dylan do his thing again.

It's going to be just like old times just, you know, with kids around. What's the worst that could happen?

18

I can't believe I'm back in a recording studio again, after all this time, and not only do I find it even harder to believe still that I'm here with Dylan and The Burnouts, but the fact that I've got Rowan's kids in tow just makes this all the crazier. I never would have anticipated this in a million years.

The studio is nothing short of high-tech luxury. The walls are padded to block out the outside world – which I kind of like, because I feel like I'm living another life right now – and the mood is just full of creativity and excitement. It's just like it used to be, in a way, but somehow so much better because the vibe is so chilled. Everyone is so happy. Mitch, the band's manager, is here, and so is Dev, the musical genius sitting behind the impressive mixing desk, who will be helping them rerecord their old tracks.

I love that the vibe is distinctly different from the old days. The entire band seems more grown-up, more sophisticated, and yet they all still give off that cool rock-star aura. Jamie, the bass player, is perched on a stool, trying to teach Ned how to play the James Bond theme on a bass guitar. Taz, the drummer, and Dylan are on the drum kit, teaching Archie the drumming basics. The sight of Archie, looking so tiny behind the enormous kit, is both adorable and hilarious.

'Hey, Dev, can you record Archie making a few sounds with the kit?' Dylan asks. 'We could use it in the recordings.'

Archie's eyes widen with excitement as he nods eagerly.

'Can we get him a cowbell?' Taz asks.

'Yes, a cowbell would be perfect,' Dylan replies – he seems almost as excited as Archie does.

'Long time, no see,' Mikey says, sitting down next to me, the two of us finally getting a moment alone.

Mikey is tall, with an athletic figure that he didn't have back in the day. His once dishevelled rocker's hair is now neatly trimmed and styled. A fashionable, well-fitted shirt complements his new mature and polished appearance and highlights his lean physique – Mikey's glow-up came around the time he made the switch from playing guitar to working as a TV presenter. He's a far cry from the shy musician he once was. We stayed in touch for a while, after he and Dylan fell out. I would see him from time to time, but nothing quite felt the same. Even the fun times felt sort of sad, without Dylan there too, it was like he had died and no one wanted to talk about it. So eventually Mikey and I drifted apart as well. He moved on to life as a TV star – finally out of his brother's shadow, as he probably saw it – and I moved on to, well, this.

'Hey, stranger,' I reply.

'Did you ever think you would see the day?' he asks, a big grin plastered across his face.

I laugh.

'Not in a million years,' I reply. 'I can't believe we're all here – and all friends.'

I dare to mention their infamous falling out.

Mikey nods knowingly.

'So, Nicole Wilde, family woman,' he points out. 'I never thought I'd see the day you grew up. They're great kids.'

'They really are,' I reply. 'Although I'm not sure

how grown-up I am, I did bring them to a recording studio. Their dad had to work. What about you? How have you been?'

Mikey's eyes come alive as he looks through his phone before he leans in and shows me photos of his wife and kids.

'I've got a family now too,' he tells me. 'I'm married – that's Nicola – and we have two kids, both girls. They're amazing, you'd love them.'

'Aww, they're so cute,' I tell him sincerely, smiling at the thought of Mikey enjoying family life. 'I'm so happy for you.'

'Thanks,' he replies. 'Jamie just got married recently and Taz, he's married, got one kid, another on the way – proper grown-ups.'

I laugh.

'It sounds like a lot has changed,' I reply.

Mikey's expression grows more serious, and he takes a moment to consider his words before he says anything else.

'Really, you know, it's just Dill who hasn't... really grown up,' he says, almost as though he's struggling to get the words out.

I nod thoughtfully. It's not just Dylan, I haven't exactly nailed adulthood myself, but I suppose I can see what he's getting at.

'The old days were a blast, don't get me wrong,' he continues while it's just the two of us. 'But we've all moved on. Sometimes I worry about him. He's struggled a lot, and I don't know if he's fully put those old habits behind him. I'm not sure anyone ever does.'

I take a sip of my tea – I never thought I'd be drinking tea in a recording studio, but here we are – and nod thoughtfully.

'Well, that's why I'm here,' I reassure him. 'I'll do my best to keep him on the straight and narrow.'

Mikey sighs.

'We've tried before, you know,' he reminds me. 'But when Dylan's in full swing, he's hard to stop.'

When Mikey says we've tried before, he's referring to a time, just before the big falling out, when we did everything we could think of to straighten Dylan out. And I failed him then, but that's all the more reason not to fail him now. He's starting from a better place, with an amazing opportunity ahead of him, so I'm hopeful this time.

I glance through the glass at him, watching him teach Archie the art of playing the cowbell, and it feels so hard to imagine the old him making a comeback. I know, he's on his best behaviour, but he's really trying, I feel like he genuinely wants to keep on the straight and narrow this time. It's only been a few days, but I can't picture him acting like he used to. Horny, drunken Dylan is nowhere to be seen. Of course, neither are the fans – yet. The real test will come when the reunion tour is announced. But we'll cross that bridge when we come to it.

19

I let out the longest, deepest, most contented sigh and smile to myself.

The car journey home has been a mixture of the boys' giddy chatter and lively singalongs.

I noticed that Dylan's vocals had changed in the studio. I wondered if it was down to some kind of magic by Dev but, no, I heard the change again in the car as he sang with the boys. I remember that his voice used to have these irresistibly sexy, raspy qualities. His raw, unrefined tone was part of his charm, it made hearts flutter and knees weak. In hindsight it was probably the result of countless late-night gigs in smoke-filled venues, too many cigarettes, too much alcohol, and everything else that goes hand in hand with rock-star life. Now, though, wow, his voice is so smooth and strong. Velvety soft with these huge bursts of power. His vocals have matured into a sound that genuinely sends shivers down my spine – I love it. His fans are going to be stunned. I suppose taking better care of his body has had this incredible knock-on effect on his vocal cords too.

Dylan pulls up outside our house and helps me get the boys out of the car. I sigh again, a little heavier this time, sad that the day has to end.

'Okay, boys,' I say as we hover by the car. 'Before we go inside, make sure to say a big "thank you" to Dylan for such an amazing day.'

Both Archie and Ned eagerly thank Dylan, their happy faces still lit up with joy.

'Thanks, Dylan! This was the best day ever!' Archie tells him. 'I know for sure now; I want to be a rock star just like you!'

I smile. Archie in particular has had a really special day. Being that little bit older than Ned, he's been able to appreciate it more. And how many kids get their music lessons from genuine rock stars in a proper recording studio? Oh, and his cowbell is going to make it into the final record, which is so, so cool.

'You certainly look the part, Archie,' I tell him.

Taz, it turns out, has become quite a successful

tattoo artist during the band's hiatus. He has these kids' washable tattoo pens in his bag so, with expert care and precision, he covered the boys' arms with super-cool temporary tattoos. He told me they wash off straight away, with little more than water. I genuinely think there will be tears when they come off, the boys love them that much.

'When can I get them done for real?' Archie asks, waiting patiently for an answer, hopeful for one that will make him happy.

'Not for a long, long time,' I tell him. 'Sorry, kid.'

'Dylan has so many,' Archie points out.

'Well, Dylan is basically an old man,' I reply – mostly to tease Dylan.

'And Nicole doesn't have any because she's always been too scared,' Dylan chimes in. 'And too indecisive. So, if she ever did feel brave enough to get one, by the time she decided what she wanted, she was too scared again.'

'You're a baby,' Archie tells me.

'I am,' I say with a sigh. 'Maybe one day I'll surprise you but, for now, it's bedtime. Say bye to Dill.'

'Bye, Dylan,' they sing, hugging him at the same time, before charging off towards the house.

'Bye, Dylan,' I say to him in a similar, childlike voice.

'Bye, Nic,' he replies, laughing at how goofy he sounds.

I hover in front of him for a second. I should hug him – the voice in my head is telling me to hug him. It would be normal to hug him, right?

'You want one too?' he asks, reading my mind.

Dylan takes me in his arms and pulls me close. God, I feel so at ease when I'm wrapped up in him.

'I forget how hard you are,' I tell him. It's only when he laughs that I realise exactly what I just said. 'Your body, I mean, your new muscles. Where has my squishy, smelly friend gone?'

'I'm still smelly,' he offers up in consolation.

'No, you're not,' I reply.

We hold eye contact for a second as Dylan keeps me in his arms.

'Nicole, I need a wee,' Ned calls out.

'And that's my cue,' I tell him. 'See you later.'

'Yeah, see you around the neighbourhood,' he replies with a laugh.

He returns to his car, to make the very short journey back to Mr Campbell's house.

'Right, come on, boys, let's—'

My voice cuts off as I see Rowan standing in the doorway.

'Oh, hello,' I say, sounding a bit like I've been

caught out, even though I haven't done anything wrong.

'Where the hell have you been?' he asks me. Then he notices the boys' temporary tattoos. 'What have you done to my kids?'

'I need a wee,' Ned says.

'It's okay, kids, go inside,' I tell them. 'I'll catch you up.'

'Well?' Rowan prompts me.

'Oh, they're *your* kids?' I reply. 'That's funny, because they were our kids when you left me looking after them this morning.'

'Yeah, I left *you* to *look after* them,' he reminds me. 'It's him, isn't it? He's done this to them. How dare he—'

'How dare he entertain your kids all day, because you were too busy?' I interrupt him. 'Bloody hell, Rowan, they're temporary tattoos, they'll wash right off – they're already fading away on their own.'

'Where have you been?' he asks me. 'Not to Jungle Jim's, I can tell you that, because I went there to find you and you weren't there.'

'We took them to a recording studio, to see—'

'He took them to a recording studio?' Rowan snaps. 'Nicole, they're children, what are you playing at?'

'I'm not understanding what the problem is,' I reply. 'You want me to look after them, entertain them for the day, so I do, but I've done it wrong?'

'Why is he hanging out with my kids?' Rowan asks. 'He's here, he's living on *my* street, he's taking *my* kids to God knows what kind of environment, he's muscling his way in at the school – don't think I don't know about that – and he's got you completely distracted, because you still managed to put the red sock back in the wash with my white shirts, and now they're totally ruined. Oh, and the icing on the cake, he's giving you long, lingering hugs on my doorstep. I should beat the shit out of him.'

My eyebrows shoot up.

'Wow,' I say simply. 'I mean, just as an FYI, for a guy who spends so much time in the gym, you are not intimidating *at all*, so you might want to work on that. And you need to grow up.'

I turn around and head down the driveway.

'Where are you going?' he calls out. 'To him, I bet.'

'Yep, to him,' I call back as I walk away. 'For another long, lingering hug.'

My blood boils as I make the short journey across the street. How dare he talk to me like that? How dare he complain about me giving his kids a great day?

Honestly, he's lucky I'm still here, still helping out, still cleaning up the mess *he* made. That's the only reason I stuck around, to get the money back that he stole from me for his stupid scheme, to make sure no one else was caught up in it, and to make sure that I left him with his reputation, his job and his house intact – all for the sake of his kids. It's mad, that he would ever dare to question if I care for them. I love them, and if Rowan will let me, I'll always be there for them in some way.

I march up to Dylan's front door and knock way harder than I intended.

'Hello,' he says, his smile dropping when he sees my face.

'Hi, can I come in?' I ask him.

'Of course,' he says. 'What are neighbours for, huh?'

I follow Dylan through the house, into the kitchen.

'Coffee?' he asks.

'Do you have anything stronger?' I ask him.

'I haven't exactly been shopping,' he says with a laugh. 'I can see what Mr C left in his cupboards.'

Dylan pulls out a bottle of whisky.

'Irish coffee?' he says with a smile.

'Perfect,' I tell him.

I take a seat at the wooden kitchen table and place my head in my hands.

'What the fuck is wrong with everyone?' I ask him, not expecting an answer.

'By everyone, I'm guessing you mean your fella,' Dylan replies.

'How did you guess?' I say, dropping my arms like a stroppy teenager.

'What can I say? My intuition is just *that* good,' he tells me. 'Also, you were in a great mood when I left you, about fourteen seconds before you knocked on my door, and he's the only person you had time to interact with.'

I laugh.

'Great intuition,' I tell him.

Dylan makes our drinks and nods towards the kitchen door with his head.

'Come on, let's take this party to the sofa,' he suggests.

I follow Dylan into Mr Campbell's lounge. It's as dark and moody as I feel. Dylan turns on a couple of lamps, which do little more than give the room an eerie glow.

'I can't turn the big light on,' he tells me. 'It's not that it doesn't work – it's so powerful it gives you a tan.'

I laugh.

'It's okay, I like this light, it's good for wallowing,' I say as I take my drink from him. I take a sip and, oof, that's strong. I'd forgotten about Dylan King measures.

'So, what's up?' he asks me.

'Oh, it's just Rowan being a dick,' I reply. 'He went mental about me taking the boys to the recording studio, and their temporary tattoos.'

'Do you want me to go talk to him, to explain what it was like there, that there's nothing to worry about – I could invite him to join us next time,' Dylan suggests.

I give him a small smile. He's so sweet.

'No, thank you, that's okay,' I reply. 'He's... he's not happy about your presence.'

'Men with girlfriends or wives never are,' he jokes. 'But I can reassure him on that one too.'

I slump down in my seat and rest my head on Dylan's shoulder.

'Ahh, Dill, it's all such a mess,' I say with a sigh. 'Can I tell you a secret?'

'Always,' he replies.

'Rowan and I aren't together any more,' I confess.

Dylan doesn't say anything so I sit up and look at

him, surprised by his lack of a reaction. I give him my best puzzled look.

'Yeah, well, I figured something was going on,' he says simply.

'How on earth did you do that?' I ask in disbelief.

'You've been messing with him,' he says through a smile. 'Pranking him.'

My jaw drops.

'And how did you know that?' I ask.

My gosh, I thought I was so clever.

'Come on, Nic, I taught you the salt and sugar swap,' he reminds me. 'We used to do it all the time on tour. It was never not funny.'

'Oh,' I say with a laugh.

'And I'm guessing it was you who put the red sock in with his white shirts,' he says.

'It was,' I reply. 'But he realised, and took it out, so I didn't actually go through with it.'

'I figured as much,' Dylan says with a laugh. 'So I chucked it back in for you.'

I snort with laughter.

'Well, I knew we were doing something,' he tells me. 'I just wasn't sure what but I had your back, like I always do. Did I miss any others?'

'I wrote "wanker" on his car door,' I confess. 'I intended to do it with a dry-wipe pen, so that it would rub straight off, except in my hurry I grabbed a marker pen by mistake – he had to take it somewhere to get it fixed.'

Dylan laughs.

'That's my girl,' he tells me. 'Can I ask why you broke up? And, more importantly, why you're still there?'

'Things were great when we first met,' I begin, the words coming without much effort, because I've always found Dylan so easy to talk to. 'And, after we dated for a while, I met the boys and I was kind of freaked out that he already had kids – their mum sadly passed away when they were really young – but they're such great kids, I liked having them around. Things just moved so fast after that, I was living with him before I knew it, and he used to talk all the time about us getting married. He would even refer to me as Mrs Nutter.'

'His last name is Nutter?' Dylan says in disbelief. 'Nicole Nutter?'

'Right?' I reply.

'You're not a Nutter, you're Wilde,' he replies with a laugh. 'But it's easy for me to say, I'm blessed – I'm a King.'

'That you are,' I reply, allowing myself a moment to smile. 'Anyway, his job is basically making money on social media, sponsored posts, ads on his YouTube videos – that sort of thing. One day he started working with this woman called Carrie who was something to do with protein powder.'

'Why is it always protein powder with guys who look like that?' Dylan asks.

'I will never understand why gym boys are so obsessed with it,' I reply. 'But Rowan was way into it. He started acting a little suspiciously, short-tempered, sneaking around. So, you know me, I start snooping around and I find out that not only is he involved in some kind of scammy scheme, but he's put money of mine into it.'

'The bastard,' Dylan says. 'Did you get it back?'

'Yes, but only recently,' I reply. 'That's why I stuck around, to get my money back, and to make sure other people got their money back. At first, when I was angry, I thought to hell with Rowan, he can sort his own mess. But not only did I worry about leaving the kids with a dad who could lose everything, I realised how terrible it would be for my business, if I had my own scandal going on inside my house, right under my nose – and that's if people believed I wasn't actually involved in it all.'

'I'm glad you didn't lose any money in the end,' Dylan says. 'That's something.'

'Yeah, I didn't lose any money, but what a way to lose your boyfriend, your home, the kids you've been raising...'

My voice trails off.

'Yeah, well, I know a thing or two about the fun and games that come with having a relationship with someone who has kids that aren't yours,' he reminds me, referring to his very brief marriage from a million years ago, when he thought he was going to be a dad.

'I've had time to get used to the idea,' I tell him. 'As sad as it sounds. And things are pretty much wrapped up now. I knew the time to leave was coming. I guess it's sort of snuck up on me. Of course, now my bestie has moved in across the street, and started working at the boys' school, I have something to lose again.'

Dylan laughs. As his face straightens up again, he wraps an arm around me and pulls me close.

'I'm so sorry all of this has happened to you,' he says. 'I would offer to go over there and punch him but, not only have I never really been any good at fighting, but I'm pretty sure as the person who is re-forming my public image, you would advise me not to do that.'

'Wow, you are learning,' I say with a smile as I snuggle in closer to his embrace. 'Did you ever think we'd end up back here?'

'What, together, talking about what a mess we're in?' he asks through a laugh. 'Yeah, of course, we've always been like this.'

I laugh too.

'That's the spirit,' I say. 'Glad to be in it again together – and in case I didn't say it before, thank you so much for ruining his shirts.'

'Any time,' Dylan says. 'Actually, I might have another offer for you. How do you fancy a night out in London tomorrow?'

'I'm listening,' I say.

'I'm going to check out a support band with the rest of the lads, you could come with us,' he suggests. 'We're going to a gig, then we thought we'd have a night out, before things hopefully get crazy again. Fancy it?'

'I would love that,' I reply. 'I think a night out is just what I need.'

'When was the last time you had a wild night out?' he asks.

I think for a moment.

'When was the last time I saw you?'

Dylan laughs.

'Okay then, we're setting off in the morning, I'll message you the details,' he says.

'Great,' I reply. 'Do you mind if I hang out here for

a bit before I go home? I can't face having it out with Rowan. I can sneak back once he's gone to bed.'

'Yeah, of course,' Dylan says as he squeezes me again. 'Stay as long as you like.'

If it were up to me, I'd never move again.

20

I'm almost embarrassed to admit it, but it's been years and years since I last attended a gig. I'd never consciously thought about it but, when I walked away from the music industry, I walked away from everything I associated with it – which included going to gigs.

I used to go to several gigs a month – I've got tinnitus to prove it – but I needed a clean break, to leave all the mess behind me, so I just stopped going to gigs. I was more selective about the music I listened to too. It is the silliest thing but, when you're friends with bands, or get to know too much about them, it can basically ruin their music for you, if you find out things you don't like about them, or come to associate their songs with bad times in your life.

For most people it's fine, you can listen to any music you want, and unless some big scandal hits the news you will be unaffected by the personal lives of those you admire musically. Being there, peeping behind the curtain, you see too much. The wholesome image so many bands and musicians project to the public is a stark contrast to the behind-the-scenes reality. I remember meeting Plastic Rap (back when they were at the height of their fame) for the first time. They had a massive female following – pretty much women of all ages too. Their entire persona was built on being good boys, loving their girlfriends, and embracing a squeaky-clean image. Unlucky for me, I had the icky privilege of witnessing first-hand that they also liked to embrace their fans, behind their significant others' backs, and the ones I saw didn't exactly look old enough to be making good decisions for themselves.

I suppose I was no different to those girls (just much older, even ten years ago), I wasn't immune to the allure of the fame and hype. When I started seeing Luke, I hoped he might turn out to be different from the rest, because I'd known him before he became properly famous, and he always seemed like such a great guy. But he wasn't – he probably never was – and his band soon dropped off the face of the earth. Well, that's what happens when all you care about is getting off your face and into the pants of any girl you can, your music career heads down the toilet. We love to see it.

Plastic Rap, frustratingly, have managed to hold on to their pristine image, still making appearances on TV shows or going viral with social media posts. They continue to peddle their wholesome lives – and maybe they've changed, now they're all married with kids – but it still makes me queasy whenever I catch them on-screen.

Hopefully, these days, it's harder to get away with all that stuff, and new bands are better across the board.

Tonight we are checking out a punk rock band called Agents of Animals, with Dylan and the boys, to see if they seem like a good fit for a support act on the tour. Honestly, I was like a kid on Christmas Eve, as I was getting ready for my first gig in forever. I wore clothes I already owned, but I put them together differently, in a way that made me feel more like the old me. A black leather miniskirt, a hot pink cami, and my trusty leather jacket. Teamed with a pair of high-heeled boots, and a heavy dose of black eyeliner and red lipstick, it's amazing how much like the old me I feel right now.

I knew almost right away, when the five-piece band came out on to the stage, that they were perfect. They remind me of a younger version of The Burnouts, in a way. Unapologetically loud, fun and totally themselves.

The atmosphere inside the venue is electric – it's only now that their set is winding down that I'm realising just how much I have missed live music. I'd forgotten everything about it, but it's all coming back to me, all at once. The air is thick with sweat, and stale beer, and my feet are stuck to the floor, and I'll probably be covered in bruises tomorrow from the lively crowd, and I've loved it.

Oftentimes, on tour, the gig was only the start of the night. Depending on where we were, what we were doing – if we needed to drive through the night and things like that – the gig itself would be like the pre-drinks, and we would almost always end up either having a huge party in the hotel, or we would hit the clubs. Tonight, seeing as though this isn't a tour, so no hotel or bus to think about, someone suggested we go to a club after and everyone said yes. Honestly, it was almost scary, the way it happened, so naturally, like none of us had ever had a day away from it.

So now, here we are, at a London club, for the first time in forever. I laugh to myself, as we arrive, because it is after 10 p.m. You forget that, when you're in your twenties, that's a perfectly reasonable time to start your night out. These days, pretty much any time after 8 p.m., the only thing I'm getting ready for is bed. I had made peace with a lifetime full of evenings where all I drank was tea, and the only thing I put my butt on was the sofa. Now that I'm single, and in places like this again, I need to find my (old) feet.

Everything still feels like a fever dream – and the colourful, strobing lights in the club aren't exactly helping me convince myself otherwise. The bass is turned up so high I feel like my heartbeat has synchronised with the music, the floor vibrating up through my feet, swirling around in my chest, and as the neon lights cut through the air, shining on us all, making everyone look like a surreal multicoloured version of the person they are outside, in the real world, it only makes things feel more surreal.

Our cluster of tables sits in a prime spot – near the bar and the toilets and, oh my God, do I sound like an old woman right now? It's also a great spot for people-watching. Everyone on the dance floor looks so young and carefree. I was going to say I wish I was on what they were on, but someone did try to sell me some of what they're on in the toilets. I'll stick to getting my buzzes in the usual way – by triggering a panic attack – thank you very much. I'm with The Burnouts – Dylan, Mikey, Taz, Jamie – as well as our new friends from Agents of Animals, and we're all having a great time.

The drinks are flowing like there is no tomorrow – and given that The Burnouts have actually experienced 'no tomorrow', you would think they might take it a little easier. I guess everyone is just excited, giddy to be back in their old lives. I'm keeping an eye on Dylan, who has had a few beers, but doesn't seem to be drunk. I admire his restraint because the old Dylan would've been off his face since breakfast.

A tall, slim woman with long brown hair and a glittery green dress does a double take as she passes our table. She glances around the group, recognition in her eyes as she looks over each of the guys. Of course, just like the good old days, her final sights are set on Dylan.

With palpable excitement, she makes a direct approach, giving life to a flirtatious scenario I've witnessed countless times. Dylan responds with his usual charm, showing polite interest.

'You're Dylan King,' she tells him.

Good one. He's never heard that before.

'I am,' he replies. 'Hello.'

She chews her lip as she looks him up and down. I suppose, like me, his new look is a shock to her too. There are no photos online of the new and improved Dylan King and, even if there were, I imagine it packs way more of a punch in person.

'I'm such a big fan of yours,' she tells him. 'Big, big fan.'

'Thanks,' he replies. 'Always nice to meet a fan.'

'Are you single?' she asks, cutting to the chase.

Dylan laughs – probably at her directness. He's always loved it when people cut through the bullshit.

She leans in closer, resting her elbows on the table, using her forearms to push her boobs together as she practically shags him with her eyes. Her giddy laughter is louder than the music, and she's twirling her hair like her life depends on it. He's polite, and his effortless charm is ever-present. I've seen thousands of girls flirt with Dylan – and him flirt back – but today something is different. The sight of her flirting with him, right in front of me, so physically close it's almost like I'm a part of it, unsettles me more than I'd like to admit. I find myself squirming in my seat and averting my gaze. It's irrational, I know, because it's nothing new, but today it's getting to me.

'Is it true what they say about guys with tattoos?' she asks in a breathy voice.

'I don't know, what do they say?' Dylan replies with a laugh.

'I'm just going to the toilets,' I say, pushing my chair out, making a dash for the big pink door nearby before anyone can say another word.

As I exit the cubicle, and wash my hands, I stand in front of the bronze-tinted glass mirror and stare at my own reflection. The dim, moody lighting casts a soft, flattering glow, but none of it can offset the fact that I have a face like thunder.

'What are you doing, Nicole?' I ask my reflection, silently having a word with myself in my head. 'What's going on? Are you jealous? Are you seriously jealous of girls flirting with Dylan?'

I take a deep breath and close my eyes, trying to shake off the irrational emotions I'm experiencing right now. I've probably had more to drink tonight than I have this year, and I clearly can't handle it any more, that's all. I just need to tell myself to stop, because I'm being ridiculous.

With a final mental shake, I square my shoulders, apply a fresh coat of lipstick and plaster a smile on my face. Suck it up, Wilde. Go out there and have fun.

As I head back to the group with my head held

high, I notice something going on. Things seem to have taken a turn with the girl in the sparkly green minidress. From here, outside the commotion looking in, it seems as though her boyfriend, a tall and absolutely furious figure, is now shouting at both her and Dylan. Oh, and just when you think things can't get any worse, I notice that someone in the crowd is filming the scene on her phone, capturing every tense moment, because everything has to go on social media these days.

My heart races as I step closer and I arrive just as the situation spirals out of control. The boyfriend, blinded by anger, grabs his girlfriend by the hair, violently pulling her closer. I watch Dylan's expression change, his brow furrowing, his jaw tightening, as something in him engages. He jumps forwards and pushes himself between the girl and her boyfriend.

'Are you okay?' he asks her, but with his attention on the girl he has no time to see it coming, the boyfriend swings his fist, and he smacks Dylan right in the face, knocking him to the floor.

My heart leaps into my throat as I rush to Dylan's side, my hands trembling as I check to see if he's all right, but the boyfriend is still here, and he's about to lash out again.

Dylan pushes me out of the way, placing himself

squarely between the angry boyfriend and me, but then the bouncers rush in and grab the guy, dragging him away as his sobbing girlfriend chases after them, complaining that the bouncers are hurting him. Unreal.

I turn to Dylan, to examine his face, and my heart skips a beat as I see his lip bleeding. He casually feels the cut with his tongue and then laughs to himself.

'You're laughing?' I say in disbelief.

'I am,' he says, grinning through the discomfort. 'We both know this isn't the first time someone's boyfriend has given me a smack in the mouth.'

'Oh, well, that's fine then,' I say sarcastically.

'Are you proud of me?' he asks jokily. 'For not fighting back?'

Now I'm laughing.

'Yes, Dylan, I'm proud of you for being on your best behaviour in a bar fight,' I say with a sigh. 'Good work.'

His smile falls for a second.

'I couldn't just watch him hurt her,' he tells me. 'And then I was worried he was going to hurt you.'

'God, I need a drink,' I say, snatching Dylan's beer from the table, and taking a big swig even though I hate the taste of beer. 'Ergh, but not this one – I swear, it tastes even worse than usual.'

'Before you go, we might have a problem,' he says seriously. 'That girl over there, I noticed she was filming everything.'

'I saw that too,' I tell him. 'Don't worry, I've got this.'

We approach the girl who is already watching the footage back on her phone, showing her friend who must have missed the drama.

'Hello, did you film what just happened?' I ask her.

'What's it to you?' she asks.

I gesture at Dylan to join us.

'This is Dylan, he's a friend of mine, and as you can see, he's hurt,' I tell her.

Dylan pouts, showing her his bloody lip. The girl smiles and giggles – my God, is he flirting right now?

'We just need to know someone filmed it, in case the police need evidence,' I tell her.

'Oh, right, yeah, I filmed it,' she says. 'I thought you were going to tell me to delete it.'

'No, no,' I insist. 'It's evidence! But, if you want a top tip, you should call the *Daily Scoop*, ask for a guy called Jasper and say you have a video for him – he'll pay decent money for something like that.'

'Really?' she squeaks.

'Really,' I reply.

'Okay, cool, thanks,' she says before getting back to her friends.

'Nic, what the hell was that?' Dylan asks me as we head towards the bar.

'That was me,' I tell him. 'Working.'

'I thought you were going to get her to delete it, not encourage her to sell it to a tabloid,' he replies in disbelief. 'At worst it looks like I'm having fights in bars. At best I got knocked on my arse because I didn't even fight back.'

'And that is best,' I tell him. 'Look, she's going to take that footage to the press, and they're going to see you, looking sober in a club, defending the honour of a woman – taking a punch for her. How could you look like anything but a hero?'

Dylan thinks for a moment. Eventually his mouth pulls itself into a smile.

'You're a genius,' he tells me. 'An evil genius. Have you always been so manipulative?'

I laugh it off.

'Come on, let's get a drink,' I say. 'I thought we were supposed to be having fun?'

'Yeah, that's what I thought,' Mikey says, pushing himself between us, wrapping an arm around us both. 'Tonight we are letting our hair down, the calm before the storm, and now we've got the fight out of the way it's sex, drugs and rock and roll from here on out.'

I laugh because he's obviously joking.

I think about what Dylan just said. Have I always been this manipulative? I've always tried to do what I thought was best, if it helped people, but I haven't always got the best results. But that's a conversation I need to have with him on another day, because tonight we party, together, for the first time in almost a decade.

Wish me luck.

21

I grip the sheets below me with both hands, squeezing so hard I feel my nails dig into the mattress.

I have woken up to the feeling of the world spinning around me. Hangovers in your thirties are really something; a cruel reminder that your body isn't as resilient as it used to be. I've had bad hangovers before, and the usual suspects are all there: the relentless headache, the desert-dry mouth, and the feeling that my stomach is trying to turn itself inside out. But this hangover has a few fresh tricks up its sleeve too. The bad back I've woken up with is just such a nice touch, honestly, I'm loving all of the little reminders that I'm getting older.

I wince as I dare to lift my head. My back actually

feels like it's on fire. Worse than that, though? I'm not even sure where I am. Panic creeps in, adding another layer of misery to my already pounding head. I sit up in what appears to be a large, unfamiliar bed. I look around with my bleary eyes, trying to find something that tells me where I am but there's nothing. It's a nice room – a hotel? No, not a hotel, I can't see any of the usual things you would expect to find. This is definitely a bedroom.

'Hello?' I croak out.

I clear my throat and try again, my voice louder this time. Of course, then it hits me, that the last thing I should be doing in a random house is calling out, alerting people to the fact that I'm here. I should be grabbing my things and sneaking out. Better to sneak out quietly than find myself running for my life later.

I turn my head and spot my phone on the bedside table. It's charging and within arm's reach. There's a glass of water next to me too. The chances I've been kidnapped are looking slimmer by the second, but I still don't know where I am.

The door creaks open. I quickly look, to see who it is, pulling the covers up to my chest and only now noticing that I'm wearing an oversized black Burnouts T-shirt from their 2012 tour.

Dylan walks in, wearing nothing but a pair of pyjama bottoms, clutching what appears to be a bowl of cereal.

'I thought I heard you,' he mumbles between spoonfuls. 'Good morning.'

'Oh, it is not a good morning at all,' I complain. 'I have the hangover from hell, and I woke up with no idea where I was, I was in such a panic until you walked in.'

Dylan shrugs, seemingly unfazed by my suffering. He's a picture of perfect health this morning, despite our wild night out last night. He plonks himself down on top of the bed next to me.

'You don't recognise your old room?' he says with a laugh.

I rub my temples and squint around, only now realising that I'm at Dylan's house.

'I do now that you mention it,' I admit. 'You've re-decorated.'

'Yeah,' he acknowledges. 'I fancied a change last year, so I redid every room.'

Now that the place looks familiar, the warmth of nostalgia goes a little way to taking the edge off my hangover.

'I don't remember coming back to your house,' I admit. 'Or much else about last night. My God, what did we do? I feel awful, and my back... Every time I move, it's like I'm lying on broken glass. Am I an old lady now? Will I complain about my back every day until I die? My auntie warned me not to wear a push-up bra in my teens, she said it would wreck my back and attract the wrong boys – she was right about the second part.'

Dylan smiles mischievously, making my heart pound even more.

'Well,' he grins, and I know it's going to be bad news, so I grit my teeth and brace myself. 'The good news is you don't have a bad back. So, you're younger and fitter than you think you are, and all that weird stuff your auntie told you is probably not true.'

'And the bad news?' I ask through a wince.

'The *other* news – not the bad news – is that you got a tattoo,' he says with a smile.

I recoil, my stomach churning.

'Oh, God, no,' I squeak. 'What have I done?'

I kick off the bedcovers and roll around like a maniac, trying to get a look at my back.

'Tell me I didn't get a lower back tattoo,' I moan as I keep trying. 'Can you get me a mirror, so I can see it?'

'You didn't get a lower back tattoo,' he tells me. I sigh with relief. 'Technically, it's closer to your bum, just above your right cheek.'

My jaw drops.

'I don't need to get you a mirror,' he tells me, placing his empty bowl down on the side before slipping off his pyjama bottoms. 'Here.'

And there it is. A tattoo of a tiger wearing a crown, on his thigh.

'We got matching ones,' he announces proudly. 'I went for the thigh, instead of the butt.'

I flop face first into my pillow.

'Why, why, why?' I groan into it.

'It was your idea,' Dylan says. 'Remember?'

My idea?

I only have to think about it for a second before a flash of last night pops into my head.

'Wilde and King,' I mutter, sitting up again.

'Yep,' he says with a nod. 'The boys and I were getting matching band tattoos, to celebrate the new tour, and you'd had that one done while I was busy. So I couldn't really say no when you told me I should get a matching one. I guess I'd forgotten what you were like when you've had a drink. You seemed pretty chill about it.'

'You got a silly tattoo done, to make me feel less stupid?' I say.

'I mean, all tattoos are silly, when you think about it,' he replies. 'And I'm covered in them anyway and... I liked the sentiment. We're bound together forever.'

I guess that's kind of nice – if not completely ridiculous.

'I couldn't tell you the last time I got so pissed,' I admit. 'I guess I can't handle it like I used to. Okay, okay, show me yours again.'

Dylan obliges, parting his thick legs to show me the tiger creeping out from his inner right thigh.

'And mine is the same as that?' I ask.

'Exactly the same,' he replies. 'Same size and everything.'

'It is cute,' I grudgingly admit. 'And I guess I have always been too scared to get one.'

'And if you ever want it removed, hit me up for the laser bill, yeah?' he replies. 'I feel bad now, I shouldn't have let you drink so much.'

'Okay, have I woken up in a parallel universe?' I ask in disbelief. 'Because I'm the one who usually keeps an eye on what you're drinking.'

'And yet it was me who helped you to bed last night,' he reminds. 'I tell you what, you didn't need singing to sleep last night.'

'Wow, I forgot you used to do that,' I reply, although it's a blatant lie. I remember it like it was yesterday. Whenever I was feeling stressed, unwell, or just couldn't drift off to sleep, Dylan would gently stroke me, or tickle my arm, while softly serenading me with lullaby versions of my favourite songs. In those moments I always felt at my absolute happiest and safest. It always worked like a treat.

I remember one time, when I was under a lot of pressure at work, I hesitantly asked Rowan if he could do it, to comfort me. However, instead of the tenderness I had anticipated, all he did was sing me a funny song as he touched me for a few seconds before promptly trying to shag me instead – it's amazing how many men think that's a cure for all problems. It was a stark reminder of the differences between the two of them – not that I should be comparing boyfriends to Dylan King – but it just made the times Dylan did it seem all the more special. It only worked with his touch.

'I used to paint your toenails too,' he reminds me with a laugh. 'You always used to say that your legs were too long for you to reach.'

'You had your uses,' I say with a smile. 'And you were surprisingly good at it.'

We naturally fall into silence. I don't know what he's thinking about, but I'm trying to push the past out of my head.

'Anyway, the good news is I can drive you home,' Dylan tells me. 'I said I would go into the school tomorrow, to start helping out with musical rehearsals.'

'Aww, that's great,' I reply, genuinely pleased on both counts. 'I'm surprised you're sober enough to drive yet. Then again, you've had a lot more practice than me.'

Dylan leans in close, our faces are just centimetres apart. It's an unexpected closeness, and for a brief moment, I'm uncertain about his intentions. My heart quickens and I hold my breath. Then he starts sniffing.

'Oh, man. Yeah, I would fail a breathalyser test just by being in a car with you,' he jokes as he pulls away. 'Maybe we'll keep the windows down.'

I laugh but I can't ignore that I felt something, having him so close to my face, but I'm scared to even think about what.

Why am I being such a weirdo? And why is the thought of going home – of returning to reality – causing a pang of sadness in me? Being here in Dylan's house, after a night out, it feels like a journey back in time, just like the good old days – only somehow even better.

'Come on then, let's go,' Dylan says, snapping me from my thoughts.

'Okay,' I reply, trying not to sound too disappointed.

I really wish I didn't have to leave.

22

I got out of Dylan's car outside Mr Campbell's house, choosing to make the last minute of the journey home myself, just in case Rowan was around.

Walking up the driveway, seeing his car there, I'm glad that I did.

I walk into the house and I'm immediately bombarded with the sound of excited little voices and the smell of Rowan's cooking.

Rowan and the kids appear from nowhere. The boys run up to me and give me a hug.

I can feel my new tattoo still, which doesn't only serve as a reminder of last night, but it feels like I'm bringing a bit more of the old me into the house. I'm not sure if that's a good thing or not. It's either something I can use to tell myself that I'm not so boring after all, or something that will remind me of a life I no longer really live.

'Let me get one too,' Rowan says.

'You're back,' Archie says.

Ned just squeezes my leg. The two of them look so happy to see me.

Then I look up and see, hanging from the banister, a handmade banner that reads:

Welcome home, Mummy!

I hold my breath as I look at it.

'Do you like it?' Rowan asks me. 'The boys missed you so much, they wanted to make you a banner and – boys, go get Nicole the presents you made her.'

'Okay,' they both say before charging up the stairs.

My heart swells at the sight of them.

'They really did miss you,' Rowan tells me when we're alone. 'I missed you too.'

Rowan ushers me into the kitchen and I can tell from his expression that he wants to talk.

'Nicole, listen, I'm sorry for how I reacted,' he starts, his voice earnest. 'I just... I admit it, I felt threatened. Seeing you with Dylan, I couldn't help but over-react, seeing him being close with the boys – come on,

he's Dylan King. But I shouldn't have acted so inse-
cure. I want to make things right, Nic. I want to play
nice and help out with the fundraiser. I want to be
better, for the boys, and I want to be better for you
too.'

I appreciate Rowan's honesty but, deep down, I
know that things between us have changed irrepara-
bly. It's not just about the way he's acting because
Dylan is here; our relationship has run its course. I
don't trust him, and you can't truly love someone you
don't trust, no matter how hard you try.

'Thank you for the apology,' I say softly. 'I appreciate where you're coming from.'

Rowan smiles, relieved that the beef is squashed –
well, the new beef, at least.

'Okay, well, I'm going to check on dinner, and the
boys have made you something,' he tells me. 'I just
want you to see how much we appreciate you.'

As he walks away to check on dinner, I'm left with
a bittersweet feeling, and more than a pang of guilt.
The kids missed me and, you know what, I missed
them just as much. I've been around them every day
for almost three years, that's a long time. I'm not only
breaking up with Rowan, I'm breaking up with them
too. And now I feel like one hell of a villain, but I can't
stay with Rowan for the kids, can I? Would he still let

me see them, if we did break up? Thinking about it, with everyone pretty much reimbursed, and only a few 'family' social posts to go, the boys are the only reason I'm still here – well, that and not having sorted anywhere to go yet, but it's so hard to pull the trigger, to shake up their world like that.

Everything is such a mess. I have no idea how I'm going to sort it.

23

The weather today is dreary and unforgiving, with relentless rain hammering down, and skies so dark I'm not convinced it isn't night-time. It feels as though this winter has lasted a lifetime and, for some reason, spring is refusing to turn up. It's one of those days when an umbrella is a futile accessory.

Of course, given how dark, cold, wet and windy it is, obviously today is the day I managed to absent-mindedly grab a coat without a hood, and it's not the kind of weather an umbrella could survive.

I make a mad dash from my car to the school entrance, my coat held over my head, but I feel soaked through within seconds. The wind cuts through my thin coat as I sort myself out to head inside, before quickly stepping through the school reception doors.

The first thing I spot is Rebecca and Lisa, the two of them deep in conversation about something. I wonder if I can sneak past them but, oh, too late, they've seen me.

'Good morning, Nicole,' Rebecca greets me with a warm (but entirely forced) smile.

'Morning,' I reply, my teeth chattering slightly from the cold.

'What are you doing here?' Rebecca asks, narrowing her eyes. 'Oh, you're here to be under Dylan.'

'Under him?' I enquire, perplexed.

'His understudy,' she explains, grinning. 'Will musical duties fall on you when his strange little holiday is over?'

'I'm just here to help out,' I reply matter-of-factly, ignoring whatever she's getting at.

'I absolutely love your theme for the fundfair!' Lisa says, changing the subject. 'I am celebrity obsessed so I had to get involved. Do you think Dylan might do a song?'

'You can ask him,' I answer with a smile. 'I think he's looking forward to it. Anyway, I'd better head in.'

Rebecca gives me a lingering look, and there's a hint of suspicion in her gaze.

'Yes, us too,' she says to Lisa. 'We have lots to do, don't we?'

'Oh, absolutely,' Lisa agrees. 'See you soon, Nicole.'

'Yeah, see you around,' I tell them.

I head to the main hall, where the stage is, and where Dylan said they were holding the auditions today. I told him I would catch him up, as I wanted to arrange some interviews for him – getting him the right press in the right places right now is crucial, with the reunion tour announcement on the horizon. I frown to myself, as I wonder what Rebecca might be up to, but the thoughts are quickly pushed from my mind as I finally enter the hall.

I hear the music first, the familiar tune of 'Fat Sam's Grand Slam'. I'm pleasantly taken aback when I realise it is Dylan up on the stage singing – I'm even more surprised when I hear that he's singing the female parts too, making his voice super squeaky for his audience. He looks like he's having a blast, like he isn't just performing for the kids, he's one of them.

The kids are completely captivated. They laugh at Dylan's onstage antics and mimic his playful dance moves. His enthusiasm is clearly infectious. I can't help but bob along to the music too, smiling as I watch him up there doing his thing.

Dylan takes his final bow, and the applause and cheers from the children roar through the hall. He grins, acknowledging their cheers, like the natural-born performer that he is.

'Okay, Miss Pallett, dancers,' he says, addressing a petite blonde teacher and her group of excited teenage girls. 'That's the song I want you to work on a routine for.'

'We'll get right on it,' Miss Pallett replies with a gleeful nod and – of course – a flirtatious smile.

Dylan's attention shifts to the rest of the room.

'Now, who is the naughtiest boy?' he asks, a mischievous glint in his eyes. 'Be brave, point him out.'

Laughter and chatter fill the hall as every finger in the room points toward the same boy, who somehow just looks like he would be the class clown. He stands up with a proud smirk.

'What's your name, kid?' Dylan enquires.

'Calvin Conley,' the boy replies confidently.

'Not any more,' Dylan tells him. 'From now on, you're Fat Sam. Apparently, that's how they cast the movie, so that's how we'll do it.'

Everyone laughs, and Calvin – or should I say Fat Sam – celebrates with a bit of a victory dance.

'Assuming you're any good, though,' Dylan quickly adds with a wink. 'Anyone who wants a big part, stand over on that side of the room. One at a time, we'll have you sing a few lines, and we'll see who is best placed for each part.'

I love how naturally Dylan handles the children, bringing out their enthusiasm and creativity. I didn't know he was good at anything, apart from music, but he seems like a born teacher, as well as an entertainer, and the kids clearly adore him already.

Dylan's eyes meet mine from the stage, and his smile lights up the room. He quickly hops down from the stage and makes his way over to me, wrapping me in a warm hug.

'Okay, this is seriously fun,' he tells me, as though I might not have realised either. 'Honestly, I'm so excited about this musical. Come on, sit down with me, help me audition the kids.'

I can't help but laugh at his enthusiasm.

'Okay,' I reply with a smile. 'We'll be like Simon and Sharon.'

Dylan's forehead furrows in confusion.

'Who?' he asks.

'I was just making a noughties *X Factor* reference,' I say with a laugh, batting it away with my hand.

'You watched *The X Factor*?' he replies in disbelief.

'I was a music journalist,' I remind him.

'Exactly,' he replies with a playful roll of his eyes.

Dylan takes his seat behind the audition table. I join him, and while I'm not sure what someone with minimal musical talents like me can offer, I am kind of looking forward to getting involved.

As the auditions crack on, we watch each kid take the stage one by one, and show us what they can do. Dylan is an absolute natural with them, encouraging every single one and offering compliments, no matter what kind of performance they put in. He scribbles notes on his pad, pencilling different kids in for various characters. He really is enjoying this.

A blonde teenage girl confidently steps onto the stage.

'Hi, my name is Ellie Pallett,' she announces. 'And I'll be auditioning for the part of Tallulah.'

'Pallett?' Dylan replies, his eyes flicking over to the dance teacher, Miss Pallett. 'Any relation?'

'Yeah, she's my mum,' Ellie tells him, giving her mum a wave.

Dylan playfully drops his jaw.

'Well, that doesn't make any sense,' he teases. 'Something isn't adding up here.'

'Oh, stop,' Miss Pallett insists with a bat of her hand, but you can tell she's loving it. Attention from Dylan is a special thing, it makes you feel like the most important person on the planet – when you have it. When you lose it, it's like coming off a drug.

'So, Ellie, who do you look up to musically?' Dylan asks her.

'Tay Magenta,' she says quickly and certainly. 'I want to be a pop star just like her.'

'Okay, Ellie, who can't be more than four years old based on how her mum looks,' Dylan jokes. 'Go for it.'

I join the laughter with everyone else, though I can't help but feel a tingle of something that is not jealousy... but it's close.

As Ellie sings, she shows that she is as talented as she is confident. She has a great voice and the kind of stage presence that is essential for playing Tallulah.

'Okay, wow,' Dylan praises as he jots down notes. 'Absolutely fantastic, Ellie. Good work.'

We sit through the rest of the auditions, pretty much finishing up as the bell rings for break time.

'Great work, everyone,' Dylan calls out. 'Someone will let you know when the next one is.'

The kids disperse, their excited chatter filling the room as they go.

'Who is that?' I ask Dylan, nodding towards a small, shy-looking boy who is lingering near the stage.

'You okay, bud?' Dylan asks him, approaching him slowly. 'Didn't fancy auditioning for a big part?'

The kid shifts on his feet, remaining silent.

'What's your name?' Dylan asks, a warm smile on his face.

'Joey Pallett,' the boy replies.

'Ah,' Dylan says simply. 'Joey Pallett of the super-talented Pallett family?'

Joey nods in acknowledgement.

'I'll tell you what, it's just me and Nicole listening. Why don't you sing for us?' Dylan suggests. 'I know I'm great, but Nicole can't sing a note, so you can't be as bad as her.'

I laugh. Joey does too.

'Are you really bad?' he asks me.

You know what, I probably am.

'Terrible,' I reply. 'Show me how it's done.'

Joey seems unsure at first but he eventually agrees. As he starts singing, his nervousness gradually gives way to a beautiful voice, one that that fills the room.

'You've got a great voice, bud,' Dylan compliments him. 'Honestly, one of the best. You should have a lead part.'

Joey's eyes widen with horror.

'What does your mum think?' Dylan asks him.

Joey just shrugs. My heart breaks for him, it must be tricky, having such a confident sister, and being talented yourself but so unsure about it.

Dylan moves to sit on the floor, crossing his legs and patting the space next to him, inviting Joey to join him.

'Do you want to hear a story, about when I was younger?' Dylan asks.

Joey nods, his curiosity piqued.

'So, I have a brother called Mikey, who started classical guitar lessons when he was, like, six – really young,' Dylan begins. 'He was really good, even from a young age, and he only got better as he got older. My mum and dad thought he was brilliant, so they wanted to do everything they could to help him. And it made me feel like they spent all of their time and their resources on him, and that they weren't really bothered about me.'

It's funny how, even when you know everything worked out for the best, it can still break your heart to see the sad look on a person's face when they talk about their past.

He's playing it down, because he is telling the story to a young teen, but Dylan's parents really did push him aside for perfect Mikey. And it's not that Mikey wasn't talented, or didn't deserve it, but Dylan deserved some attention too, not being left to his own devices, inevitably getting himself in trouble, starting to drink and smoke at an early age – I often wonder if that's where his problems with drinking originated, using it to escape when he was a teen.

'So I did what kids do,' Dylan continues. 'I acted up, I was disruptive at school, because if I couldn't be the really good kid, then maybe I could excel at being the really bad one – I don't recommend that, by the way.'

Joey laughs.

'Anyway, one night, when I wasn't much older than you, we went out for my auntie's birthday, to the pub,' he continues his story. 'I was bored, there were no fit girls there, and I wasn't allowed a dr...' Dylan's voice trails off briefly, as he rethinks endorsing underage drinking.

'Basically, there was nothing fun to do,' he says instead. 'But then the DJ started taking karaoke requests. You know the song from *The Lion King*, the Elton John one?'

Dylan sings a little bit of 'Can You Feel the Love Tonight' and Joey nods in recognition.

'Yeah, I sang that,' Dylan continues. I give him a reassuring smile to show my support. 'I don't, er, I don't think anyone knew I could sing. My mum was sobbing, my old man looked like he was going to cry too. I had the room, every single person, all eyes on me. I didn't even know I wanted to be a singer until that night, and then I couldn't imagine ever doing anything else.'

Joey listens intently, captivated by Dylan's story, obviously seeing similarities with his own life. I know it was hard for Dylan, growing up in his brother's shadow, which is probably why he was so willing to be the frontman of the band, singing, leaving the writing and playing to Mikey, letting him take the credit.

'The reason I'm telling you this,' Dylan concludes, 'is because I know how hard it is when you have a sibling who finds it easier to step forward.'

Joey's shoulders slump again.

'My sister doesn't even like me,' he tells us. 'She doesn't think I'm cool – no one does. It's my birthday today, and I'm having a party tonight, and she says she won't come because no one else is going to come, because I'm a loser.'

I notice Dylan's facial features tighten.

'That's not very nice,' he remarks, shaking his head.

Miss Pallett joins us.

'Teenage girls,' she says with a sigh. 'I'm trying to get her to be nicer.'

'Miss Pallett, you have two talented kids, it turns out,' Dylan says, lightening the mood.

'Please, call me Jessica,' she insists, an unmistakable hint of flirtation in her voice.

Oh, boy, here we go again.

'And we're hoping some people will turn up to the party, aren't we, Joey?' Jessica says, rubbing her son's shoulder.

'Can I come?' Dylan asks like it's the most normal thing in the world.

Joey's eyes widen. So do Jessica's, to be honest.

'Really?' Joey squeaks with delight. 'You would come to my party?'

Dylan nods with a friendly smile.

'Of course,' he replies. 'Can I bring a friend?'

Joey turns to Jessica.

'Mum, can Dylan come to my party, and can he bring a friend?' he asks her.

I can't help but laugh at how funny it sounds, Joey asking his mum if his new friend can come over.

'Dylan can bring anyone he likes,' Jessica tells him. 'In fact, Dylan, if you give me your number, I can send you the details.'

Oh, smooth. So nicely done.

Dylan promptly hands her his phone – a little too promptly, maybe – and Jessica keys in her name and number.

Once Jessica and Joey head off, it's just me and Dylan.

'I can't believe you're going to a teenager's birthday party later,' I tease him.

'We're going to a teenager's birthday party,' he corrects me with a chuckle. 'You didn't think I'd go without you, did you?'

I laugh and roll my eyes in mock exasperation.

'Oh, great,' I say sarcastically. 'Can't wait.'

But, now that I think about it, is it weird that I can't?

Ex in the City

24

Standing in the village hall, with Dylan, at a teenage boy's birthday party was not something I ever thought would happen this year – or ever.

It's certainly not one of our usual haunts, or our usual crowds, but here we are.

Joey's mum, Jessica, has gone all out, renting the village hall but, heartbreakingly, there are only five other kids here. There's a DJ playing music and the disco lights are on but no one is home – well they are all quite literally at home, that's the problem.

I lean in close to Dylan because, even over the music, in an otherwise empty room I worry my voice will carry.

'This is so sad,' I say softly. 'I can't believe Ellie hasn't even shown up. She's his sister, and she's popular – she could've packed this place with kids if she wanted to.'

'Kids can be cruel to each other, but hopefully, they grow out of it,' he replies. 'In the meantime, I'm determined to make sure Joey has a good birthday.'

Jessica and Joey make their way over to us.

'Thanks so much for coming,' Jessica tells us both, before turning to Dylan. 'This is probably the quietest party you've ever been to, I'll bet?'

'Back in the day is a different story,' Dylan replies. 'But these days no one invites me to their parties, so thanks for letting me come.'

Dylan gives Joey an encouraging smile.

Jessica, not wasting an opportunity to flirt, tilts her head.

'Speaking of back in the day, I would love to hear your stories sometime,' she says. 'Even if it has to be away from little ears.'

'Mum, I'm fourteen,' Joey reminds her with a groan.

Yeah, unfortunately, I know what she's suggesting too.

Dylan, always the gentleman (these days, at least), nods and maintains a friendly tone.

'I've probably forgotten any stories worth telling,' he replies. 'But I'll bet Nicole can tell you a few.'

Jessica isn't interested in what I have to say. She flashes me the briefest of smiles before turning her attention back to Dylan.

'Well, I'd still love to hear it from the horse's mouth,' she continues. 'And we were wondering if you might sing tonight. I would love to see you up there, doing your thing – we both would.'

She quickly adds on those last few words, I'd imagine to offset the flirty-sounding voice she said the bit before in.

'Usually, I would love to,' Dylan replies. 'But I made a promise to my friend that she could sing tonight.'

'But Dylan, you said Nicole can't sing,' Joey points out.

Fantastic to be reminded of that fact again.

'Oh, no, she can't,' Dylan agrees with a shudder. 'I was talking about my other friend.'

Before the conversation can go any further, a bulked-up figure in a black suit walks into the village hall, towering above the few kids that are here, terrifying pretty much all of them.

'He's singing?' Joey asks, even more confused now.

Dylan grins and nods towards the door.

'No, she is,' he replies.

My jaw drops with everyone else as we witness the unexpected and unbelievable arrival of pop superstar Tay Magenta. She struts in, dazzling in a glitzy pink catsuit, her pink hair cascading in bouncy curls that have a life of their own. It's amazing how she can walk through a village hall the same way she walked the catwalk during Fashion Week, and still look just as flawless.

'Happy birthday, Joey,' Tay chirps, approaching the birthday boy, who can only manage to gawp at her in awe.

Dylan doesn't miss a beat, stepping in to greet her with a hug and a couple of showbiz air kisses.

'Tay, hi. Thanks for coming,' he says.

'No problem,' Tay says. She turns to Joey. 'Dylan said I could come to your party, thanks for inviting me.'

As Joey and Jessica begin chatting with Tay, I turn to Dylan, completely gobsmacked.

'Tay Magenta is a friend of yours?' I say in disbelief. 'And you got her to come to a kids' party?'

'Sometimes I think you forget I'm Dylan King,' he replies. 'Not to hit you with a "don't you know who I am" – but do you remember, for your birthday, when I hired out that science museum you love, just for the two of us to walk around, and you couldn't understand how I'd blagged it?'

I laugh. It was a museum I used to visit as a kid, full of interactive things for kids to do, to learn all about all areas of science – but, crucially, it was for kids. One of the most depressing things about growing up is realising that, one day, you're not allowed to visit one of your favourite places any more. So Dylan – being Dylan – got them to open it for a night, for my birthday, and we spent hours in there, just the two of us, having a laugh, playing with all the exhibitions.

'Fair enough,' I reply.

'To answer your questions, yes, she's a friend of mine,' he explains. 'And she owed me a favour, so she was happy to do it.'

My inner curiosity nags at me, but I decide to let it go. After all, this is an incredibly kind gesture. It doesn't matter what Dylan did to make it happen.

'I can't stay too long, unfortunately, but I thought I could sing a couple of songs if you'd like?' Tay tells Joey.

Joey, for the first time today, is beaming with confidence.

'Yes, please!' he replies.

Tay grins back at him.

'I'll go set up,' she says.

Jessica's gratitude could not be more apparent as she throws herself at Dylan and plants a lingering kiss on his cheek.

'Now, see, all the kids that didn't come are going to miss out on this,' Jessica tells Joey. 'And they're going to think twice about the choices they make in the future.'

Joey ponders this for a moment.

'I'm going to call Ellie,' he says. 'She loves Tay Magenta. She would be so sad if she missed her.'

I smile.

'Okay, let's go call her, quick,' Jessica says, leading Joey away to go call his sister, before she misses the show of a lifetime.

'See, they're not all bad,' Dylan tells me as he smiles widely, clearly getting one hell of a serotonin and dopamine hit from his good deed. 'I still want some kids of my own, you know. I think about it a lot.'

'Me too,' I dare to admit. 'I do actually really like looking after Archie and Ned. When I was younger, I always felt pretty certain I didn't want kids, but now that I've seen what it's like... *boring* life isn't so bad after all.'

Dylan smiles.

'I'm starting to see that,' he replies. 'But boring life

doesn't have to be boring. You're about to attend the world's smallest Tay Magenta gig – she played the O2 arena last week.'

'There is that,' I reply with a laugh. 'But perhaps boring life *is* boring, without you in it.'

'Yeah, I'll drink to that,' Dylan chuckles. 'Well, I would if I wasn't at a kids' party in a village hall.'

I can't help but grin like a maniac as I look at him. It is moments like these that remind me just how great Dylan is. He really would make a good dad one day – is it weird that makes him seem even more attractive?

25

I'm in London again which, if I'm being honest, I could seriously get used to.

I'm only here for a few hours, with Dylan and the rest of the band, but I very much feel like I'm back in my old shoes and I'm loving it.

Oh, and I'm quite literally in my old shoes. I'm currently admiring the shiny black pair of Louboutin heels that are gracing my feet. They're not mine, although, if I keep them on any longer, I could be tempted.

'These would go great with my outfit for the fundraiser,' I tell Dylan.

'I love that you're going as Cher,' he says. 'She's an icon. I'm not sure who to go as.'

'I mean, the theme is celebrity, and you are one,' I point out. 'Surely you go as yourself.'

'Well, that's boring,' he says with a laugh.

We're in a private dressing room area of a huge department store, where Dylan, Mikey, Jamie and Taz are meeting with a stylist. It's not by choice, obviously, this is something their management has organised for them. It just seemed like a funny thing before but, now that we're here, the stylist seems to be implying that she's here to make them cool again – to get them with the times.

Tara, the stylist, has a reputation that precedes her. Still, you can be as great as you want, but when you're in a room with rockers who don't like to be told what to do, I'm wondering how far she'll even get with them. I'm surprised they've taken it seriously thus far.

I'm only supposed to be here for moral support, for Dylan, but with a mixture of clothes and shoes – many of them just my style – it would be rude not to get involved.

Tara looks like a stylist, you can just tell by how effortlessly trendy she looks. She wears oversized cat-eye glasses and has long, dark hair that cascades in loose waves down her back. Her outfit is a mix of vintage and modern, with a chic black turtleneck, high-waisted jeans and a statement belt. She looks like she just stepped out of a fashion magazine – a French one – so it's clear she knows her stuff. If the boys don't want to take tips from her, I certainly will.

So far we've been gathered around while Tara explains to us what's cool and trendy at the moment. She's mentioning fabrics, patterns and styles – things these guys do not care about. There are racks upon racks of clothes behind her, each filled with a wide variety of outfits. Tara keeps emphasising the need for a fresh look, something that will help rebrand the band, and take them to the next level. I see the boys wince every time she says it, because to them they are cool, they are top level, and a belt isn't going to change that, right?

'All right, guys,' Tara says with a confident smile. 'So, I'm going to take a quick break, but I want you to try on different pieces and experiment with your new look. Let's say goodbye to the old and hello to the new. I'll be back to see your creations shortly.'

As soon as Tara leaves the room, the boys waste no time doing what she suggests – of course, not one of them takes it seriously. They eyeball the racks of clothes with a mischievous gleam in their eyes. The four of them, always up for a laugh, start rifling through the array of garments, and not one of them grabs anything they would actually wear.

Taz picks out an outrageously patterned floral shirt and holds it up to himself, smirking as he poses for the others.

'What do you think, lads? Can you see me behind the kit in this?' he asks.

Jamie, in his quest to push it even further than Taz, heads straight for the women's rail where he spots a neon-green dress with feather boa straps hanging from a hook.

Without hesitation, he drapes it in front of his body, parading around as if he's on a catwalk.

'That actually suits you,' Mikey tells him. 'Perfect for helping a forgettable bassist stand out.'

'Ooh, someone thinks that, just because he's been on the telly, he's a big shot now,' Jamie teases him in return. 'I suppose you're too good to try on something silly – I bet you do this sort of thing all the time *on TV.*'

You've got to love how Jamie is using Mikey's success to mock him. That's a special talent.

'Well, that's where you're wrong,' Mikey replies as he grabs a pair of tight-looking leather trousers.

He heads behind the curtain to change, but within moments, we hear muffled swearing.

'Uh, guys, I think I'm stuck!' Mikey's voice calls out in a mild panic from behind the curtain.

'Yeah, all right, pull the other one,' Dylan calls back. 'We're not falling for that one.'

Mikey whips open the curtain and the sight of him standing there, in a pair of leather trousers that are too small to fasten, with a solemn look on his face, is enough to send me into hysterics. The other boys are loving it too.

'I thought you had to keep trim for the telly,' Jamie teases.

'I am,' Mikey insists. 'It's just... I guess these are women's trousers?'

Well, that just makes everyone laugh harder.

'Can you help me out of them, before the stylist comes back?' he begs.

'Yeah, hang on, just let us take a photo,' Taz says, looking around for his phone.

Mikey closes the curtain again.

'Nicole,' he calls out from behind it. 'Will you help me – *please*?'

My eyes widen with horror.

'Erm... okay?' I reply, not sounding all that into the idea.

I step into the small cubicle with Mikey. He smiles at me pathetically.

'Okay, have you tried wriggling?' I ask.

'Yeah, it's not working,' he replies.

I hear sniggers from the outside.

'What if I grab them, and you jump up and down?' I suggest.

'Mmm, yeah, grab it,' I hear Jamie moan in a sex voice.

Mikey grunts as he jumps.

'My balls,' he practically cries.

The boys roar.

'Careful with his balls, Nicole,' Taz calls out.

It makes what I'm trying to do all the more difficult, having a bunch of comedians behind the curtain.

'You just hold super still,' I tell him. 'I'll yank them.'

I, of course, instantly regret using the word 'yank' because Jamie is straight in there with the obvious joke.

'That's it, that's it,' Mikey says as I make progress, and I do wish he would try a little harder to make this not sound sexual. 'There we go!'

And... they're off.

My God, I'm roasting now. I quickly whip back the curtain, to get some air, only for Tara to see the two of us emerging, both red-faced, Mikey all sweaty and – regrettably – without any trousers on.

'I understand people in your industry have... these

urges,' Tara says through gritted teeth. 'But can you please... not... thank you.'

Her voice gets higher with each word.

'Don't worry about the rest of us,' Jamie tells her. 'This just classic them – they do this all the time, can't take them anywhere.'

My eyes snap in Dylan's direction. I can see his jaw clenching and he's fidgeting, tapping his thumb with each of his fingers, but worst of all is the fact that he can't even look at me right now.

There's an awkward conversation Dylan and I need to have, about what happened between me and Mikey, and I know what you're thinking but it's not that. It's quite the opposite really.

I walk over to Dylan.

'Can we go for a quick walk?' I ask him quietly. 'I need some air.'

'Sure,' he replies.

We duck out and head down a few stairs, eventually popping out on the homeware floor. For a minute or two we browse, over in a quiet corner where no one seems to be looking – I suppose the stuff over here is kind of kooky. I pick up various large candles, all of them in what have to be purposefully phallic shapes, as I wonder how I'm going to say what I need to tell him.

'Okay, we need to have an awkward conversation,' I say.

'Which one?' Dylan asks as he carefully places down the unusual ornament he was just examining – probably trying to work out what it is supposed to be.

Because of course there are two awkward conversations we need to have.

'The Mikey one,' I clarify.

Dylan takes a deep breath. I brace myself.

'Look, Nic, it's fine,' he tells me, not exactly sounding like it's fine. 'Do I love that you were with my brother? No, obviously not, because – well, it doesn't matter why now. But it was a long time ago. We've all grown and changed and all that shit. When we had the chat, about the band getting back together, Mikey and I decided that we just wouldn't talk about the past. I figured you and I could do the same.'

'Okay but, here's the thing, I wasn't completely honest with you back then,' I confess. 'And you're right, we've all grown and changed, so I'm hoping you'll understand.'

Dylan stares at me, an almost terrified look in his eye. It feels like it takes me a lifetime to start talking again. I just need to blurt it out.

'Dill, nothing ever happened, between Mikey and me,' I tell him. 'We both lied to you.'

His terror changes to confusion. His brow wrinkles and his jaw drops slightly.

'Nic, I'm not a baby,' he insists. 'And I'm over it. You don't need to pretend it didn't happen for my benefit.'

'I only pretended it *did* happen for your benefit,' I go on. 'Right, just listen to me for a second, hear me out until the end.'

I need to explain, from start to finish, and I need to make sure I recap every last detail for him, because I don't know how sharp those memories are for him now.

'It was just before you guys called it quits with the band,' I explain. 'We had our... we went on our holiday, after our respective break-ups.'

'Awkward conversation number two,' he says.

'Yep, awkward conversation number two,' I reply, laughing just a little. I love that, even when he's serious, he's still funny. 'When we got back from holiday, and with all the bad press you were getting – Dill, you were in a really bad way. You were a mess, you were drinking probably the most I'd ever seen you drink, you didn't care about the band, or yourself, or anything. You and I were in a bad spot, and there was so much tension building between you and Mikey, and every gig you did only left your fans feeling disappointed. The Burnouts were over, no matter what I did, and I see that now but, at the time, I just felt like I needed to do something. We were all talking about you, all the time, any chance we got, trying to work out what to do with you. That night, on the last tour, Mikey and I were talking, trying to figure out how we could get you into a rehab. People kept walking into the dressing room, so we went into the bathroom.'

'And then I walked in,' he says.

'And then you walked in,' I confirm. 'And you were drunk, and the first conclusion you jumped to was that something was going on between me and Mikey, that we were carrying on behind your back. So I just thought, seeing how bothered you were about it, that I would tell you that you were right, that me and Mikey were together, because I knew how much you always hated coming second to Mikey – I thought it might shock you into doing something – and Mikey went along with it. And I guess it worked in a way, because you did go to rehab soon after, but you also didn't speak to either of us ever again until, well, now.'

Dylan looks at me with suspicion.

'But I walked in on the two of you at it in the bath-room,' he says.

'We were just talking,' I tell him. 'You were wasted.'

'No, that last night, we were in Liverpool, and I came to find you after the soundcheck and—'

'Dill, we were in Birmingham,' I remind him. 'You were wasted.'

'But it doesn't make sense,' he says. 'I spoke to Mikey briefly, maybe five or six years ago, and you were still together – you must have been together for years?'

I shake my head.

'I was so sure – I'm sure someone said your name,' he replies, racking his brain, looking frustrated that he can't remember.

'His wife is called Nicola, right?' I point out. 'And their eldest is at least four...'

'Oh my God, I've been such an idiot,' he says. 'I thought it was you. Mikey called me up one Christmas out of the blue, years ago, and said that his girlfriend thought she had overheard my voice in the background of a phone call – I assumed it was you, encouraging him to reach out, to reconnect with me, but the last thing I wanted was to see the two of you together, so I never met up with him. I even told the people around me that I'd figured stuff out with him, and with you, just to stop talking about it all, to bury it at the back of my mind again. I don't think he even said your name, I think he just said "girlfriend" and I assumed the worst, that his girlfriend was you. Did I torture myself over nothing?'

Poor Dylan. It must be awful to realise that you're not exactly a reliable narrator, not even when it comes to talking about your memories.

'I'm guessing that was Nicola. Dylan, I owe you a huge apology,' I tell him. 'I honestly thought that my meddling would help. Needless to say, I've worked on my methods a lot since then. I'm so sorry. I'm sorry for lying to you, I'm sorry I hurt you... I'm just sorry. I just wanted to help.'

He turns to face away from me and composes himself for a second. I feel sick with nerves as I wait to hear what he has to say. God, I hope he isn't furious with me. I really was only trying to help him. The tears that have been threatening to fall, that I've been trying to hold back throughout my explanation, finally find an escape.

Dylan turns around, grabs me and pulls me close.

'I'm the one who is sorry,' he tells me as he hugs me. 'I'm sorry for what I put you all through, I'm sorry you felt like you had to do anything about it. You did help me. You stopped me making one of the biggest mistakes of my life because, honestly, I really thought I was doing better then. I thought I was drinking less, I thought I was behaving, and I really thought I was going to win you back. But I would have ruined your fucking life, and that would have been too much for me to take. But look at us now, that's all that matters. You did the right thing, okay?'

He relaxes a little, letting me move back so we can look at each other.

'I'm sorry you had to go through all of that alone,' I tell him.

'I think I needed to go through it alone, to do it for myself,' he reassures me.

I can see every single emotion behind his eyes. The sadness, the relief, the gratitude.

Dylan places a hand on my face and wipes away a tear with his thumb.

'You've had that bottled up for a while, hmm?' he says with a smile.

'Just a bit,' I say, laughing with relief, happy to see that he's okay.

'I get why you did what you did and, looking at it through "present eyes", which is probably the only other rehab thing I remember – aside from the obvious one – I'm actually glad to hear it,' he says.

'Yeah?' I reply.

'Yeah,' he says, the picture of casual coolness again. 'I thought you were my brother's ex. Now I know you're not, that changes things.'

'It does?' I say, my breathing quickening.

'It definitely makes awkward conversation number two a lot less awkward, right?'

I laugh.

'Maybe,' I reply.

'Oh my God, you're Dylan King,' a voice screeches.

We quickly part and turn to see a gang of four women, all with Dylan firmly in their sights. I worry for a second, that they're going to notice the crying girl standing next to him, but then I realise that they're all crying, all so overwhelmed to be in Dylan's presence, so I fit right in.

As Dylan poses for photos with each of them, I take a step back. I feel so relieved – I don't think I've ever known relief like it. I was stupid, at the time, thinking I knew best, that I could somehow trick him into becoming a better person. Since then, I've tried harder to help people, to genuinely make them better people, rather than just to spin things so they look good. Pretending to date his brother – the one he always wanted to be more like – felt like the only way out of a bad situation at the time.

I'm so happy it's all out in the open now. The only thing that is left to worry about is awkward conversation number two. But we'll save that one for another day.

26

My life, at the moment, is very much divided into two halves.

There is the half when I'm here, at home, making dinners and doing the school runs. I'm surrounded by all the mums and the manicured lawns and the bull-shit. Then there is the other half, the old me, who gets to hang out with musicians, and spend time in London, and have the most fabulous days – like I used to when I was younger and cooler.

Flip-flopping between the two is so bizarre, but there is one constant in my life, whichever version of myself I am, and that is Dylan. When we're in the city, in recording studios and seeing stylists, it feels like old times. However, when we're here in the village, doing the school runs and helping out with the musical, things feel so effortless too. Wherever we are, whatever we're doing, if we're doing it together then you can guarantee we're having a good time.

As I suggested, much to Rebecca's annoyance, the theme for the evening is 'celebrity'. This fundfair is all about the glitz and glamour of Hollywood, making attendees feel like a celebrity, for one night only (unless you're Dylan, of course). As guests approach the school hall, they're greeted by 'paparazzi' who eagerly snap their photos on the red carpet. It feels like a star-studded event, even before you step inside, although beyond their main door is still a mystery, as I hover by the car, waiting to go in.

'James Dean' and 'Marilyn Monroe' walk past me, saying hello as they go, before making their way along the red carpet.

I smile to myself. I don't usually look forward to these things – in fact, I actively dread them – so I can't quite believe how up for tonight I am. I've gone all out with my Cher costume, channelling her iconic 'If I Could Turn Back Time' look. I stopped shy of fully committing to the bit here and there – mostly with my hair which, even though I could achieve the big, bouncy curls required, I wasn't willing to dye it from blonde to black, so I have a wig, but that's all good because it's keeping my head warm, and I still have my coat on while I'm waiting.

Rowan had a meeting, so he said he would be arriving late. Honestly, I'm finding it harder to care than ever. We couldn't be more like strangers right now – in fact, I briefly forgot that he would be coming at all. I guess, when I was at the school in relation to the boys, it all felt very much tethered to Rowan. Now, though, with Dylan being here, and the musical, this feels more like a me and Dylan thing.

Dylan also had somewhere to be, so I got ready at home, and arranged to meet him here, outside, so we could walk the red carpet together.

I'm relieved to see his car pull up, because it's quite chilly out here, but as he steps out of the car, I am nothing short of speechless. He practically struts over to me, clearly incredibly proud of himself.

'So, what do you think?' he asks me.

I open my mouth to speak but nothing comes out other than a spluttery, indescribable sound – like a car that won't start.

'Come on, what do you think?' he prompts me again.

'I think you've lost your mind,' I tell him with a cackle. 'No pun intended.'

'Well, with you being Cher, I thought it might be

cute if I matched,' he explains. 'So I figured Meat Loaf would be a good shout. And I was thinking about my favourite Meat Loaf looks, and then I decided Eddie from *Rocky Horror* was my favourite. So, here I am.'

'Here you are,' I say, shaking my head in amusement. 'In the sort of clothes that people have seen you wear a million times, but with the addition of a terrifyingly realistic head wound.'

'Yeah, that's where I was,' he replies proudly. 'I paid a special effects make-up artist to make it super realistic.'

Dylan is wearing a pair of blue jeans, a tight-fitting black T-shirt and a sleeveless black leather jacket with silver stud detailing. He almost certainly, without a doubt, owned all of these things already. And even though he is wearing Eddie's exact outfit – which, on another man here, would be glaringly obvious – he just looks like Dylan King with a grossly fresh forehead wound.

'Well, you didn't waste your money,' I tell him, still not quite believing my eyes. 'You could definitely convince me that you'd just had a bit of slapdash brain surgery.'

'Aww, thanks,' he replies. 'I'm loving the wig – the dark hair really suits you.'

'Why, thank you,' I reply.

I do kind of love the wig. My black hair is wild and curly, cascading over one shoulder – helping me to very much look the part.

I slip off my coat and throw it into the car, ready to head inside.

'Oh my God, Nicole, look at you,' Dylan says.

'Do I look all right?' I check.

'You look stunning,' he tells me. 'I mean... wow, that outfit. Are you allowed in a school in an outfit like that?'

I laugh. So, obviously, Cher's outfit in the video for 'If I Could Turn Back Time' is very much something only *the* Cher could pull off, and I didn't fancy walking into a school in a thong, so it's sort of my own interpretation. I'm wearing big black boots over a pair of black stockings, which connect to the suspenders hanging from my black bodysuit. The bodysuit has a black mesh panel, that forms a V-shape down the front, but it sinks nowhere near as low as Cher's does, and I've got a black bra on under mine, to keep everything where it is supposed to be. The whole look is finished off with a black leather jacket, so Dylan and I do indeed look like we have coordinated our costumes.

'If you go in there, in that outfit, you will be covered in seamen in a matter of minutes,' he tells me plainly.

'I think you'll find the men in the music video were sailors,' I correct him with a laugh.

'I think you'll find we're talking about different things,' he jokes. 'Come on, let's go.'

As we approach the red carpet, ready to be papped (which is something of a sore spot for us), I notice Rebecca and her new sidekick Lisa stepping outside, to check on things. Rebecca is dressed as Princess Diana, because of course she is, while Lisa has opted for Britney Spears in her '...Baby One More Time' school uniform.

Noticing us approaching the red carpet, they head over to greet us, and as they get closer, they both turn the same shade of white at the same time.

'Oh my God, Dylan, what happened?' Lisa says, running to him, taking his head in her hands to get a better look. 'We need to get you to a hospital, right now, this is—'

Dylan takes her hands and holds them.

'Relax, relax,' he says with a laugh. 'It's just make-up. It's part of my outfit. I'm Meat Loaf, in *Rocky Horror*.'

'Wh-what?' she says. 'It's not real?'

'It's not real,' he reassures her. 'Relax. Rebecca, I said it's not real, don't look so worried.'

'I'm not worried about you,' she says as she looks me up and down, scowling.

'Me?' I say with a laugh.

'Nicole, you have come in your pants,' she says simply.

'Nah, I think that's just the way I'm standing,' I dare to joke.

Her blood boils. Dylan finds me funny, at least.

'Don't you think that's a bit provocative?' she replies.

'I didn't really think about it like that,' I reply. 'I just wanted to be Cher and this felt like her most iconic look, so...'

'And you,' she says, turning her attention to Dylan. 'What are you doing? Why would you not come as yourself?'

'I wanted to dress up too,' he insists. 'I'm me every other day of the year.'

Rebecca sighs heavily.

'Go on, go in,' she tells us. 'Nicole will catch her death out here in that.'

Going off the look on her face, I can't say that I feel like I'll be all that safe inside, wearing this.

Dylan and I head down the red carpet, routinely stopping for photos, posing in different directions. The rest of us are just cosplaying at being a celebrity but, for Dylan, it's all second nature. He walks the carpet like a pro, like he hasn't been away from it for a minute.

Stepping into the party room genuinely takes me aback. I can't believe this is the same school hall we were standing in the other day, it's so glitzy, like a genuine award ceremony. The transformation is nothing short of extraordinary and, while I may not have had a hand in putting it together, I'm so happy that my idea has come to life so well. This is so, so much cooler than the usual, stuffy black-tie fundraisers I usually have to try to stay awake through.

The room is a vision of red velvet and sparkling gold. Long, flowing curtains of deep red velvet adorn the walls, hiding anything remotely school-looking, and the tables and chairs are obviously hired in because they're not the kind of tables and chairs kids sit on – not even by private school standards.

The tables are adorned with white linen cloths with gold accents, laid out with silver cutlery and crystal glasses. Waitstaff weaves through the crowd, offering trays of champagne and delectable canapés fit for the Hollywood elite. I love it, I absolutely love it, and it's not just me. The atmosphere is great, easily surpassing anything I've ever seen at a school event. Laughter and chatter blend with the funky music being played by the live band on the stage. The large projector screen is down alongside them, on the stage, with images of real celebrities being projected onto it – which only emphasises just how ropey their doppelgangers in this room look in comparison. And, yes, I do include myself in that. I might be rocking this outfit, but I'm not super slim or leggy like the real deal.

'I'll go get us some drinks,' Dylan says.

He turns to head towards the bar, only to come face to face with a woman dressed up as Tina Turner, who screams when she notices the wound on his head.

'It's not real, it's part of my costume,' he reassures her.

She scowls at him, for giving her such a fright, before getting back to what she was doing.

'Is this going to happen all night?' Dylan turns to ask me.

'Yes,' I reply.

'Cool,' he says simply.

As I scan the room, I look at all the other parents and staff members, who have all embraced the celebrity theme with gusto. I honestly never thought I'd see the day. This lot always take themselves so seriously, and yet here they are, all dressed up and having the time of their lives.

There's 'Elvis Presley', wearing a bedazzled white jumpsuit that he definitely didn't have hanging in the back of his wardrobe. Not to be outdone, 'Elton John' is propping up the bar, in a huge pair of sunglasses and a suit covered with feathers. Oh, a special shout out to Martin, Rebecca's husband, for his fantastic white trousers and white vest Freddie Mercury get-up.

Dylan hands me a drink – some kind of cocktail – and as I taste it my eyes roll into the back of my head. My God, that's good – why can't these events always be this fun?

Dylan and I begin making our way around the room full of people. We chat, drink and nibble on the delicious canapés. Dylan is undeniably the star of the show tonight, everyone wants a piece of him, and it reminds me of what it used to be like, being around him, knowing he commanded the attention of every single person (and the taken ones too) in the room. Sometimes it would make me feel like a spare part, like I might get lost in his shadow, but tonight it's different, it's like we're a team – every bit the duo we appear to be.

'We've got a very special guest in the house tonight,' the lead singer's voice booms through the room, commanding everyone's attention. 'Well, we've got a lot of special guests in tonight, but one, in particular... Meat Loaf! And I heard a rumour Cher is with him, so, without further ado, this is "Dead Ringer for Love".'

Dylan's eyes light up with mischief as he takes both my hands and pulls me towards the dance floor. The rhythmic beat of Meat Loaf's iconic hit fills the room, and Dylan – ever the showman – instantly transforms into his character, lip-syncing to the lyrics, giving it all the intensity and confidence the man himself would have. His commitment to the performance is nothing short of brilliant.

By the time Cher's part rolls around, I can't help but join in the fun. I strut, spin and lip-sync alongside him. Together, we're the ultimate duo – for one night only we *are* Meat Loaf and Cher – lost in the infectious energy of the music. The rest of the room practically fades away as we enjoy the moment. As the song finally comes to an end, I fall about laughing, and Dylan sweeps me into his arms. This is the kind of pure, carefree fun we used to have all the time, I've really missed it. Tonight, he's like the old Dylan again – well, the *old* old Dylan – the one who knew how to enjoy life without going too far.

Rebecca, suddenly standing on the stage with a

microphone in hand, taps it a few times, sending a screechy feedback noise through the speakers. You could be mistaken for thinking it was her first time holding a microphone, given how terribly she handles it, but unluckily for me I can tell you that it isn't. Rebecca almost always finds her way to an amp.

Everyone in the room stops what they are doing, listening to hear what she has to say.

The evening is an undeniable success. I'm interested to see how Rebecca acknowledges that without giving some kind of praise to me and Dylan, because that is the last thing she will want to do, believe me.

'I just wanted to take this opportunity to thank you all for coming,' she begins. 'Each and every one of you looks like a genuine celebrity – I hope you've had an A-list night.'

The room ripples with applause.

'Love you, Rebecca,' a man dressed as Gene Simmons shouts out.

She smiles and curtsies, very much channelling Lady Diana this evening.

'With the theme being celebrity, we thought perhaps we should honour our own celebrities, right here,' she says, gesturing to the screen next to her. 'Many of the residents of Little Harehill have been featured in the press many times, for all sorts of reasons.'

The screen shows a newspaper page featuring James Burns, Thom Burns' dad, who famously leapt into a canal to rescue a stranded dog. The crowd applauds his heroics.

'The amazing and heroic James Burns,' Rebecca says as she claps him. 'Let's see who is next.'

The next slide showcases Deanna and her choir, and the headline from the time they performed for members of the royal family. The audience claps again.

'Didn't they do us proud,' Rebecca announces. 'Next slide, please.'

My heart stops when I see the familiar front page up there on the screen. I haven't seen it since the day it was printed, back in 2014, but I remember every single detail.

Underneath the headline, 'Dylan goes Wilde', there is a photo, of me and Dylan, lying on the pavement, him on top of me, the two of us looking into one another's eyes.

See, this is what I was worried about, without the explanation, this looks bad – really bad. The reality is that the two of us went on a night out and, both a little worse for wear on the walk back to the hotel, Dylan fell down, dragging me down with him. When it happened we were on the floor for less than a minute, and we spent most of it laughing, but the picture is from only a split second of that time, and of course, the way the tabloids spun it, it made it seem like (a recently married) Dylan and I were having an affair, rolling around on the floor together, on our way to a hotel to spend a night together.

The room comes alive with chatter and everyone stares at us, some laughing, some judging. Neither feels great.

I seethe. This is classic Rebecca, I expect no less but, still, what a horrible thing to do.

'And here is the man himself,' Rebecca announces, her voice echoing through the hall.

All eyes turn to the back of the room, to where Rebecca is pointing, and both Dylan and I are taken by surprise to see that she isn't pointing towards us. There, at the back of the hall, is Rowan, strutting in with an exaggerated sense of cool. He's dressed in black skinny jeans, a white shirt and a loosely tied black tie – a look that used to be Dylan's signature style. His hair is deliberately dishevelled, and dark circles have been strategically applied beneath his eyes. In his hands, he carries a bottle of Jack Daniel's and a cigarette, just to hammer the point home. He's supposed to be Dylan.

Dylan maintains his composure, his gaze firmly fixed on Rowan, but I catch those subtle signs of tension in his body language – the faint flaring of his nostrils, the clenching of his jaw.

'Go to the car,' I tell him. 'I'll catch up with you. Let's just get out of here.'

Dylan gives a silent nod. He walks past Rowan without exchanging a single word or even a glance. Rowan has such a smug expression on his face, a real shit-eating grin, because he's clearly so proud of himself. His cocky exterior crumbles when I catch his eye and he notices my barely-there Cher outfit.

'Nicole, what are you doing?' Rowan demands. 'You're practically half-naked.'

I arch an eyebrow. Right, because that's the conversation that's needed right now.

'What am I doing? What are you doing?' I ask him. 'Did you and Rebecca plan this together?'

'Well, when were you going to tell me about you and Dylan?' he replies angrily.

'That photo was nothing but a set-up,' I tell him honestly. 'Why didn't you just ask me about it?'

'Why didn't you tell me in the first place?' he claps back.

I sigh, exasperated.

'It's none of your business, is it?' I say. 'Definitely not any more.'

'I don't understand how you can be so cold,' he tells me and, yes, he genuinely feels like the wronged party right now.

I stare at him for a second. I can't believe he's serious – and I definitely can't believe he would come here dressed up as a drunk Dylan.

'And I can't understand how you can be so cruel,' I reply.

Without another word, I grab a bottle of champagne from the table next to me and make my exit from the room.

'Wait, where are you going?' he says, following me. 'To him, huh?'

'Yep, to him,' I reply.

'You're making a fool of yourself,' he warns me. 'Look at you, look at your outfit, this isn't you. You're not yourself right now.'

I stop in my tracks and turn around, so that I can look in his eyes when I say this.

'Rowan, I am nothing but myself right now,' I tell him. 'This is me, the real me, the one I've been keeping locked away for years. She's been screaming for me to let her out and, guess what, here she fucking is.'

'You buy a slutty outfit and you think you're suddenly this strong, sassy girlboss?' he replies.

Oof, if I wasn't angry before, I would definitely be now.

'Well, that's where you're wrong, fella, because I already owned this slutty outfit,' I reply with a laugh. 'This is me. The genie is well and truly out of the bottle now. So, enjoy.'

I know, it's not very mature of me, but I use my free hand to give Rowan the finger before I storm out. I'm relieved when I realise he isn't following me.

I pop the cork on the champagne before I hop in Dylan's car, slumping down in the passenger seat, before taking a big swig from the bottle.

'I didn't realise suburbia was so fun,' he says sarcastically. 'Where to, miss?'

'Let's go back to yours,' I tell him. 'And let's burn this entire village to the ground.'

27

'Okay, here we go,' I say, swigging from my champagne bottle before returning it to the bedside table. 'Let's do this.'

We're sitting on Dylan's bed, surrounded by Mr Campbell's notebooks, the ones bursting with his meticulous notes on all of my neighbours. While it is odd, and slightly unsettling, that these things exist, they are exactly what I need to feel better right now. I wasn't going to do it, flipping through these is a real invasion of privacy, but here we are. Look what they've driven me to.

'She thinks she can just broadcast my secrets to the entire school,' I mutter, sorting through the notebooks, assembling a pile of notes on Rebecca and

Martin. 'And she thinks she's so untouchable. Let's see what secrets she has, huh?'

Dylan chuckles, picking up one of the notebooks and flipping through it.

'Yeah, imagine if she knew you had Mr Campbell's very own take on the tabloid right here,' he replies. 'I'm looking at some of them, and sometimes it's nothing but speculation.'

'Well, that's exactly like a tabloid,' I reply. 'That newspaper clipping they showed about us was a complete work of fiction anyway, it's win-win, it levels the playing field.'

That night, back in 2014, was a time when Dylan was really struggling. I was living in Leeds, he was in London, and while we saw each other as much as we could, and talked on the phone all the time, it was around this time that his drinking was getting worse, and he found himself in a bit of a mess.

Everything is clear to see, when you're looking back at it, but when it's all going on right there in front of your face it can be harder to make out.

Things took a turn when Crystal Slater came on to the scene, telling Dylan that she was pregnant with his twins, and his record label hired that absolute moral crusader of a moron to handle his publicity – Charles, the guy who managed to talk Dylan into marrying Crystal, even though he didn't love her, because it was the 'right thing to do'. Of course, in a twist of events that surprised absolutely no one, it all turned out to be a grift, the kids weren't his, and his marriage ended almost immediately.

The picture of us that wound up on the front page of the *Daily Scoop* was taken after he got married, but before the babies came. He turned up at my office one evening, in a panic, saying he couldn't handle it. So, I took him on a night out, and I gave him a pep talk, and I told him to go give family life a go. I got through to him, he was willing to go back and try, but that picture hit the front page before he got the chance. It makes me so cross because he was really struggling that night, he was in a really bad place, mentally, but that doesn't matter to a tabloid like the *Scoop*.

There were a few stories about me after that – me, a nobody – it was almost as though the *Scoop* were trying to break me. They tried to break Dylan, many times – in fact, it was stories in the *Scoop* that brought about our falling-out. I really, truly hate them, and I hate Rebecca, for putting that photo up for everyone to see, and I'm going to find something out about her right now.

I take another swig from the bottle of champagne. Okay, let's do this.

'Right, let's start with this one,' I say, clearing my throat, ready to read aloud. '"Rebecca and Martin Rollins are up to something. Guests to the house are frequent, in groups, and not their usual crowd."'

'Well, that's interesting,' Dylan says.

'Indeed,' I reply, skimming the page for the next juicy bit. '"It all makes sense. It's the pineapple, the pineapple is the key – and it's where they hide their key too. That ornamental stone pineapple on their doorstep, so unassuming, and yet a clear signal to those who know. *Rebecca and Martin Rollins are swingers.*"'

I practically scream the last sentence.

'No!' Dylan says.

'That's what it says,' I tell him, smiling the widest smile I have ever smiled. 'Hang on, let's see.'

I skim the pages, a little more than tipsy, but not at all mistaken. Mr Campbell's notes are crystal clear, and his mind was totally made up on the pair.

'So, da da da,' I say, skipping over a page or so. 'Okay, so: "Can a swinger cheat? I'm sure that's the very point, in groups, and all is forgiven. But there is one man, the one with the beard, who is visiting more frequently – visiting alone, and while Martin is at work. I have never trusted that woman."'

I take another swig, jigging my body with joy, delighted to learn that Mrs Perfect might not be so perfect after all. I mean, if you want to swing, do it, be you, have at it – and congratulations on finding more than one person who wants to sleep with you because, historically, I've always found getting one good one to be a challenge – but don't come over all moral and smug and judge other people. People in glass houses shouldn't throw big stone pineapples.

The champagne swishes around in the bottle a little too violently and fizzes up. Well, that serves me right, for taking so much joy in someone else's chaos. Unsurprisingly, placing my mouth over the bottle doesn't help to contain it, and I spill it all down my jumpsuit.

'Shit,' I say, jumping up. 'Is this karma?'

Dylan laughs.

'I mean, were you planning on sharing this information with anyone?' he asks.

'Nah,' I admit. 'I just thought it might make me feel better, to know their dirt too. They don't need to know that I know.'

'There you go then,' he replies with a smile. 'Somehow I didn't think you would.'

'What can I say? I'm a softie,' I tell him. 'I'm also soaking wet.'

Dylan whips off his T-shirt and throws it at me. I

use it to try to soak up some of the champers but it's no good. I'm soaking and I'm sticky.

'I'll nip to the bathroom,' I tell him, wobbling on my feet a little. 'Feel free to put all the books back – it turns out I'm not as spiteful or as vengeful as I'd hoped.'

'Okay,' Dylan says with a chuckle. 'Can you bring me the face wipes, from the bathroom, please? The girl who did my make-up gave me them to remove my scar. I'm probably safe to take it off now, right?'

I laugh.

'Yeah, it's still creeping me out,' I tell him. 'I'll be glad to see the back of it.'

I head into the avocado-green bathroom where I quickly strip down to my underwear. My jumpsuit – what little there was of it, anyway – is soaking wet, there is no salvaging it without leaving it to dry. So I run some toilet roll under the tap and do my best to wipe down my sticky body, and then I dry it, and then I just stare at myself in the mirror for a second and laugh. This really isn't how I saw tonight ending. I guess I'd better ask Dylan for a T-shirt or a hoodie, and maybe some trackies if he has some, so that I can put some actual clothes on. But, to ask him, I need to head back out there in my underwear, but it's not a big deal, it's Dylan, we were best friends, he's seen me in my underwear before – it's just par for the course, for everyone, on tour. Hmm, why do I feel nervous then? I zhuzh my hair a little – it looks a bit flat, from being inside my wig all evening – and check to make sure my make-up still looks okay. Then I grab Dylan his face wipes and head back to the bedroom, as confidently as I can, because if I don't make it weird, then it isn't weird.

As I walk back into the room, I notice the look on Dylan's face immediately. I tip my head, curiously, but then I realise this is about more than me spooking him with my bra. Something is really wrong.

'What?' I prompt him. 'What is it?'

'Come here,' he says, patting the space on the bed next to him.

I do as he says in an instant, handing him the face wipes, which he promptly uses. Oh, God, what does he have to tell me that is so bad he doesn't think he should do it with face paint on?

'What's up?' I ask him again. 'You're freaking me out.'

'I don't know how to tell you this,' he begins softly. 'I was moving the journals when a photo fell out of one. It's of Rowan.'

'Right, okay,' I say. 'So, what, Mr Campbell knew about the scam? Do you think he told anyone?'

Dylan takes an open journal from the bedside table.

'Do you want me to read it to you?' he asks. 'Or...'

'It's okay, I'll read it,' I say anxiously. He's really scaring me now.

I take the book from him – the log on me and Rowan – and read. Looking at the dates, it's obvious this is about the scam, it's dated not too long before I found out for myself. It says:

Nicole, kind Nicole, one of the only good ones on the street. These logs are for me, to keep a watch over the neighbourhood, and for future generations long after us to learn from. They were never meant for sharing and yet I must share my findings with Nicole, because Rowan is deceiving her. She needs to know. Of course, I can't tell her, so, next time she brings me some shopping I will invite her in, and I will place the photograph in her bag, and she will have all the proof she needs. Rowan is be-traying her. He is having an affair.

My heart sinks as those last five words blindside me. This isn't about the scam at all. Rowan was cheating on me.

'There's a photo?' I prompt Dylan, my voice cracking.

'Yeah,' he says softly.

'Can I see it?' I ask.

'Are you sure?' he replies. 'You two are already over, right? You don't need to see, you know he's a bastard.'

'Yeah, I just... I think I need to see how much of a bastard he is,' I reply.

Dylan takes the photo out from under his pillow and there he is, Rowan, standing on our doorstep, locking lips with none other than Carrie. So my intuition was right, he *was* having an affair with her, they just also happened to be running a scam too. Incredible. Just when I think he can't hurt me any more.

'How could I be so stupid?' I say.

'You weren't stupid,' Dylan insists, taking my hand in his. 'You trusted someone, there's nothing wrong with that – he's the stupid one.'

'I mean, yeah, he's a fucking idiot,' I agree. 'But I knew he wasn't right for me. I knew he wasn't the one. He was nice, he had a job, he had kids, he was a pillar of the community. He seemed like a catch, the kind of guy you were supposed to settle down with, and yeah, things were pretty flat between us, but that's realistic, isn't it? He didn't set my skin on fire when he touched me, but I thought that was normal, I thought that only happened with...'

I pause for a second. I can't say that.

'I didn't think you could have fire, with the kind of guy you were supposed to spend the rest of your life with,' I say instead.

'Sometimes the wrong ones look like the right ones,' he tells me simply. 'It's easy for me to look at him and see a terrible person. The kind of guy who would rip you off, cheat on you – turn up to a party dressed as an addict for a laugh.'

I hold my breath for a second. I've never heard him use the A word before.

'I'm so, so sorry for that,' I tell him. 'I had no idea he was going to do that – I didn't ask him what he was wearing. I don't even talk to him any more. But that was so, so unforgivably cruel of him and I will never, ever forgive him. Are you okay?'

'I'm fine,' he tells me, squeezing my hand. 'There will always be people who write you off, based on your past mistakes, even when you're trying to change. I'll spend the rest of my life trying to be better. What does bother me is that, in the face of all of this, you're worrying about me.'

I sigh, lying back on the bed, exhaling deeply as I try to push all of the stress out of my body.

'I suppose, because I knew I wasn't in love with him, I shouldn't care,' I say. 'But, going off Mr C's dates, Rowan did it when we were still together, when – okay, I wasn't the happiest – but I thought we were happy. We were settled and committed, and while that picture was being taken I was probably looking after his kids.'

I close my eyes to try to stop the tears from escaping but it's no good. I feel them run from my eyes, down to my ears.

My eyes still tightly closed, I feel Dylan lie down next to me. Then I feel his hand on my bare stomach. As he gently strokes my skin, he sings to me quietly. It's his soft, paced-down take on 'The Power of Love' by Huey Lewis and the News – one of my favourite songs.

It's been years since he did this, since he sang me to sleep when I was having a bad day, and not only does it work just as well as it used to do, instantly calming me down, but there it is, that feeling, that fire when he touches me, like he's holding a naked flame against my skin.

And I've never felt it with anyone but him.

28

I'm awake, and not just because it's morning, but because I am well and truly awake – my eyes have been opened.

After giving myself the time to feel sad last night, I've woken up with a clarity that's surging through me like a triple shot of caffeine. It practically fuels my steps as I march across the road to Rowan's house.

The funny thing is that, before, when I broke up with Rowan over his ridiculous scam, I often wondered if I'd made the right call. Back then, part of me questioned whether I was too harsh or if I was just looking for an excuse to call things off because the butterflies and the fireworks weren't there. But now, after knowing he cheated on me, there's no going back. What Rowan did, the whole package of arse-holery, has killed any lingering feelings I had left for him. I've been cheated on before, I didn't care for it, and I vowed I'd never put up with it again. So I have whizzed through the stages of grief, and now my mourning is complete (I highly recommend the fast-track service), and all that is left to do now is to tell him to go fuck himself. One final time.

This morning, waking up in bed with Dylan, it didn't feel strange at all. It felt oddly comforting, like he's my protector, one who isn't going to let anything bad happen to me on his watch.

I'm grateful that today is the big day, the day the band hits the road for their mini-tour to support their big announcement, and I'm going with them. Escaping this place, getting away from Rowan for a few days while I figure out my next move, is exactly what I need right now. Time and space to devise a plan. But for now, it's time to end this once and for all.

I stride into the house, making my way straight upstairs. Rowan must hear me from the kitchen because he is hot on my heels, I'm only in the bedroom for a few seconds before he appears.

'Decided to come home, did you?' Rowan says, sarcasm oozing from his words. 'I take it you stayed with *him*, and those are his clothes you're wearing.'

'You're not as stupid as you look,' I reply. 'Where are the kids?'

'They're still asleep,' he replies.

'Okay, I'll make this quick,' I say as I grab a suitcase and start stuffing it with my things.

'Whoa, okay, what are you doing?' he asks, genuinely puzzled, and clearly alarmed by the sight of my suitcase. 'You're the one who was keeping secrets from me – I should be throwing you out.'

'You think?' I reply, pulling out the photo from my pocket and lightly slapping it onto his chest, right over his heart. He takes it, his expression darkening as he looks at it, as he realises what it is.

'It's not... it's not what it looks like,' he stammers.

'As incredible as it would be to hear you come up with a remotely plausible explanation for this photo, I'm really not interested,' I say, my tone ice-cold.

'Okay, look, maybe I overreacted about the newspaper thing,' he tries to explain. 'I was helping Rebecca and Lisa with the slideshow for the fundraiser, and it came out that Lisa remembered you from the news, because she was such a huge fan of Dylan's. I was hurt that you didn't tell me, and I went along with the plan, but, okay, I appreciate what you're saying, a photo can look bad, even when it isn't.'

I return from the en suite with the bathroom essentials I need, giving him a filthy look that quickly transforms into a burst of laughter.

'Okay, but here's the thing,' I begin, my tone somewhere between amused and exasperated. 'In the picture of me and Dylan, we were on the floor, okay? We were on the floor together, fair enough, but I can think of a whole bunch of reasons why that might happen that aren't remotely sexual – including the truth, which is that we fell. But in your photo, the one of you and Carrie, you are kissing. Kissing. Your lips are touching. There's no excuse, and even if there was, guess what? I don't care. You could have been sucking venom from a sting on her lips to save her life, and I would not care. It wouldn't make me want you again. You have behaved so terribly, and so disrespectfully, at pretty much every opportunity. So, I've cleaned up your mess – you're welcome – and now I'm going to go. I'm going away for a few nights, with Dylan, and then I'm coming back to get the rest of my things, and then I'm gone for good. It's time we ended this.'

'You can't do that,' Rowan protests, his voice trembling.

'Watch me,' I tell him firmly. 'Perhaps Carrie will wash your shirts – if you can find her – and maybe Rebecca will do the school runs for you. But I am not playing this stupid game any more.'

I head back downstairs, struggling with my suit-case, Rowan still right there behind me.

'Let me help you,' he says, grovelling. 'Why don't you take your trip, cool down, have a think about things?'

'Okay, sure, I'll go on my trip, and I'll think about how you cheated on me,' I reply with a snort.

'I mean think about us, about our family, and our life, and if you're sure you want to walk away from it,' he pleads.

I put my suitcase down on the doorstep and turn to look him square in the eye.

'The only thing I'm going to be thinking about while I'm away is just how good revenge sex feels,' I say with a smile. 'See you later.'

Turning on my heel, I grab my case and head down the driveway.

Okay, so that's not strictly true, but the look on his face when I said it, damn, I really hit him where it hurts.

It's not entirely untrue either, though; I'll be thinking about it – but the chance would be a fine thing.

29

Standing at the bottom of Mr Campbell's drive, with Dylan at my side and our suitcases in tow, I can hardly believe what I'm looking at, and I've seen some things in my life.

I don't imagine our quaint little street has ever seen a tour bus parked on it, but here one is. Mr Campbell, with his penchant for snooping on his neighbours, would have loved this, peering out at what was going on through his telescope. I can't help but wonder if anyone is looking, like Rowan or Rebecca, but I'm far too dignified to give in to the temptation of looking to check.

Mitch, the band's manager, greets us with a warm, enthusiastic smile as we approach the bus. He's a tall, lanky guy with shaggy hair and a perpetually stressed-out look on his face. Then again, I don't think I've ever met a band manager who didn't look like they were on the verge of a meltdown.

'Nicole, Dylan, welcome aboard!' he says excitedly, in a way that makes you feel like you're part of something big.

'I'm sure it's too late to back out now,' Dylan jokes, his excitement mirroring Mitch's.

I offer a genuine smile and nod, my anticipation building by the second, but not quite as fast as my nerves.

We step on board and the bus door closes behind us with a soft hiss. Wow, it really does feel like there's no turning back.

It's been a long time since I was on a tour bus. I'm actually amazed by how little they've changed over the past decade. It's almost comforting, in a strange way, because it makes me feel at home, like it hasn't been all that long since I was on one last.

Through the door, on the lower level, you step into the kitchen area. Everything is made from a dark, shiny wood that doesn't do much to help how dark the bus seems. The artificial light illuminates the space but there's something about that tour bus darkness –

something that makes you feel like it's a secret space, for getting up to no good.

I cast an eye over the kitchen. It has everything you could want or need on board a bus. I am especially delighted to see that there is a coffee machine – a proper one – which is going to make this whole process so much easier. Next to it there is a living space, with sofas and a TV, although no one is sitting there currently.

'Everyone is up in the back lounge,' Mitch tells us. 'Let's head up.'

We follow Mitch up the steep, windy staircase, past the tiny bathroom, and along the walkway where all the bunks are. I run my hand across the curtains, my mind darting back and forth all over the place, as different memories from different tours come flooding back – some bad, some good. I really, truly never thought I would ever set foot on a tour bus again, to the point where even the crappy curtains are making me smile.

Finally, we reach the back lounge, which is probably the biggest communal seating area on the bus, where we find Mikey, Taz and Jamie. They're all looking at a TV, watching Taz play PS5, and they're all drinking beer – in fact, the number of empty bottles around already is actually quite impressive.

The boys are laughing and chatting animatedly, clearly all super excited to be here too, already straight back into the swing of things.

'Hey, guys,' Mikey greets us with a grin as we take our seats. 'Now the party can really start, huh? This is really happening.'

'Yeah,' Dylan replies. 'Glad to be here.'

'Hey, Mitch, grab Dylan a beer,' Mikey calls out. 'One of the special ones, from the back. Do you want anything, Nicole?'

I smile and shake my head.

It feels surreal to be sitting here with The Burnouts – The actual Burnouts, hitting the road again, when no one ever thought it would happen.

As we settle into conversation, I can sense the gentle hum of the bus's engine and the subtle vibrations beneath us. We're moving. This show is officially on the road.

Mitch places a bottle of beer in Dylan's hand before sitting down to join us.

I try not to pull a face but, come on, we all know Dylan is trying to drink less – is what is basically a breakfast beer really the way to go? Hopefully it's just the one.

'So, to recap the details, folks,' Mitch starts, now that everyone is here. 'We're headed to Manchester, for the first leg of our secret show mini-tour. We've purposefully spread rumours, hinting that it might be The Burnouts making a comeback. After tonight, the cat's out of the bag – The Burnouts are officially back, and we'll be playing more secret shows in Leeds, Paris, and the grand finale in London, where we'll announce our big reunion tour later this year.'

'Fucking yeah,' Mikey says with an almost aggressive level of excitement. 'Come on, lads, I'll drink to that.'

The boys all raise their beer bottles, clinking them up high. The band members exchange excited glances, and the reality sinks in. The Burnouts are back. It feels surreal and exhilarating and completely terrifying. And the journey has only just begun.

30

As the tour bus slows down, approaching the venue in Manchester, we all dive toward the windows, eager to catch a glimpse of the crowd – and to see if there even is a crowd because the fear is (according to the boys) that no one cares about them any more. The excitement – and the nerves – on board the bus are palpable. The boys have swapped partying for feeling petrified. God, I really hope people turn up for them.

The windows, designed to allow us to see outside but keep the crowd's prying eyes at bay, mean we can all look outside, to see what's going on, without anyone spotting us.

I sigh with relief. The queue of fans goes on for as far as the eye can see – it even turns the corner; the fans at the back of the line might even be in a different postcode.

'Good news must travel fast,' Jamie remarks, peering out of the tinted bus window. 'It looks like your rumour did the trick, Mitch.'

It isn't just that the line is long, every single person there looks almost too excited to function, and you can tell they are all here for The Burnouts. Some people are wearing band T-shirts, some are holding signs – oh, there's a girl with the band's name written across her cleavage, it's nice to see we're still doing that in 2024.

Jamie is right, the strategically circulated rumour about The Burnouts making a secret comeback has created the hype, and when these four men appear on that stage it is going to make their year.

'Look at them, they haven't forgotten us,' Mikey says, his eyes twinkling like a kid on Christmas morning. You would think he had just won the lottery, although I suppose in a way he has. If this many people will turn up for a secret show, just think how many tickets they'll shift on an arena tour.

'Mate, I'm shaking like a leaf in an earthquake,' Taz, who is usually the laid-back one, confesses.

'Come on,' Mikey says, giving him a nudge. 'This is what we wanted. We're going to smash it.'

'It's easy for you to say, TV boy,' Jamie jokes. 'Some of us were banished to obscurity.'

'Are you okay?' I ask Dylan.

He puffs air from his cheeks.

'Yeah, I'm good,' he replies. 'I was hoping for a crowd, but not expecting one, I can't quite believe it.'

'Was it always this many girls?' Taz asks. 'Like, it's almost all girls out there.'

'Girls?' Mikey says. 'You mean women. They're mostly thirty-somethings, possibly married with kids. I mean, look over there – that woman has a teenager with her.'

'It's a mix of ages,' Dylan says. 'That's kind of cool. I'd never really thought about different generations listening to our music while we were off the scene.'

I smile – that is nice.

'We still clearly have an adoring female fan base,' Jamie says. 'It's a shame we're all taken.'

Ew, that's less nice.

'Dylan isn't taken,' Mikey reminds him.

'Then Dylan will clean up,' Jamie says.

'Well, that won't be much different to old times, will it?' Mikey jokes as he pats his brother on the back.

Dylan just laughs it off.

'Get ready, mate, you're going to get mobbed,' Taz adds.

'No one is getting mobbed yet,' Mitch interrupts. 'This is still a secret gig, so we'll be sneaking you guys in while the crew bus distracts the crowd.'

'They know we're here,' Mikey points out.

'It's a secret gig,' Mitch tells him with a laugh. 'Come on, we're almost there, let's not ruin the surprise now.'

Mitch glances at his phone for a few seconds.

'Right, come on, this is our window to sneak in,' he tells us all.

It's like a military operation as we all make our way from the bus to the back door, quickly and carefully, making sure that no one sees us. Finally inside the fortress of the venue (have you ever tried to meet your favourite band before or after a show? It's hard to even catch a glimpse), we all start to relax.

We head through the backstage area, towards the dressing rooms, none of us in need of a tour guide. We've all been here various times in the past and it shows.

'Okay, get yourselves settled in there, get some food – I'll be back when it's time for your soundcheck, which shouldn't be long,' Mitch says. 'Don't get too drunk too quickly, please.'

'Erm, we are grown men now,' Mikey protests.

'You were grown men before,' Mitch says with a laugh. 'I still had to wipe your arses.'

'Fair,' Mikey replies.

As I follow Dylan into the room, I smile, immediately noticing that it hasn't changed one bit since the last time I was here. There are still the same tired-looking old leather sofas dotted around – and they were worn the last time I sat on them, so they're positively knackered now. Over the years, every band that has played here has graffitied the walls with their autographs, the dates, doodles – all sorts. It's like a rock and roll museum exhibit, although, with some of the drawings and choice messages, it might be for the best that the general public doesn't see this.

I cock my head and smile as I notice the table of food. The boys in the band might have matured but their tour rider certainly hasn't. The table is laid out with crisps, sweets, biscuits – honestly, it's like the buffet table at a kids' party, although you couldn't mistake where you were for a kids' party, thanks to the mountain of booze. There are crates and crates, piled high, all filled with what looks like any alcoholic beverage your heart might desire.

As the others gather around the food, tucking into their pre-show fuel, I notice Dylan slipping away, stepping outside the room. There is something about the look on his face, an emotion I can't quite decipher.

I slowly back away from the others too, heading out without them noticing, so that I can make sure Dylan is okay. He is uncharacteristically quiet. Back in the day, he would have been the loudest, the one cracking the jokes, the one eating everything on the table and working his way through the crates of beer.

I just about miss catching up to him, as I see him turn the corner at the end of the corridor, but I think I know where he's going.

I head through the stage door and, just as I expected, there he is.

Dylan is standing at the centre of the stage, a lone figure under the bright spotlights, gazing out over the empty room. It's a cavernous space when it's empty, but it won't stay this way for long. Soon it will be overflowing with adoring fans.

I walk up to Dylan, silently approaching him as he stands there, motionless, frozen like a statue. He's lost in his thoughts, and at first, he doesn't notice me.

I clear my throat softly to let him know that I'm here, I don't want to make him jump.

'Oh, hi,' he says as he spots me.

'Hi,' I reply as I stand alongside him.

I look at him, offering him a smile, giving him the chance to tell me what's on his mind.

'Nic, I never thought I'd be back here,' he says seriously. 'I always wanted it, but I never thought it would happen. I somehow feel like I'm at the moment I've been hoping for all this time, and somehow completely unprepared.'

I flash him a reassuring smile, trying to calm his nerves and give him a boost of much-needed confidence – something he used to have in bags.

'Dylan, you have nothing to worry about,' I tell him. 'Everyone out there is here because there is a chance it could be you. They don't even know for sure, and they're queuing around the block.'

He nods, and gratitude begins to replace his lingering doubts.

'You're right. It's just... it's been a while, you know?' he explains. 'I don't want to sound ungrateful for the opportunity. I just hope I don't let anyone down, that they don't walk away saying I haven't got "it" any more.'

I place my hand on his arm as I wonder whether lightening the mood might be the key.

'Dylan, the last time you were on this stage you threw up into Taz's lap and almost impaled him with the pointy tip of a hi-hat cymbal,' I remind him. 'You didn't have "it" that night, and everyone still loved you. Just imagine when they hear you now, your voice stronger than ever – and since you reappeared in my life I haven't seen you be sick once, I'm starting to worry you're an imposter.'

'You're right,' he says with a grin. 'Thanks for the pep talk.'

'I think people are going to love the new Dylan even more than the old one,' I say. 'I know I do. I mean, because he doesn't vomit on me, obviously.'

I'm quick to add that last part on because I didn't mean that sentence to sound as intense as it does. Way to go, Nicole, batting around the L word like it's nothing.

'I may have changed in some ways, but I'm still the same old me,' he tells me with a smile. 'I'm still talented, cool, charming, irresistible...'

'Modest,' I say with a laugh, adding to his jokey list.

'Yep, modest, let's not forget that,' he replies. 'I'll be charming the pants off everyone in the room before they know what's hit them.'

'Oh, I never said *that*,' I tease him. 'Not everyone in the room. Your charm doesn't work on me, boy.'

He gives me a knowing smile.

'Okay, go on then, prove it,' I prompt him. 'Prove you can charm me.'

He pauses for a moment.

'I charmed you once before,' he dares to say.

'But that was then, and this is now,' I continue. 'I know, we're friends, but you can at least show me what you've got. For sport.'

What am I doing? I'm flirting with him. Jesus Christ, Nicole, you never change. A few seconds with a man on a stage and you're weak at the knees.

His laughter fills the air as he leans in a little closer, our faces just inches apart.

'Well, if we weren't friends, it would probably go something like this,' he says, and then all at once his smile drops into something serious. He places his hand on the back of my neck and leans in closer, his lips lightly touching my ear.

'I would tell you that I was going to have you – again – before the night was over,' he whispers. 'Because the more you tell yourself that it's a bad idea, the more you want it, and when you give in to that feeling, you'll see how meant to be this is.'

I hold my breath as Dylan lingers next to my ear for a second or two. What do I do? What can I do?

He pulls away, quickly, all at once, and it feels like he takes a part of me with him.

'...but we are friends,' he reminds me through a smile, his features softening again. 'So I would never say that.'

My mouth is so dry I feel as though I could choke.

Dylan takes my hand and smiles as he gives my arm a playful shake, to show me that sexy rock-star Dylan has retreated, and that my best friend is back.

'Here you are,' Mikey calls out as he joins us.

Taz and Jamie aren't far behind him. Then Mitch appears, and some roadies, and some sound and lighting techs – we couldn't be less alone right now. Actually, scratch that, I've just remembered this room will soon be full of fans – more than 2,500, if the place sells out.

I don't know if I'm devastated or relieved that we were interrupted.

'I'll get out of the way,' I say, taking my hand back.

I sit on the edge of the stage and hop down into the pit below before heading out into the wide-open space where the crowd will be later.

'You doing all right?' Mikey asks Dylan as he slaps him on the back. 'You're not losing it, are you, bro?'

'I'm good, mate, I'm good,' Dylan reassures him.

'You need one of your special beers,' Mikey tells him with a laugh as they all take their positions. 'Honestly, don't look so worried. There are thousands of fans outside and pretty soon they're all going to be in here, screaming your name. You're Dylan fucking King. I bet there will be at least one or two of them screaming your name a bit more privately later.'

Taz, right on cue, supplies Mikey with a drum sting – *ba-dum-tss* – for his oh-so funny joke.

'Uh, Dylan, uh, uh,' Jamie grunts in a high-pitched voice.

'All right, come on,' Dylan says, laughing it off. 'Let's get this soundcheck checked off the list.'

'Yeah, let's do it, lads,' Mitch encourages them. 'Tonight marks the start of The Burnouts comeback, you're going to be bigger and better than ever. You thought things were crazy before – you haven't seen anything yet. I'm taking you guys to the fucking top and beyond.'

Suitably hyped up, Taz counts them in before they break into their first song. Seeing Dylan up there, performing the old songs, with all the charm and charisma he had before – except now he is not only about a million times hotter, but he seems to have me grabbed by the knickers too – is great for about five seconds, and then reality sets in.

It should be great, that things are shaping up to be as good – if not better – than the old days but... I don't know. Is that good for me? There's a part of me that worries things might go back to how they used to be, and that Dylan will soon belong to the fans again, and then who knows how things will go? The fame and the hype and the temptation can carry people away – sometimes past the point of no return. I've been through that before, and I don't want to lose him again.

31

'Come on,' Mikey bellows out, punching the air. 'We're the number one trend, everyone online is talking about us, about how we're back – we fucking smashed it.'

After an exceptional first show – honestly, every single one of them has seriously refined their talent since the last time they gigged together, it blew me away – we were rushed away from the venue and bundled on to the tour bus to head to the next city before the fans even had a chance to leave.

We're almost at Leeds, where the boys will be playing their second secret show tomorrow – not that it's much of a secret any more, of course.

'Yeah, we smashed it,' Jamie replies. 'Honestly, that might have been the best performance of my life.'

'Yeah, my forearms are throbbing,' Taz adds. 'Totally worth it, though. I played my heart out.'

You can tell that the excitement and adrenaline from the gig are still coursing through their veins. I can't even imagine what it must feel like, to get that buzz, one that can only come from performing on stage in front of a sea of adoring fans.

'What do you reckon, Dylan?' Mikey prompts him. 'Bit of all right, wasn't it?'

Dylan laughs. I can tell you how he's feeling going off the look in his eyes alone.

'Best feeling in the world,' he replies with a smile.

'And this is just the first night,' Mikey reminds him. 'It's only going to get better from here. We're definitely going out to celebrate tonight.'

I smirk to myself, thinking, once again, that I might not be cut out for nights out starting after 10 p.m. any more. My days of partying until dawn feel like a lifetime ago – honestly, I don't know how I did it.

'Well, the plan is to check into the hotel first,' Mitch reminds them. 'But, yes, we can go out to celebrate – so long as you remember that you have another show tomorrow. Let's not go too crazy on night one.'

'Oh my God, tits!' Jamie calls out. 'The first tits of the tour – look out of the window.'

Mikey is straight over there, peering out of the window as the bus grinds to a halt.

I look to see where we are and see that outside the hotel there is already a group of eager fans, hoping to catch a glimpse of the boys.

'How do they know we're staying here?' Mikey asks no one in particular.

'Because you always used to stay here,' I remind him. 'Fans remember details like that. They will know every move you're going to make – probably even before you do.'

Dylan furrows his brows, deep in thought.

'Who was that girl who used to follow us around?' he asks.

'Oh, yeah, that crazy one – you found her in your wheelie bin,' Mikey says with a laugh.

'Cherry,' I remind them, my eyes widening with horror.

They all say her name at the same time, and the memories flood back.

'She was unhinged,' Mikey says.

Cherry wasn't very nice at all. She definitely had issues. When she wasn't rifling through bins in search of treasure, she was resorting to desperate measures, like throwing herself in front of the tour bus or sending her horny fanfic to my work email address in the hope that I'd pass it on to Dylan.

'Straight in, boys, unfortunately,' Mitch tells them as he ushers us from the bus. 'No time for tits.'

'There is always time for tits,' Mikey replies.

Mikey really has changed over the years, I can't get over it. He used to be so shy and he took everything far too seriously, but now he's gone a bit too far in the other direction, and he isn't even charming with it, like Dylan was, he's coming across as arrogant and sleazy. I'm not so sure it suits him.

I breathe in the subtly fragrant air of the hotel lobby. Okay, this part of the lifestyle I have *definitely* missed.

It's all sparkling chandeliers and polished marble floors – and every member of staff looks fit to serve the royal family. A pianist plays a soothing melody on a grand piano over by the bar, which only adds to the boujee atmosphere.

Mitch is over at the check-in desk where a seriously well-dressed member of staff is helping him check us in. Eventually he returns with the key cards – practically a deck of them – for the band, the crew and then, well, me.

'Here you go, Dylan,' Mitch tells him as he hands

him a couple of cards. 'This one is yours, this one is for Nicole. Then, Mikey, this is for you...'

Eventually everyone has a key for their room – not that it seems like most of them are planning on going to them just yet.

'Okay, boys, the hotel is going to arrange your transport to the club,' Mitch announces. 'I want the closest thing you can manage to best behaviour, yeah? Especially you, Dylan, I know what you were like.'

Dylan gets a few cheers and claps from the others – those who were there, or read a newspaper at the time. I just sigh. I remember what he was like too.

'Yes, lads, let's go,' Mikey says, clapping his hands together. 'Lads and Nicole – sorry, Nicole.'

I laugh it off. I always did feel more like one of the boys.

'Don't worry about it,' I reassure him. 'I think I'm going to get an early night anyway.'

'What? Really?' Mikey replies in disbelief, because going to bed early on tour is just not the done thing at all.

'Yeah, I'm tired, and I have work to do – someone needs to make sure there's good press from tonight,' I say with a smile.

Dylan hands me the key card he's been holding.

'Here's your key card,' he says. 'If you're sure?'

'I'm sure,' I reply confidently.

After a round of goodbyes, I make my way to the lift. It's true, that I should do some work, but the thought of watching them get swarmed by eager fans while I get pushed to the sidelines isn't the night I'm after. I know, this is why we're here, this is what I signed up for but, still, there are parts of the 'good old days' that I'm pretty sure I've grown out of.

As the lift doors slide open to my floor, I let out a long yawn – which proves to me that my decision to not go out partying was the right one. I step into the corridor and locate the door to my room, fumbling with my key card, eventually letting myself inside.

'Wow,' I say to myself – and you know something is really good (or really bad) when you find yourself talking out loud *to yourself*.

This isn't just a room; it's a lavish penthouse suite – one with multiple rooms.

The first thing that strikes me is the sheer opulence. The first room is a huge open-plan living space, kitted out with plush sofas, fancy furniture and striking contemporary artwork. A gleaming modern kitchen area with stainless-steel appliances and polished granite countertops sits at one side of the room – with floor-to-ceiling windows at the other. Oh, and everything you could possibly want in between, like a piano and a cinema screen.

Back in the day, this is exactly the kind of space we would always get, for at least a few nights of the tour, so that we could have huge parties. They would always be these big, beautiful rooms... and then the boys would destroy them. There is no chance of me doing that, not unless I have some sort of clumsy accident, which now that I think about it wouldn't be unlike me, so I'm not going to tempt fate with that one.

Venturing deeper into the suite, I discover that there are two bedrooms, but it's the larger bedroom with a super-king-sized bed that calls my name. The brilliant white sheets look so inviting, I can't wait to climb in – after removing my make-up not once, but twice, lest I leave grubby brown and black marks on the pillows. The en-suite bathroom is a dream of white marble and shiny gold fixings, and the bath looks so deliciously deep – it would be rude not to.

I head back into the bedroom and then step out onto the balcony, despite the chilly air that immediately nips at my skin, to take in the city. The Leeds skyline stretches before me and while it brings back so many memories, from when I lived here, I can't help but feel a little freaked out by how much it has changed.

Leeds was so different ten years ago, with only a handful of iconic landmarks dotted around the otherwise seemingly flat skyline. But now, towering skyscrapers have sprung up all over, totally transforming the cityscape. Somehow it just looks like the future – even though compared to somewhere like London it is still tiny – but that's probably just because I can't get my head around how somewhere that was once so familiar has been totally transformed.

Just about being able to pick out my old haunts – my flat, my office, the various venues I used to always be dashing to – allows me to look back in time, and I can't help but wonder, if I really could turn back the clock, and make different choices, and carve out a different path for myself – would I do it? I suppose everyone thinks that, don't they, but the likelihood is that I would just find a different way to mess it all up.

It's almost not worth thinking about, because it's never going to happen, but I don't suppose that will halt my imagination, especially not when I'm here, literally looking out over my past, all on my own.

I hover for as long as I can stand the cold air before deciding to head inside for a bath. Oh, it's going to feel all the more glorious, now that I'm a bit chilly.

I'm only back inside about five minutes when I hear a knock at the door.

'Room service,' a voice calls out as I approach it.

I definitely didn't order any room service but, now that I've remembered it's a thing, I'm definitely going to do it.

I open the door, ready to sadly send the staff member on their way – and probably crack some kind of lame joke about how they will be returning shortly – only to find Dylan standing there, a plastic bag in each hand.

'Hello,' he says with a smile.

'Erm, hi,' I say, laughing. 'I thought you were going out – you're the last person I expected to find lurking outside my room.'

Dylan laughs as he steps inside.

'So, first of all, confession time, this isn't your room, it's my room,' he explains.

'Noooo,' I whine – playfully, but I am low-key devastated. 'I should have known this beauty was too good to be true. I'm assuming I took your card by mistake?'

'Oh, no, I gave you the wrong one on purpose,' he explains confidently, like it's the most normal thing in the world. 'And then I nipped to the shop next door, to get the things I needed to make you dinner.'

'I thought you were going out to celebrate with the others,' I say again, not that I'm complaining.

'And I thought I would rather hang out with you,' he tells me with a smile. 'There will be plenty of chances to party but, I don't know, I would rather celebrate this one with you.'

My body warms up, all at once, as Dylan's gesture gives me a strange, tingly feeling. I don't know what it is but it's definitely a good sensation.

I guess, for the boys, this is the start of a new chapter, the beginning of their second act, and all being well, tonight will be the first night of many. For me, this is a one-night-only (well, technically three nights, but you know what I mean) kind of deal, I'm just here with Dylan, because I've been helping him out. This isn't my life any more, and soon enough I will be back to reality. So it's really nice that he's celebrating with me tonight, seeing as though I will be going home soon. Wherever that is.

'Thanks,' I say with a smile.

We look into each other's eyes, only for a second or two, before Dylan heads for the kitchen.

'So, what are we having?' I ask him.

'The best thing you've ever eaten,' he says confidently. 'But a much shitter version, because it's made by me.'

I laugh.

'Remember in LA,' he prompts me.

I freeze. Every time I remember it, it feels like I'm being hit by a car.

It feels like so long ago, and it was so surreal, that it honestly feels like a movie I watched – one of my favourite movies, that I think about all the time. It's one of those memories where you look back and think to yourself: there is *no way* that happened to me.

Dylan and I became best friends on pretty much the day we met. We had this instant, undeniable connection, this sudden big love for one another that hit us from the word go. I will never be able to explain it but, looking back, it was clear that we both knew that we wanted to be together in some way. He was Dylan King, I was a journalist. He was – according to the press – a serial shagger, a man incapable of a meaningful relationship. I was – what I now can look back at and say with ease – a dummy, who had this silly idea of what she wanted her life to be like.

I idolised celebrities, I wanted to be with one, to be one myself – and Dylan was never going to be an option. So we friend-zoned one another almost instantly, but definitely mutually, and then settled into a friendship, and it really was a great one. In fact, we were so close that, when Dylan finally got his divorce from his grifter of a wife, and I found out that Luke, my boyfriend, was shagging his way around Europe behind my back, we decide to go on holiday together. Honestly, it was just what I needed, it gave me the time and space to forget about Luke-bloody-Fox, and it seemed to do Dylan the world of good too. He hadn't seemed healthy when he was with Crystal, or in the immediate aftermath, but escaping to the US for a road trip with his bestie seemed like it changed him. While we were away, it was probably the best I've ever seen him – not including the present day, obviously. We had the best time, and I could feel us growing closer and closer by the day, almost as though – without the shit back home – we could just be us, and our true feelings could finally come to the surface.

So, on our last night there, we went for dinner – and had the most amazing grilled cheese sandwiches and fries, which I really did say was the best thing I had ever eaten – and then we went for a gorgeous night-time walk. And then he kissed me, and while I was totally stunned, I was somehow, confusingly, not at all surprised. It was like we both knew this moment was coming and, when it finally arrived, it was even better than I had imagined it. We spent the night together – the whole night – and then I woke up in his arms, very much feeling like things had changed, like our relationship was going to be so different from there on out. And it turned out that it was going to be different, just, you know, not for the better. We landed back in London, all over each other, like love's young dream. The second I looked up from kissing him, in the airport, the front page of the *Daily Scoop* caught my eye, and they were running this huge feature on the women Dylan had slept with, while he was still married to Crystal.

Looking back, with rational eyes, it seems as though Dylan and Crystal called it quits, and so he went right back to his old life *before* they were divorced. But back then, to me, the girl who had just thrown away years of friendship by sleeping with her best friend, it just seemed to me like he was never going to change and that I had made a huge mistake, so I tried to style it out, to walk it back. I'm pretty sure I just laughed, kissed him on the cheek, told him that he was never going to change and that was fine, we would always be friends. Yep, I know how stupid that sounds, and all it did was pretty much kill our friendship, and then the band broke up, and then – well, I guess you're up to date from there.

Sex with Dylan was nothing short of incredible. It was like we'd had years and years of foreplay that all built up to that moment, and I had never (then, or since) experienced anything like it. That feeling of my entire body being on fire, of my skin burning wherever he touched me, but in the most amazing way. Even something as simple as him kissing my neck felt like a nuclear explosion.

I need to stop thinking about it because it gets my knickers in a twist, even now, and despite little hints here and there, the two of us haven't actually had a serious conversation about it. I'm not even sure we need to, but that memory is going to haunt me for the rest of my life, for better or worse – I suppose it's a bit of both.

I watch Dylan pottering around in the kitchen, grabbing the things he needs to make me a sandwich, somehow looking so normal in some ways, but making me feel almost star-struck in others. Dylan King is making me a sandwich. *The* Dylan King.

'Oh, there's a present in that bag for you,' he prompts me.

I smile and cock my head curiously as I peer inside. I laugh as I reach in and take out a bottle of red nail polish.

'I thought, seeing as though I'm running around after you, you might make a joke about me painting your toes,' he explains. 'It was just a cheap one, that they were selling off at the checkout, but I thought if you did mention it, it would be funny to have one.'

'You thought of everything,' I say with a laugh. 'I'll get us some drinks.'

I pop the bottle in my pocket so that I can pour myself a drink – a vodka and orange from the bar – and ask Dylan if I can get him anything.

'A beer, please,' he says. 'The one with the blue label. I know you don't know beer.'

I laugh.

'I know I don't *like* beer,' I reply as I hand him his drink, but then something catches my eye. 'Shit, the pan is smoking.'

Dylan grabs the pan from the hob, which only releases more smoke from under it.

'Okay, this isn't my fault,' he says, coughing and laughing. 'This must be a new pan – there's a huge paper label underneath it.'

'Geez, you can't get service these days,' I joke, but then I start coughing too.

'Go out onto the balcony for a minute,' he tells me. 'Get some air, leave the door open to let the smell out. I'll wave this towel around, before the smoke alarm starts.'

I do as I'm told, heading outside, taking a seat on one of the comfortable outdoor sofas. It's a large, private terrace off the living space. I notice an outdoor heater above me so I click it on.

I don't hear the smoke alarm, which is good for us, but kind of worrying generally.

Eventually, Dylan joins me with our drinks in his hands and a blanket tucked under his arm.

'I didn't burn the hotel down,' he says proudly.

'Yeah, you didn't!' I confirm with faux encouragement.

'I did make it stink, though,' he replies as he hands me my drink and takes a seat next to me. 'Maybe we should give it a minute to air out, before we go back in.'

'Sure,' I reply, taking the blanket, covering myself with it. 'I don't mind that this isn't my room now.'

Dylan laughs as he gets under the blanket on the sofa next to me.

'How do we flag that the smoke alarm didn't go off, without admitting that we almost started a fire?' I ask. 'It's odd that it didn't go off.'

'You know what musicians are like, for tampering with smoke detectors,' he reminds me. 'Would you be surprised if a previous guest had messed with it?'

'I wouldn't be surprised if you had stayed here in 2014 and done it yourself,' I point out through a chuckle. 'Of course, I would have been here, and I would have stopped you.'

'Do you ever miss it?' he asks. 'The lifestyle, the

touring, running around in a whirlwind of chaos with me?'

I laugh.

'There are plenty of things that I miss,' I tell him with a smile. 'I miss the glamour of it all – all the nice places we would go, all the cool free stuff we would get. I miss eating Hawaiian pizza in your bunk while we watched that Tom Green movie everyone but us hated. I miss going out for dinner with you, and the way people would move heaven and earth to give us what we wanted, even if it was chicken nuggets in a five-star fish restaurant.'

Dylan laughs as he recalls the evening I'm referring to.

'I miss being in your orbit,' I continue, a little more seriously. 'I miss the feeling of being around you. I miss the way you make me feel about myself, because, I don't know, you make me feel like there is something there worth liking, even when I don't think it myself. I miss having you to talk to. I miss having someone so on my wavelength that we always knew what the other person was going to say or do – before we knew it ourselves. Someone who knows me well enough to finish my...'

'...Sandwiches?' he jokes.

God, that's exactly the same joke I would have made too.

Dylan looks into my eyes – not just into them, through them, peering into my soul.

'I miss you too,' he tells me. 'I miss the way you can make anywhere feel like a home, whether it's a hotel room or a tour bus. I miss your calming influence on me. I miss having someone who will tell me when I'm being a dickhead. I miss the smell of your perfume, the way it would always linger in a room after you'd gone, always leaving me wanting more. I miss having someone around who always likes me, even on my bad days. I miss watching you sleep, when you would drop off while we watched movies together, or when I would sing you to sleep if you'd had a bad day. I even miss painting your bloody toenails.'

My breathing is heavy and my heart is pounding, but even now I can laugh at that.

'Did Rowan used to paint your toenails for you?' he asks curiously.

I shake my head.

'Did you ask him to?' Dylan replies.

I shake my head again, only this time I reach into my pocket and take out the bottle of nail polish. Then I place it down on the table in front of Dylan, like a chess master making their final move, as if to say: Checkmate.

Dylan picks up the bottle and gets down on the floor in front of me. First he takes off my heels, then he gently takes one of my feet in his hands, lifting it into the air.

I can tell by the way he took off my shoes, and the way he's touching me now, even though it's only my foot, where he wants this to go. I show him that I want it too by using my free foot to run up and down his leg as he kneels in front of me.

Dylan's expression doesn't change at all. He lifts my foot to his face and begins to kiss my ankle. He slowly works his way up the inside of my leg, each kiss lasting longer, and being more passionate than the previous one. By the time he gets to the top of my thigh, he stops and looks up at me.

God, I want him – I need him, even. I don't care if he shags me and then never speaks to me again (well, obviously I do, but you know what I mean), I just can't spend another platonic second with him.

I lean forward and kiss him on the lips, slow and sensual for as long as I can take it, but this feeling in-side me is too frantic not to give in to. As we kiss, he stands up, picking me up in his big, strong arms before he sits back down on the sofa and sits me down on top of him.

He's got me now, I'm his, for whatever he wants. As I reach down and whip away his belt, I think about how, since the second he walked back into my life, doing this has been all I could think about – although, if I'm being honest (and I know it sounds bad), I can think of a few times, with Rowan, when I just closed my eyes and let my mind drift right back to LA.

It's just like I remember it being, only better, that full-body fire from head to toe. Here, now, in the moment it's hard to care about what this means for tomorrow. Tonight it's all about the fire – it's a good job the smoke detector is broken.

32

My eyes begin to open, ever so slowly, and then all at once when I suddenly remember where I am.

I'm in bed – in Dylan's bed – with my head on his chest, and his big arm wrapped around me, holding me in place, and I've been here since we fell asleep (which, admittedly, probably wasn't that long ago).

I notice his phone is ringing on the bedside table, which must have been what woke me up. A few seconds later it wakes him up and he finally releases me, leaning over to answer it.

'Hello,' he says, half asleep. 'Oh, hi, Mitch... Yeah, I was asleep... Yeah, I know, but I bet they're all in a worse state than me... What, really?... Okay, yeah, a signing sounds good... I'll meet you in the breakfast room... Okay, bye.'

I feel like I work out everything I need to know from Dylan's half of the conversation – well, everything except where I stand with Dylan, after last night. I'm terrified, waiting to find out.

'Well, time to get up,' Dylan says, his face serious and his tone abrupt, but his face dissolves into a mischievous smile. 'But not just yet.'

Dylan springs into action, climbing on top of me, pressing his body down on mine as he gives me a big squeeze.

I let out an excited little squeak, not only because I love to feel his hands on me, or because I'm loving the one-on-one attention he's showering me with, but because this feels real, he isn't going anywhere, he's here, in bed with me, the morning after. That's got to mean something.

'I don't want to get up,' he says with a pout. 'I'd rather have breakfast in bed and spend the whole day here, with you, in this bed – although I could be convinced to move to the bathroom for a few rounds.'

I laugh. I can't deny that I'm tempted to stay in bed with him too, but the reminder that the others are waiting for him – and that he has work to do – nudges me back to reality.

'As much as I'd love that, it sounds like you've got fans to meet,' I remind him.

Dylan leans in, planting a gentle kiss on my lips.

'I thought you were my biggest fan,' he jokes.

'Well, after last night, you might just convince me,' I reply.

'I'll have to try a bit harder, then,' he says as he leans in for another one – this time he doesn't stop.

I could definitely get used to starting my day like this.

33

I stand in the wings, my eyes glued to Dylan onstage. He's giving it his all, and the crowd is loving it, drinking up every last drop of their encore. Dylan cradles his microphone stand, clutching it like it's the most precious thing in the world. He leans into the mic, ready to unleash one of their classic hits.

Dylan looks ridiculously sexy under the blazing stage lights. Beads of sweat glisten on his forehead and run down his neck, and it reminds me of last night. Our heated moments together still linger in my mind, and – not to sound like a psychopath –I can still remember what his skin smells like, and it gives me the raunchiest flashbacks.

I can't help but let my mind wander, letting myself

get lost in the music, watching him out there. I imagine lots of people in the audience are doing the same thing, I'm certainly not the only one who finds Dylan irresistible.

The sea of fans before the stage is filled with hundreds of women who would love nothing more than to get their hands on him. Exhibit A: the pairs of knickers that have found their way onto the stage during the performance.

My mind drifts to the earlier events of the day, when the boys did their signing. The hysteria around them was as intense as ever – worse, even. It was a madhouse, with hordes of eager fans lining up to meet the band and, as always, most of them had eyes only for Dylan.

I watched from the sidelines, my heart heavy with mixed emotions. One after another, women approached Dylan, their flirtatious smiles and batting eyelashes impossible to ignore. I lost count of the number of phone numbers they slipped him.

It was torture – especially after last night. It's strange because I rarely felt jealous when I was with Luke, in fact, I don't remember feeling it at all. Despite the relentless attention Luke received from female admirers, I never questioned his loyalty. He was mine, and I was his, and we trusted each other. But then of course, on the first tour he went on without me, he slept with anyone who was willing, so I suppose I'm not all that trusting in these situations any more.

It is also probably worth reminding myself that Dylan isn't mine because, wow, listen to me – already. We had one (incredible) night together, but the last time we attempted something like this, it ended in disaster. I can't let myself get carried away again.

The Burnouts' performance leaves everyone buzzing as they finally leave the stage. The echoes of their music are still reverberating in the air as we're ushered outside, towards the tour bus, so that we can get out of here before the venue lets the fans out too. There is nothing freakier than sitting on a bus that is being swarmed by fans, hoping they can't get in, knowing you can't get out, the bus being unable to move an inch.

As we approach the waiting tour bus, we notice something – a crowd of women, largely in their twenties, who are dressed more for a night out on the town than for a rock concert. It's not just that their revealing dresses and glamorous make-up make them look less like most of the other fans, who all seem to be opting for band merch or nostalgic fashion – the kind of thing they were wearing last time around – it's also the fact that real fans will still be in the building, if they were at the show.

I hang back, observing from a distance as the boys are immediately swarmed.

A confident blonde in a short red dress presents Mikey with her cleavage.

'Mikey, will you sign my left boob?' she asks him.

'Of course, darling, I'd be delighted,' Mikey replies playfully as he obliges.

'Dylan?' the blonde says.

'Go on, bro, do the other one,' Mikey says, nudging him.

'Sure,' Dylan says with a laugh, taking the pen, giving her his autograph.

I never understood the autographing of body parts. Surely it just washes off – unless of course you're Cherry, the superfan, and you get it tattooed over. I always used to prefer getting CDs signed, but I appreciate that makes me sound old and outdated.

'So, what are you doing now?' the blonde asks them. 'Are you going out-out?'

'Nah, we're throwing a huge party at the hotel, in Dylan's suite,' Mikey tells her. 'He's known for throwing legendary parties.'

'Can we come?' the blonde asks, trying her luck.

'Of course you can,' Mikey replies. He turns to Dylan. 'Right, mate? The more the merrier.'

'Yeah, sure,' Dylan says.

'Okay then, but we need to move so, everyone on the bus,' Mitch calls out.

Excitement fills the night air as the crowd of women excitedly piles on to the bus as Mitch herds them inside.

As I walk behind the boys, still a few paces away, I notice Mikey gives Dylan a knowing look.

'I'm doing this for you, bro,' I overhear Mikey encouraging Dylan with a wink.

I pile on with everyone else and find a spot on the sofa.

'Do some of us need to go in the bunks?' one girl suggests cheekily. 'So that we all fit.'

'There's plenty of room, and the party is only a five-minute drive away,' Mitch tells them with a laugh. 'Let's go.'

I slump back in my seat, like a moody teenager.

I can safely say that this aspect of tour life is one that I don't miss, not one bit.

34

I thought people were supposed to calm down as they got older?

I know I have. In fact, Rowan used to tell me I had BGE – big grandma energy – but I think lots of women, as they arrive in their thirties, realise that there is a lot of value in embracing their inner granny.

Don't get me wrong, I know I'd let things get a bit stale, and that my life before Dylan turned up was positively dull, but I'm not talking about that. What I'm on about are the little things, things that you wouldn't necessarily dream of embracing in your twenties.

I mean, I would go out, multiple times a week, in absolutely minimal clothing – no matter what the weather. I would wear heels that made my feet ache, and talk to men who made my brain hurt, and I would ride out my hangover like it was a badge of honour.

These days, however, I have thoughts like: there's a lot to be said for a good cardigan. I love a cardy, a big pair of fluffy socks, a huge cup of tea and a book. Imagine doing that on a cold November night, instead of traipsing out in the cold, in uncomfortable clothes, to get drinks spilt down you, and random men dry-humping you – unsolicited – on the dance floor.

Don't get me wrong, I have been loving reliving my youth, and hanging out with the boys, going on nights out – but I'm starting to think that the reason I have been enjoying it is because it has felt special, a break from reality, something different for a change.

Thinking back, to the so-called good old days, I remember that nothing was special. Crazy nights, every night, getting drunk and staying that way for the whole tour – it's like anything where, if you overdo it, it sort of ruins it. It's sort of like when you have a gigantic bar of chocolate, and it's amazing, but the second you eat too much it's hard not to look at it, angrily, like it's trying to ruin your life. Too much of anything is almost always a bad thing.

Of course I'm the only person here, at the party, who thinks this way. I never thought I would be the one sitting in the corner, watching everyone, feeling exhausted, willing time to go faster so that it can be over and we can go to bed.

Last night, Dylan's suite was the sleek, boujee pad – this stunning love nest, where we had sex in every room, and we woke up to sheer luxury. Tonight it has been transformed into a den of hedonism – and a total shithole of one at that.

An array of multicoloured strobe lights darts around the room. The air is heavy with the thumping bass of music, laughter and the kind of conversation that makes you want to ram cocktail sticks into your ears.

People from all walks of life have gathered here. The guests are as diverse as the music because, for the last hour, Dylan and Mikey have been taking requests, Mikey playing the guitar while Dylan sings, and honestly they've covered a bit of everything.

Over at the bar area there is a self-designated mixologist, who is concocting the strongest drinks, and everyone is loving them, but the more they drink, the more boisterous the party gets.

The living room area, previously pristine, is now filled with dancing bodies, twisting and gyrating to the music.

The balcony door is wide open, allowing some

fresh air to enter – it's boiling in here – but only the smokers are stepping out there.

As Dylan sings 'Livin' on a Prayer', I notice the blonde – the one who invited herself and her friends to the party – invade the makeshift stage and hang off Dylan's neck, as she joins him in screaming into the microphone. They're just singing, just having a good time – I'm being ridiculous.

As the song ends, it's Mikey who spots me. He comes over and sits down next to me, wrapping his arm around me, pulling me close. He holds my head on his chest, a little heavy-handedly, but he's very drunk, he's not exactly in control of his motor skills.

'I never thought I would see Nicole Wilde looking grumpy at a party,' he says.

'Then you never looked hard enough, back in the day,' I reply. 'You guys have always been a pain in the arse.'

'You love us really,' he says, peppering my head with kisses.

I look over, to where I last saw Dylan, only to see him looking back at us. The blonde girl is telling him a story, and she couldn't be more animated, but he's looking over here, watching – almost as though he's keeping an eye on us.

The blonde girl, unhappy that he isn't watching

her tell her tale, takes his face in her hand and turns him toward her.

'Back in a bit,' I tell Mikey.

I grab my drink and take it outside, to get a break from the music, and the smell of sweat, and the floor show.

As I pass the outdoor sofa, the spot where Dylan and I started heating things up last night, I can't help but stare at it. There is a man sitting there though, and I accidentally make eye contact with him, so I quickly avert my gaze and head over to the glass balustrade, resting my forearms on it as I look out over the city.

Hang on a minute, that guy, the one on the sofa. He looks familiar, in fact, he looks like...

I feel a tap on my shoulder.

'Jake!' I squeak, grabbing my old friend, pulling him in for a hug, but then I push him away just as quickly, to look him up and down.

'Nicole Wilde,' he says with a laugh. 'Some things never change.'

'You change,' I tell him, not quite making sense, but he knows what I mean.

I'm stunned. I used to work with Jake, when I first started out. He was the tech guy and he was so shy, and quiet, and nerdy. He didn't care about the music industry, or celebrities, and he used to love making fun of me for how into it all I was. We were good friends, back in the day, but back then he was very much the kind of guy you would expect to work in a techy role – from the plaid shirt to the neat haircut – but not any more. Bloody hell, has everyone had a glow-up but me over the last ten years?

Jake's look has totally evolved. His hair is dark, long on top, and blown back. He's rocking the designer stubble, honestly, is there any man on this planet who doesn't look ten times hotter with facial hair? He's wearing black jeans, a T-shirt and a black leather jacket.

We never fell out or anything like that but, when I moved to London, and we no longer worked together or even lived in the same city, we just naturally drifted apart.

'What are you doing here?' I ask him.

'Taz invited me,' he replies. 'We stayed in touch – he did the ink on my leg.'

Jake places his foot on a nearby plant pot and rolls up his trouser leg to show me his tattoos. Every inch of his leg – from his ankle to his knee – is covered in the most intricate design. I can't resist dropping to my knees, to take a good look.

'Wow,' I say, taking it all in.

'Erm, hi,' Dylan says with a laugh as he joins us.

'Oh, hello,' I say, still on my knees. 'You remember Jake, right?'

'Of course,' Dylan says as he reaches out to shake his hand. 'All right, mate?'

I should probably get up from the floor, shouldn't I?

I return to eye level, standing between them.

'We were just catching up,' I tell him. 'It's been a minute.'

'Yeah, no worries, I was just coming to say we're going to play beer pong in the bedroom, on that long desk – in case you're looking for me,' he explains. 'I didn't think you'd fancy it, seeing as though it's beer, and technically sport...'

He laughs.

Dylan and I haven't spent a second together at this party – in fact, this is the longest we've interacted since we got here. Everyone wants a piece of him. They want him to sing them a song, to talk to him, dance with him. Oh, and of course most of them are women.

'Dylan, come on, strip beer pong,' the blonde bellows out of the balcony doors.

I turn to look at him.

'It's not strip beer pong,' he insists with a laugh. 'But, even if it were, I'm too good at it to lose.'

'Yeah, no worries, that's fine,' I say – not exactly sounding like it's fine. 'I was actually just going to ask Jake if he wanted to get out of here?'

The boys both look at me for a second. I turn to Jake, pretty much ignoring that Dylan is even standing there.

'Do you want to get out of here?' I say again. 'We could go somewhere quieter, where we can actually hear one another without having to stand in the cold – it would be good to have a proper catch-up.'

'Yeah, sure,' he says. 'I'd love to.'

'Go enjoy your strip beer pong,' I tell Dylan. 'I'll catch up with you later.'

Jake and I make a move, heading for the door, but Dylan takes my hand, holding me back for a moment.

'Hey, you know you can trust me, right?' he says with a smile. 'This isn't going to be like it used to be.'

'Dylan,' I hear the blonde screaming from inside.

'Yeah, okay, sure,' I reply. 'I guess I'll see you in the morning.'

'You're not coming back later?' he replies.

'Nah, I think I'll just go to bed,' I reply. 'After I hang out with Jake for a bit.'

'Okay, cool,' Dylan says. He leans forward and kisses me on the cheek. 'See you later.'

I head inside, catching up with Jake, happy to have

found an escape from the party that doesn't simply involve going and sitting in my room, on my own, worrying about what is happening at the stupid party.

I want to trust Dylan, really, I do, but I've been here before and, so far, everything looks just like it used to, to me.

I guess I'll just have to hope for the best and see what things are like in the morning.

Great.

35

Rubbing my temples to ward off the headache, I wake up in bed, in my own hotel room, with the slightest hangover – well, I didn't drink too much last night, but it turns out it doesn't actually take much these days.

The room is silent, the only light seeping in through the blackout curtains, where I didn't quite close them properly, but I can tell it's at least morning.

The 'slight hangover' intensifies a little, as I lift my head, reaching out to grab my phone. I need a bucket of water, a cup of tea and a big hug.

I felt a bit better last night, after bidding goodbye to the chaotic party, in favour of going for a catch-up with Jake. We ate pizza, had drinks, and we lost track of time as we chatted for ages, bringing each other up to date on our lives, and reminiscing about old times. But then, as I left him behind to return to the hotel, that niggling sense of unease lingered as I wondered how things were playing out at the party. Still, I tried my best to push it from my mind. I made myself a cup of tea, I got in bed and I watched TV until I fell asleep. I just kept telling myself not to worry about it, that he might not be doing anything all that bad.

The last thing I did, before I fell asleep, was to have a word with myself. 'Don't be so mental,' I'd muttered under my breath, trying to calm my ridiculous imagination. It's not the end of the world. Relax. Let Dylan do his own thing. He's said you can trust him, so trust him.

It's going to be strange, getting up, going down to breakfast, and then cracking on with the tour because the reality is that I am never going to know what went on last night. I'm sure everything will feel fine, and everyone will reassure me that it was fine and I'm supposed to, what? Believe them? Yep, I'm just going to have to believe them. Which, ladies and gentlemen, is the very definition of trust. I just need to trust him.

I squint at my phone, rub my eyes, and then try again.

What the hell?

The notifications seem endless, to the point where

I wonder if something might be wrong with my phone. I haven't seen it like this since... oh God.

I begin scrolling through the notifications. Multiple missed calls from Dylan and Rowan scream at me from the call log. The various messages and pings from different social media apps are relentless – more and more coming through as I'm staring at the screen.

But, amid it all, on thing stands out more than the others, a news alert for Dylan King. The headline reads:

Dylan King goes Wilde on tour.

My heart sinks, and a wave of sickness washes over me. Why is this happening again? Why do people have to drag my name into it? I'm not taking any blame for what the idiot does on tour. Okay, I'm the person who is supposed to be keeping his image on track, but I will murder him if this has repercussions for my business because I am not the ringmaster of this shitty circus.

With trembling fingers, I open the article, and for a moment, I'm suspended in a bittersweet haze. The blonde in the photo isn't me – a small relief, but one that is most definitely short-lived.

My heart shatters when I read the subheading:

Dylan King in drug-fuelled romp with old
flame... and it's only day two of the tour.

The photo shows a blonde woman, from behind,
sitting on top of a dark-haired man. You can't see their
faces, or any real distinguishing features, but you can
tell that they're both naked, on a bed, having sex. If I
didn't recognise the hotel room, I would definitely
spot Dylan's leather jacket on the chair next to the bed
– and the article has gone to the trouble of pointing it
out, showing that it is the same one he wore on stage
last night, so that's super helpful. Empty booze bottles
and various illegal substances are clearly visible on
the bedside table. The photo has sex, drugs and rock
and roll – that's bingo.

It isn't me in the photo, I know that much – obviously. But my eyes squint at the man in the background, blurred and distant. Is there a chance it's not
him? My heart races. Please don't let it be him for, I
don't know, about fifty different reasons.

I skim-read the article which – you've got to hand
it to the *Daily Scoop* – they've got online lightning-fast.
I miss the days when you could only be exposed in
sync with the news cycle because this is online already and... oh my God. They've got a quote from
Dylan.

I close my eyes for a second, scared to look, because for all of my worrying about what happened last night, and the question marks I was going to have to accept if I wanted to trust him, I can't be sure if reading what he has to say is going to make it better or worse.

I read it, and it makes it worse, so much worse.

In response to the question, asking him if it is him in the photo and how he feels, Dylan said: 'What I do on tour is my own business. Photos like this are unacceptable. No one should have their privacy breached like this.'

Well, that's that then. If it wasn't him, he would deny it. He's not wrong, that the photo is a huge breach of privacy but – honestly? – I'm glad it exists, and that it was printed. It was so, so stupid of me to think that a man like Dylan could change. I love him, so much – too much, probably – but he's never going to be the kind of man I can be with.

As devastated as I am, I should be grateful for the clarity. I'm too old for this shit. I've outgrown this lifestyle, the silly boys, the crazy nights. I shouldn't be here, participating in this crap, I should go home. Well, the closest thing I have to one right now.

36

Rowan greets me at the front door. It's late – the boys will most definitely be asleep – but from the look on his face I can tell that he wants to talk, so it's probably for the best.

I open my mouth to say something, but nothing springs to mind. Before I have a chance to figure it out, Rowan grabs me and pulls me close. He hugs me, and it is warm, and comforting, and everything I need right now.

I relax in his arms, his familiar embrace soothing me.

'Come on,' he says as he releases me. 'Let's sit down, in the lounge. Let's talk.'

I abandon my bags in the hall. I'm knackered, after one hell of a draining day.

The first thing I did, after I saw the messages, was call the hotel and see if I could book my room for another night – which thankfully I could. It wasn't that I wanted to stay another night, far from it, but I was too scared to leave the room. I worried that there might be paparazzi lingering around, and that I might bump into one or, worse, that I might bump into Dylan or anyone else on the tour.

So the plan was to hole up there, to wait it out for a few hours, wait for it to get dark and then head home with minimal attention. I guess it worked, no one spoke to me, although I was paranoid the whole time, wondering if people were staring at me, if they recognised me from the online article. Anyway, I'm here now.

'Let me start by saying this,' Rowan begins, taking a deep breath. 'I have, well and truly, monumentally fucked up. I've been stupid. I got caught up in some stupid scheme, I put myself, you and our entire family at risk. And I let myself get manipulated by Carrie – she didn't want me, it was all part of the plan, to get me involved. But still, there are no excuses, and no apologies that will ever come close to making this right, and I am certain that you will never forgive me.

But I'm willing to try, to spend every day, for the rest of my life, making it up to you. I love you, the boys love you – we will love you forever. But, if you decide that we are not what you want, that's okay too. There will always be a place for you here, even if it's just to visit. You can see the boys anytime you want, no matter what. But I hope you come back to me, I hope you stay, I hope you give me another chance.'

I give him a slight smile. It's a huge relief, to hear that I can see the kids no matter what happens, because the thought of suddenly up and leaving them, of never seeing them again, it's one of the reasons I stuck it out as long as I did.

Wouldn't it be nice to believe him, to forgive him, to try to get our family back on track? If being with Dylan again – even briefly – has taught me anything it's that the fireworks just aren't worth it, they're not realistic – or, at the very least, they come at a huge cost. I want to believe that the people we ultimately settle down with are the big, amazing loves of our lives, the ones who give us fireworks, who set our skin on fire with their touch, the people who the butterflies just never wear off with... but the kind of people who give us the above are never the ones who actually settle down.

If you want the explosions then you need to accept

the noise, the mess, the casualties. Maybe I was silly, to dismiss Rowan so quickly, to feel so apathetic when we were together – even before the mess. It doesn't change what he did, and I don't think I can ever forgive him, or get that trust back. It's almost funny, in a world where it seems like no one can be trusted, who do you give your heart to? Perhaps it's best I don't give it to anyone.

'Rowan, even if I could forget about all of that, I still can't get over what you did at the fundraiser,' I tell him. 'You're telling me you made a mistake, that you got caught up in a moment. But what happened at the fundraiser was different, it was cold and calculated and cruel.'

'I didn't know what else to do,' he says. 'I was ambushed, by the mums, when they presented me with all this information about you and Dylan. I was hurt that you didn't tell me, and watching the two of you getting closer again terrified me – not just because I thought I was going to lose you, to him, but because I was scared he was going to hurt you. And I suppose he has.'

'Hmm,' I say simply. 'You saw the article then.'

'I did,' he replies. 'And, look, I'm not exactly happy about that article being out there, but I know you, so well, and I know you would never touch a drug.'

'Thanks,' I say softly.

It is nice, that he knows me like that, that he can just look at it and know that it's not me.

'I know you won't have touched them, and, as far as Dylan goes, look, I hurt you, I cheated on you – I don't like it, but if we can say we've levelled the playing field—'

'Wait, what do you mean?' I interrupt him.

'I mean, you sleeping with Dylan, I don't like it, but it seems to me like he set his sights on you from the day he arrived here, and I don't blame you, for going for it,' he explains.

'You can tell that's me in the photo?' I check.

'Well, *I* can, Nicole, I know your body like the back of my hand,' he tells me with a smile, like it's some kind of compliment. 'But I don't think anyone else is going to know for sure and, even if they thought they did, I don't care. It's our business, not theirs. I can find a way past this, if you can.'

I sigh. Obviously I plan on clearing my name but, I don't know, part of me hoped that Rowan really would know, deep down, that I would never be involved in a 'drug-fuelled romp' at a party.

'I think I need to get some sleep,' I tell him. 'Clear my head.'

'Of course,' he replies. 'But think about what I said. Whatever you want to do, I respect it.'

Rowan takes my face in his hands and places a light peck on my lips.

I head back to the hall, grab my case and head upstairs.

It makes me sad that he couldn't just tell from looking at that photo that it wasn't me. It was so clearly the blonde girl, the one who invited herself and her friends to the party – although I spent most of the night, while I was there, looking at the back of her head, so perhaps that's why it is so obvious to me.

Could I track her down? I'm sure I could channel my inner journalist, if I wanted to, although I didn't get her name, so I wouldn't know where to begin – and do I even care? It would be good (to say the least) to clear my name, but what's the point? I cleared my name before, and people still dragged it up years later, and as far as Dylan goes, well, if it's another decade before I see him again, I can't say I'll be disappointed.

37

I'm woken up by the sound of my phone vibrating on the bedside table.

For fuck's sake, I'd only just managed to cry myself to sleep.

I reach out and grab it. It's Dylan, aka the last person on earth I want to talk to right now. I let it ring out before placing my phone back down on the bedside table.

I close my eyes again, for about five seconds, before it starts ringing again.

This time, when I grab it, I reject his call in temper, and place it back down.

Then I hear a message come through.

I snatch up my phone, all amped up, ready to

reply to him, to tell him to piss off, and to never contact me again, but then I notice what his message says:

Look out of your window, I'm outside.

The next thing I notice is the time – 3 a.m.

I jump out of bed and hurry over to the window. He can't be serious. And yet he is, he's standing there, outside the front door, gazing up at the house.

I call him from my phone.

'What the hell are you doing?' I ask him.

'Nic, can we talk?'

'No,' I say emphatically. 'I don't want to talk to you. Please, just go, you're going to wake the neighbours. Don't you think you've embarrassed me enough?'

'Please, Nic, just let me explain,' he begs. 'Come across the road with me, hear me out, and if you're still furious then I promise to piss off and you never have to talk to me again.'

I want to say no, to tell him to piss off again, but I can't. I sigh.

'Okay, fine, you've got five minutes,' I say. 'I'll just get my clothes on.'

I throw on a tracksuit and head downstairs, meeting him on the doorstep.

'Hi,' he says softly.

'Hi,' I reply through a frown. 'Why are you here, at 3 a.m., being an arsehole?'

'Because I need to explain,' he tells me. 'And I couldn't find you earlier, so I thought maybe you had come here, but there was no sign of you. I just woke up, looked out of the window, and saw that your room was lit up – sorry, I should have known you were sleeping with the lights on. You always do when you're anxious.'

'Wow, Mr Campbell would be proud,' I tell him as I pull a face.

'Erm, thanks, I think,' he says with a laugh.

Once we're inside Mr C's house, we take a seat on the green sofa.

'I know how this all looks but you have to believe me, it wasn't me in that photo,' he explains.

'Well, if it wasn't you, then why didn't you deny it?' I ask in disbelief.

'Because it was Mikey,' he tells me simply.

'Mikey is married with kids,' I correct him.

'Exactly,' he replies softly. 'He fucked up, big time, and the last thing I wanted was for his wife and kids to find out about it by reading it online, seeing that photo.'

I stare at him, holding my breath, waiting for him to continue.

'So, I took the fall – sort of – and when he's had a chance to talk to his missus then we can see about how we set the record straight,' he continues. 'I wanted to tell you, but I didn't even know, until we got a call from the *Scoop*. I don't even know who the girl was but I knew it wasn't you – I'm sorry they jumped to that conclusion.'

'You know it wasn't me?' I ask curiously. 'How do you know it wasn't me?'

'That wasn't your body,' he replies. 'Even from the back, and even though you have the same hairstyle and colour, I can tell.'

I smile.

'Plus, it's a pretty recent development, but you have the tattoo of a tiger wearing a crown on your lower back,' he reminds me.

I can't help but laugh – then I start crying.

'Dill, I thought it was you,' I admit. 'I was so quick to believe it – to think the worst of you.'

'And so you should,' he says, wrapping an arm around me, pulling me close for a hug. 'I was a dick – I was going to say in a previous life but, no, it was this one – so I can't expect you to just accept that I've changed, but I *have* changed. No girls, no drinking – no nothing.'

'Except I've seen you drinking,' I remind him with a frown.

'Have you?' he replies. 'Have you seen me drunk?'

'You've not been getting hammered, thinking about it, but you have been drinking,' I say. 'It's scary, if you've forgotten, or if you think you can convince me that you haven't.'

'I've been drinking alcohol-free beer,' he tells me. 'I haven't had a real drink in a long time. I don't want one either. It's nice to have something, on a night out, on tour, that makes me feel like I'm blending in but, honestly, I couldn't care less.'

'So you haven't been drinking,' I confirm. 'And that wasn't you in the photo.'

'No,' he stresses with a laugh.

'So, have you made any mistakes?' I ask him, confused.

'Maybe one,' he replies. 'I fell in love with my best friend, although, when I think about it, I'm not sure how much of a mistake it is.'

'We can't do this,' I tell him simply. 'We can't live like this, right? You're back on the wheel, you're touring, the band is going to be bigger than before. Nothing has changed.'

'*I have*,' he tells me. 'It's great, to be touring again,

but it's a one-off. None of us want that life full-time any more and, the more time I spend here, with you, the more I realise that the life you have might be the one for me. I like being around the kids, I like working at the school – why can't I have the best of both worlds?'

'You want to settle down?' I say, still not quite able to believe my ears.

Dylan just laughs.

'Nicole, I already have.'

'But what about the tour?' I reply. 'Won't it be cancelled, with the recent scandal?'

'Okay, I haven't been completely honest with you,' he starts. 'The tour was always happening, there was never any threat that if I didn't sort myself out it wouldn't happen. I just wanted to see you, to spend time with you, to show you that I'd changed. If I had called you up and told you that I was a whole new person, would you have believed me?'

'No,' I reply firmly. 'But I would have wanted to see you anyway.'

'When we were together, the other night, it felt right, didn't it?' he says.

I nod my head.

'I felt like I'd come home,' he tells me. 'You're my home. I don't care where that is, or how we do this, but it has to be you. I have to be with you.'

'I am not a happy woman,' I tell him. 'I go through the motions, every day, and I feel this huge hole in my heart, and I have no idea how to fill it. Sometimes I think I see it, as I glance around, just these little glimmers of – almost like déjà vu – and it ruins my day. And just when I had decided that I would probably never feel real happiness, you came back into my life. Suddenly everything had meaning again and that hole, well, I thought you were distracting me from it, but I guess it turns out you were filling it. You're my happiness, my missing piece of the puzzle.'

'Nic, I don't care what we do,' he replies. 'I don't care if we run off on tour and you stay right by my side, watching every move I make – because I never could do any of it without you, and I don't want to start out now. Or fuck the tour, I won't do it, I'll buy this house – I know how fond you are of the décor. I don't care what we do, where we do it, or why. I just need my best friend back.'

'Me too,' I say with a smile. 'But I think he might be more than a best friend.'

Dylan can hardly contain his smile as he leans in to kiss me.

'That's all I need to know,' he replies.

'But listen, don't blow off the tour,' I insist. 'Where are the others?'

'Paris,' he replies. 'We have a show there in, oh, about sixteen hours.'

'Dylan, no, what are you doing?' I say. 'You should be there.'

'I still could be,' he says, raising an eyebrow. 'Fancy going to Paris?'

I smile.

'I'll get my things.'

38

The hum of the jet engines is like music to my ears, reminding me that I am flying to Paris in the sheer luxury of a private plane.

A private plane is one of those things that I've seen on TV and in movies plenty of times and yet I'm still totally taken aback by it all. The soft carpet, the plush leather of the seat, the scented air – the food and drink! I was already on cloud nine but, now that I'm taking my first flight on a private jet, I really do feel on top of the world. It feels so surreal, sitting here, with Dylan. We feel a million miles from the world below – even if, in reality, we're probably less than ten. For a moment, it seems like we're suspended in time, miles away from any of life's complications, and being here alone in the cabin really does make it feel as though no one else exists. I love it.

'I could get used to this,' I admit, my gaze darting excitedly between the stunning view outside the window and the man of my dreams next to me.

'I guess now you can,' Dylan says with a laugh.

'Oh, yeah,' I reply, practically cackling with joy. 'I can't believe I am on a private jet to Paris. I know we've got the gig, obviously, but do you reckon we could stick around for a bit? I would love to explore, to be a tourist even just for a day. It's been so long since I last had a holiday.'

'We can stick around for as long as you like,' he tells me, wrapping an arm around me, giving me a squeeze. 'We could visit the Eiffel Tower, the Louvre, we could take a stroll along the Seine – oh, and I know some amazing places to eat.'

'Amazing,' I reply. 'I want to do it all, to see all the sights, to eat absolutely everything.'

'Well, we can kick off with coffee and croissants when we land, and then take it from there,' he suggests. 'And don't worry, I called ahead to tell the authorities that you were coming, and they agreed to let you into the country so long as I promised to make sure you behaved this time.'

I laugh.

'You keeping an eye out for me – that's rich,' I say with a snort. 'You're never going to let me forget that, are you?'

'Never ever ever,' he tells me.

'Okay, well, I promise to behave this time,' I tell him.

'Oh, I really hope you don't,' he replies, pushing me back onto the sofa, climbing on top of me as his lips meet mine.

I gasp, the gentle turbulence only adding to the thrill of it all.

Dylan pauses kissing me for a second and looks into my eyes.

'I can't believe we're here,' he tells me simply.

'You mean on a private jet to Paris?' I reply.

'That's not what I mean at all,' he says with a smile. 'But yeah, sure, that too.'

'We're on our way to Paris,' I practically squeal, because I still can't believe it.

'Tops optional?' Dylan asks.

'Tops optional,' I reply, grabbing at his T-shirt to pull it over his head.

Well, we're not technically in Paris yet. But I'll behave when I get there, I swear.

39

12 DECEMBER 2024

'Okay, so why did you get married?' Dylan asks me, his voice dripping with disdain.

'Love,' I reply, emphatically.

'Oh, well, if it was for love,' he replies sarcastically.

I sigh with a mixture of sadness and frustration.

'Right, fine, that's it, forget it,' I rant. 'I'm done with you, I don't want anything from you...'

We both stop in our tracks and turn to the two kids who are staring at us.

'Your voice needs to sound like that,' Dylan tells Joey, who is playing Scrooge. 'You think your nephew is an idiot. And, Albi, when you're playing Fred, you should play it like Nicole just did. You're frustrated with your uncle – you think he's a dull old fart.'

'Dylan,' Miss Pallett calls out, interrupting him. 'Dylan, can we run something by you?'

'Yeah, sure, I'll be there in a minute,' he calls back, then he turns to the boys who are standing in the centre of the stage, eager to get back to their rehearsal. 'Run it through a few more times, I'll be right back.'

I walk with Dylan, to the edge of the stage, and down the steps.

'This is so non-stop,' he tells me, exhaling deeply. 'I love it.'

'I love that you've got the kids interested in Dickens,' I reply.

'Who knew all it would take was a bit of fun modernisation and satire?' he replies. 'Right, keep an eye on those two for me, I'll go see what Miss Pallett needs.'

'Sure,' I reply with a smile.

I never would have thought, in a million years, that I would see Dylan working in a school, managing their summer and winter productions, but here he is, and he's committed – so committed, in fact, that he bought a house here in Little Harehill. I think in a strange way, Mr C's house holds sentimental value for him, and I find it hilarious that he is the kind of guy who will buy *a house* because it's sentimental.

The place looks great, now that it has had some

intensive modernisation, and even though Dylan said that his plan was to get him through the tour (which was an absolute smash, and sold so many tickets they had to add extra dates) and me through my separation from Rowan, and then sell the place in the new year, I don't know, something tells me that we might be sticking around in Little Harehill longer than we thought.

Living across the road from Rowan, Archie and Ned really has been helpful in helping with the transition. Sure, it was weird at first, but the fact that I wasn't ripped away from the kids – that Rowan never stopped me seeing them, and that I didn't just take off – has helped them get used to the idea. To be honest, I think they're both so jazzed to have Dylan living across the street that they don't really mind that their dad and I are no longer together. Kids are smarter than we think. I'm sure that, even though I did my best to keep playing happy families, the boys must have picked up on the fact that Rowan and I weren't happy.

Oh, speak of the devil.

I notice Rowan walk into the hall with Archie and Ned, who charge ahead of him, running towards me, each grabbing one of my arms to greet me. He smiles widely as he catches them up.

'I am still loving this hair,' I tell Archie as I ruffle his growing locks.

Now that he's decided he wants to be a drummer in a band when he grows up, he is very much embracing his inner rock god.

'I want it even longer,' he tells me. 'And I want tattoos and piercings.'

'Hmm, I would stick with the hair for now, make sure it's what you want,' I tell him with a laugh. 'You can head through to the music room and start practising now, if you want. Dylan is nearly done.'

'Cool,' he says, charging off, drumsticks in hand.

'What have you done to him?' Rowan jokes. 'He hasn't touched a football in months.'

'It's nice to see him enjoying it,' I reply. 'And, for what it's worth, his longer hair really does suit him. Anyway, look at you, all dressed up. Going somewhere nice?'

Rowan is wearing black trousers and a white shirt. His hair is neat and I can smell his aftershave from here. Definitely not his usual attire for picking the kids up from school.

'Erm, I was, I'm not now, though,' he says, lowering his voice. 'I actually had a date but Ned's after-school club is cancelled so...'

'So leave him with me,' I insist. I turn to Ned. 'Hey,

Ned, fancy being the director of the play? You get to sit in that cool chair over there, and tell everyone what to do.'

'Yeah,' he says excitedly, before running right over there.

'Nicole, are you sure?' Rowan says.

'Yeah, of course,' I reply. 'I'll take them both back to ours, after practice. Just pick them up whenever – you know we love hanging out with them.'

'Thank you,' he tells me sincerely. 'And not just for this, for everything, because I don't think I ever thanked you properly. I was so hung up on what I was losing, when I thought you were leaving me, that I never appreciated just how huge it was that you actually stuck around to help me clean up the mess I made, and that you're still around now, for the boys, it means a lot.'

'I love them,' I tell him simply. 'And, despite everything, I care about you too. We're both doing what it takes, to make this fresh start work for everyone so, go, enjoy your date, let me take care of the kids.'

Rowan steps forward and briefly kisses me on the cheek.

'She's got big shoes to fill,' he tells me with a smile.

'Size sevens,' I joke awkwardly.

Rowan laughs and says goodbye.

I head back to the stage, to join Joey and Albi, who pretty much have their dialogue down now.

'Perfect,' I tell them.

'Yeah, absolutely spot on,' Dylan adds, joining us. 'Go on, lads, get home. I'll see you tomorrow.'

Joey and Albi, pleased with themselves, slap each other a high five before heading off.

'Archie is in the music room, ready for his drum lesson, and I told Rowan we would watch them for a bit this evening – he has a date,' I explain.

'Then I'd better do this now,' Dylan tells me, taking me by the hands, pulling me behind the thick, heavy stage curtains.

Dylan takes my face in his hands and kisses me.

'Have I told you that I loved you lately?' he asks me.

'I think you tell me every time you make eye contact with me,' I tease. 'It's starting to get a bit old.'

'Really?' he asks with a smile.

'Not really,' I reply. 'I love it, and I love you too.'

Dylan kisses me again and, as far as backstage kisses go, this is the last sort I ever expected, but the best it can ever be.

I feel so fortunate, every single day, that Dylan and I were given another chance. Sometimes I tell myself that we were meant to be, that this was all predetermined and that everything that has happened since the moment we met was all leading up to this moment, so that we could finally be together. It's a nice thought, and so romantic, but I don't think that's how things really play out. It took work to get us to this point, where we could finally be together, and happy, and that's not down to fate. I'm so, so proud of Dylan for straightening himself out. He is living proof that it's always worth trying to do better, and to be better, and that you can always get your life back on track. No person, or relationship, is a write-off if you're willing to put the effort in to make it work, and you're never too old to make a change. Be someone adaptable, someone who goes out of their way to find happiness. You will never be younger than you are today, and the past versions of yourself that you look at in the photos may look like they are so much better than you are now, but there is one thing you have that they don't: experience, and the privilege of growing older. Yes, those days are behind you, but there are so many ahead of you, and who knows what they might hold?

Shake up your life, seek out the person who makes you the happiest, get the stupid tattoo, travel to Paris if it's what you want.

Oh, and it's always tops optional – of course.

ACKNOWLEDGEMENTS

More than a decade ago, when I was running around with musicians, I never thought such a strange job/hobby could turn into something so wonderful, and yet here I am, writing the acknowledgements for not only my 30th book, but the tenth anniversary of my first publication day.

When my first book came out back in February 2014, I don't think I expected anyone to read it, so to be releasing my 30th story out into the wild – having sold over 1 million books – feels amazing.

I've had so much fun revisiting Nicole – the very first character I came up with – and Dylan. They're my original OTP – it's nice, to feel like they're in a good place now.

Thank you so much to Boldwood Books, my brilliant publisher – especially my editor, Nia, for helping me fit my anniversary project into our schedule.

I am so fortunate to feel so supported by my lovely

author friends – Sarah, Rebecca, Belinda and Sam. Thanks for always being there.

Massive thanks to everyone who has bought, read and reviewed my books over the last ten years. It means so much to me, that so many people are enjoying my stories. Writing has seen me through some difficult times, so whenever someone reaches out to tell me that reading one of my books made a tough time easier for them, it all feels so worth it.

Huge thanks to Kim, my amazing mum, for everything she has done for me. There is absolutely no way you would be reading this now, if I hadn't had so much love and support from her over the years, and thank you to Pino, for your support and for telling absolutely everyone about my books. The same goes for Aud, my wonderful gran, one of my favourite people on the planet. I am also so fortunate to have had so much support – varying from technical to emotional – from James and Joey, who always have my back, no matter what. And then there is Joe, my amazing husband, who rocked up in my life somewhere between book four and book five, and not only gave me the support to keep going, but the love to keep me feeling inspired to write happy-ever-afters.

Thank you so much to everyone who has supported me over the past decade – here's to the next ten years.

ABOUT THE AUTHOR

Portia MacIntosh is a bestselling romantic comedy author of over 15 novels, including *My Great Ex-Scape* and *Honeymoon For One*. Previously a music journalist, Portia writes hilarious stories, drawing on her real life experiences.

Sign up to Portia MacIntosh's mailing list for news, competitions and updates on future books.

Visit Portia's website: https://portiamacintosh.com/

Follow Portia MacIntosh on social media here:

facebook.com/portia.macintosh.3

x.com/PortiaMacIntosh

instagram.com/portiamacintoshauthor

bookbub.com/authors/portia-macintosh

ALSO BY PORTIA MACINTOSH

One Way or Another

If We Ever Meet Again

Bad Bridesmaid

Drive Me Crazy

Truth or Date

It's Not You, It's Them

The Accidental Honeymoon

You Can't Hurry Love

Summer Secrets at the Apple Blossom Deli

Love & Lies at the Village Christmas Shop

The Time of Our Lives

Honeymoon For One

My Great Ex-Scape

Make or Break at the Lighthouse B&B

The Plus One Pact

Stuck On You

Faking It

Life's a Beach

Will They, Won't They?

No Ex Before Marriage

The Meet Cute Method

Single All the Way

Just Date and See

Your Place or Mine?

Better Off Wed

Long Time No Sea

The Faking Game

Enemies to Lovers

Ex in the City

LOVE NOTES

LOVE IN EVERY CHAPTER

WHERE ALL YOUR ROMANCE
DREAMS COME TRUE!

THE HOME OF BESTSELLING
ROMANCE AND WOMEN'S
FICTION

WARNING:
MAY CONTAIN SPICE

SIGN UP TO OUR
NEWSLETTER

https://bit.ly/Lovenotesnews

Boldwood

Boldwood Books is an award-winning fiction publishing company seeking out the best stories from around the world.

Find out more at www.boldwoodbooks.com

Join our reader community for brilliant books, competitions and offers!

Follow us
@BoldwoodBooks
@TheBoldBookClub

Sign up to our weekly deals newsletter

https://bit.ly/BoldwoodBNewsletter